BRONTË FALLS

AN INSPECTOR CHARLES BRONTË THRILLER

Tom Marsh

Grosvenor House
Publishing Limited

This book is published by
Grosvenor House Publishing Ltd
Link House
140 The Broadway, Tolworth, Surrey, KT6 7HT.
www.grosvenorhousepublishing.co.uk

A CIP record for this book
is available from the British Library

Paperback ISBN 978-1-83615-059-6
Hardback ISBN 978-1-83615-060-2
eBook ISBN 978-1-83615-061-9

To Janet, my muse, my love and my best friend, without whose continuous, positive feedback and support I would never have had the confidence to bring this book to completion.

Thank you, Janet.

Preface

The telling of a story is a complete pleasure; I do love spinning a good yarn. I love a fast-moving thriller, in an exciting environment with dramatic, likeable characters. This is where Inspector Charles Brontë comes into his own.

Brontë is moulded from the same Yorkshire gritstone, as the wild moors where he plies his trade: the detection, capture and incarceration of bloodthirsty killers. Though influenced by events in the deep south of the United States of America, the action takes place in and around the South Yorkshire Moors.

Be aware, this novel is a work of fiction. Names, characters, places and incidents are the product of the author's imagination and are used fictitiously. Any resemblance to actual events, locales or persons, living or dead, are entirely coincidental.

What have these lonely mountains worth revealing?
More glory and more grief than I can tell
The earth that wakes one human heart to feeling
Can centre both the worlds of heaven or hell

Emily Brontë.

Prologue

Charlottesville, North Carolina.
The United States of America.
The twenty-fifth of December. Christmas Day.

Jackson Hamilton Adams III sat watching *Home Alone* for the umpteenth time. He'd seen it at least once a year since its first release. Back in the day he had watched with his children, but they'd all grown up now and had children of their own. He saluted the TV with a glass of Wild Turkey Bourbon and spoke out loud to the actors.

'You can be too old for a lot of things, Kevin... but you're never too old to be afraid.'

His laughter was interrupted by the doorbell, which he found strange; no one ever came visiting. Leaving the film running he stepped silently into the hall, stood by the outside door and listened. Nothing.

'Hello!?'

Still no reply but... Jackson was quite sure he heard shuffling on the porch.

'I can hear you. What do you want?'

A little more shuffling and then a voice.

'You, Counsellor, I want you.'

'Yeh, well, y'all might wanna go ske-daddle 'fore I call the police, ya hear?'

'But Counsellor, I haven't given you your Christmas present.'

He thought about this.

'I don't need no present, boy. I have all I need.'

'I aint no boy, Counsellor, and you're sure gonna want what I got here for ya.'

Jackson Hamilton Adams III, cracked open the door and peered out. The night was warm and the skies clear. By the light of the moon he could see perfectly well who was standing on his porch. Jessica bloody Rabbit!

Not the cartoon Jessica Rabbit, but a real live, living and breathing one: same red hair, same red dress, same banging body.

'What's my present?'

'Can't you guess, Counsellor?'

'I can guess, and if I'm right, which I'm sure I am, it won't be no free present, ma'am, that's for sure.'

'Then you'd be wrong there, Counsellor. What I got for you ain't gonna cost you a nickel nor a dime.'

He thought this over, opened the door a little more.

'You'd best get yourself on over here.'

Stepping aside, the wonderful Mrs Rabbit slinked past into the hall, green eyes flashing. The counsellor dropped the latch and turned to face her.

'OK! Where's my present?'

The apparition slid her hand through the split in her long red dress, her hand sliding down her thigh.

'Be patient, Counsellor, it's right here.' She listened for a moment. 'You're watching television?'

'*Home Alone*,' he smirked.

'And are you?'

'Always.'

'Excellent.'

'Who can I thank for sending this... little gift?'

'An acquaintance of yours, one of your happy customers.'

She wriggled closer to him, withdrawing her hand from beneath the silk dress: a hand that clutched an evil looking spike, light flashing off the sharpened tip. Jessica plunged the weapon straight through the counsellor's Adam's apple, skewering him to the door. Blood and unintelligible croaks spurted from his mouth, his eyes wide in terror. A muffled, gurgling scream escaped around the sides of the steel and Jessica Rabbit whispered huskily in his ear, 'Merry Christmas, ya filthy animal.'

Her laughter echoed round the empty hall.

Chapter One

Fourteen months later.
Raleigh, North Carolina.
The thirteenth of February. Shrove Tuesday.

Capability Goldman jabbed manically at the air conditioning button on the dash of his 42 Mustang with a heavily nicotine-stained finger. He cursed out loud with each jab.

'Bitch... bitch... bitch... bitch... BITCH!'

The air conditioning responded to neither the jabbing nor the cussing. The North Carolinian sun beat down on the big Ford, heating the interior to the temperature of a backyard barbeque grill, cooking Capability like a pork-belly roast, the sweat running down his face resembling molten fat. There was no relief from the heat through open windows either. The Mustang crawled so slowly amidst the Mardi Gras revellers there was no air movement at all: if anything, the open windows only made Capability hotter and allowed in the sickly smell of the dogwood flowers, which made his temper even worse.

In this manner, Capability made slow progress to the *Raleigh Corrective Institute for Women*. If the manic paraders didn't get out of the damn way he was in danger of missing the day's event: an execution by lethal injection. Not his own of course. He was not looking forward to witnessing the spectacle, but he felt he owed it to see this thing through to the bitter end. That is exactly what this would be, he thought, a very bitter end. He couldn't have been more wrong. Bitter, it certainly would be: end, it most certainly would not.

The Mustang was going nowhere fast; dancers and drummers blocked the whole road, Capability thumped the horn with a sweaty fist. Unlike the aircon the horn was satisfyingly operational, blasting out loudly. Nobody moved: nobody reacted. The blaring horn was completely ineffectual but satisfyingly loud nonetheless. So, satisfying. Capability blasted it again and again, just for the sheer pleasure. As expected, no one batted an eye: believing it all part of the Mardi Gras cacophony.

A cacophony raised by a gobsmacking array of men and women of every possible shape, size and colour. Diverse as they were, they all had one thing in common: the abundance of naked flesh on display. Each dancer, irrelevant of gender, was clad only in patent leather bikinis and false collars and cuffs. Nothing was left to the imagination; nothing offering even a modicum of modesty. To add to the macabre effect, the face of each dancer was painted with a skull.

'Jesus!' said Capability to nobody, 'why the deuce, does every bugger lose the bloody plot every Fat Tuesday?'

He hated everything about Mardi Gras: the parade, Easter, the Lord, even the nearly naked beauties.

'Yes siree, you guys are less to do with heaven than ye' are hell,' he called through the window. Hitting the horn again just added to the chaos. A black head with a white skull span around and glared at him.

'Hey!' shouted the skull. 'Cut the horn, grandad, or I'll stick it up your fat white ass.'

But before she could fulfil her promise, a gap appeared in the throng and Capability was through and away, blasting his horn as he went, the skull-faced woman making do with fisting the hood of the Ford and flashing him the middle finger as he passed.

'Asshole!'

***

Within the corrective institute, Capability sat himself at the very back of the viewing theatre, not because the room was full, quite the opposite. He was the only person in the room. He'd sat at the back as he didn't want to be too close to the spectacle that was to be played out before him. The air conditioning whirred away and the sweat on his back began to cool rapidly, making him shiver: it felt like someone walking over his grave.

God, he hated executions.

Suddenly, he was not alone, a thin Asian guy made his way to the front seats, taking centre stage. Thankful for the distraction, Capability, strove to suss out his fellow spectator. Now this was a twist in the tail, he thought. Learning nothing from the back of the guy's bald head, he turned his attention to the clothes. These told him nothing either. He wore only a cheap grey trench coat that covered everything. Strange choice of clothing for a day like today. His skinny wrists stuck out of large white cuffs and his scrawny neck stuck out from an overly large white shirt collar, all in all giving him the appearance of a nodding dog on a truck's parcel shelf. He was wondering what business the guy had there, and what his connection to the prisoner was, when there was movement behind the viewing window.

'Oh shit!' he whispered, not quite under his breath. 'Here we chuffin' go.'

The bald Asian guy reacted too, took a deep breath in, which he quickly and noisily released like a truck's air breaks. 'PSSSSHHHH!!'

The clinical room before them held a gurney that matched perfectly the blue of the slowly disappearing curtains. Strapped to the gurney was a woman dressed in a white prison onesie. She lay statue-like, fists clenched, eyes tightly shut, her forehead wet with sweat.

Capability hardly recognised the person that lay there before him as the so-called Ice Maiden. She had been strong and determined at her trial, unrepentant and proud. Her long red locks and green eyes had grabbed the attention of every man and woman in the room. Now she looked old and tired, the red hair shaved off, leaving a smudge stubble: a complete shadow of her former self.

Over one bloody month, this so-called Ice Maiden had been on a killing spree methodically and viscously, plunging an ice-pick into the brains or necks of a number of Carolinian citizens; five blood-soaked corpses were left in her wake: a care worker, a married couple, a counsellor and a county judge.

She had been caught red handed, literally standing over the dead body of the county judge, clutching the ice-pick in her blood-soaked mitt, the sticky redness running down her fingers and dripping into a pool on the sidewalk.

It was not just the choice of weapon that had given her the infamous tabloid nickname, the Ice Maiden, but also the cold bloodied brutality of her crimes. Capability had come up with that catchy moniker which had won himself exclusive coverage of the story for the Raleigh Tribune. The majority of the paper's readers had 'the Maiden' down as, 'just another psycho nutjob', which is exactly how Capability had written it up. He could fathom no reason for the killings; she had no connection with the victims and had never come into contact with them prior to mushing their brains with a piece of cocktail equipment. Five inexplicable, random acts of indiscriminate barbarity.

The second hand of the wall clock jerked slowly and silently around the dial, designed specifically to be silent so the condemned could not hear their last seconds ticking away. That would have been too cruel, so the clocks were silenced. The Ice Maiden's fists clenched as the staff connected tubes to the cannulas already inserted in her arms. Capability had seen this all before and was fully aware that only one cannula was necessary to carry out the execution; the others being reserved as a backup in case of failure. To enable prison officials to determine, accurately, the time of death, the condemned was hooked up to a heart monitor with a green flashing display and a slow metronomic bleep as seen and heard on every medical TV melodrama ever made.

Beep... Beep... Beep.

It was ironic that the needles being used during the procedure had been sterilised. The prison couldn't risk the chance of infection. There was a chance, miniscule though it may be, that the prisoner could receive a stay of execution; under this unlikely scenario the prison did not want suing for negligence.

There was not going be a stay of execution today; not in this case.

Capability would rather have been anywhere other than here, but he had reported on the story from its gory beginnings. It was his duty to see it through to this inevitable conclusion.

Beep... Beep... Beep.

He watched the two guards taking three syringes each and securing them to intravenous lines, the reporter knew all about the injection, a cocktail of drugs given in a set sequence designed to kill. The first to render unconsciousness, the second to cause paralysis, making it impossible to breathe. The final infusion would cause severe pain to the now paralysed prisoner, interrupting the electrical activity of the heart muscle, causing it to stop beating and bringing about the inevitable death. Capability sat and waited for three plungers to be plunged.

Beep... Beep... Beep.

The prison workers tilted the Ice Maiden's gurney up to face the window so she could see into the viewing area—if her eyes had not been so tightly shut, that is. In complete silence one guard walked to a switch on the wall. Once the switch was depressed Capability could hear the guard's heels clicking on the tiles as he walked back to take his position by the gurney, where he addressed the almost empty viewing theatre.

'The condemned is now permitted to make a final statement.'

The Ice Maiden's eyes opened and connected with Capability's for a split second but quickly moved on, searching the room, at last finding the only other visitor in the room; from that moment the Ice Maiden kept her eyes rooted on the Asian guy—bright sparkling green eyes that did not deviate from the strange bald man. Not once did she look to see who else may have come to witness her last words, or come to see her gasp her last breath.

Then she spoke.

'My veins are ready to run with fire. My heart beats faster than I can count its throbs. I am not talking to you now through the medium of custom or even mortal flesh. It is my spirit that addresses your spirit; just as if both had passed through the grave and should fall into the pit, to be burning there for ever.'

Beep... Beep... Beep.

'My very soul demands you take deadly vengeance and it will be satisfied. When we are struck at without reason, we should strike back again very hard; so hard as to teach the person who struck us never to do it again.'

She then mouthed three words; words that could be seen, but not heard.

'I... love... you!'

Beep...Beep...Beep.

There was a deafening silence as the gurney was lowered and the Ice Maiden was laid out flat once more. The executioners injected the drugs into the cannula one after another. The body twitched and rattled against the gurney. For minutes it continued to bleep; minutes that felt like hours. Body twitching, monitor beeping.

The monitor pronounced death with one long, harrowing, beep.

Beeeeeeeeeep!

The bald head on the front row dropped forward in silent prayer.

And then silence.

The warden confirmed the death.

'Cardiac activity has stopped at twelve-oh-three.'

She switched off the beep and drew the tasteful blue curtains across the window.

Capability was distracted by his fellow visitor jumping up and running up the stairs two at a time, scurrying like a rat up a pipe. Holding a handkerchief up to his eyes, most of his face was covered and he was out of the exit before Capability could get a proper look. Stirring himself into action, Capability was up on his feet giving chase, dragging his girth up the steep stairs, making breathing difficult.

Having followed the case since the first bloody corpse was found on the steps of the Unity Church of Raleigh Creek, he thought this execution would be the end of the story, but not now it seemed; now there was a loose end. A loose end intent on getting out of the way as fast as its little legs could carry it.

Who the feck are you? Capability thought. He seriously needed to catch this guy up, but he had to stop to catch his breath halfway up the steps.

'Jesus H Christ!'

Exiting the theatre, he rushed down the exit corridor between metal detectors and through the huge swing doors out into the midday sun, the heat smashing into him like a truck.

There was no sign of the little guy among the fancy-dressed Mardi Gras parade or among the half-naked dancers who were still waggling their bits at the excitable spectators. Capability jumped up and down in a futile attempt to see over everybody's heads.

'Damn it,' he swore. 'Double bloody damn it!'

Running down the courtroom steps, his feet became ensnared in discarded clothing throwing him down the steps, almost breaking his neck. Looking down, his ankles were all caught up in a discarded cheap grey trench coat. Capability laughed.

'Looks like the Jackalope's out on the lam and that'll be end the end of that.'

He couldn't have been more wrong.

Chapter Two

Eight months later.
Yorkshire, England. The United Kingdom.
The thirty-first of October. All Saints' Eve. Halloween.

Nigel Flett sat alone in the damp cottage he called home, situated in the small village of Hewenden Bridge, close to the more picturesque village of Haworth. He didn't like the cottage, it reminded him too much of his father, who he hadn't liked very much either. For as many years as he could remember he had only used three of the cottage's seven rooms: the kitchen, the dining room and the bathroom. He cooked in the kitchen, the bathroom needs no explanation and he lived and slept in the dining room because it had the benefit of a coal fire.

Nigel had never got around to clearing his mother's old stuff out of the house. There was a painting of a big-eyed boy crying, on the chimney breast. Standing in the corner, a teak sideboard holding a crystal cut sherry decanter, a silver serving plate and matching carving knife and fork set.

The rooms he did not use, which he had left to stagnate, had gradually succumbed to the neglect and were covered in mould and toadstools. Nigel really didn't give a damn about the run-down condition. The room his mother had been most proud of, the one she called 'the lounge', was in the worst condition of them all; this pleased Nigel no end. This room boasted peeling bay windows with broken panes of glass, through which the room had been infested by a creeping ivy which covered the walls, which every winter had become infested with roosting starlings. Nigel was frightened of the starlings. He hated their threatening murmuring and sulky moodiness, but he loved the way they defiled the house. He had also grown accustomed to the acrid smell of their guano, which masked some of the worst odours produced by his own tainted lifestyle.

Nigel was sitting in his dining room surrounded by pile upon pile of hoarded junk. After years of not throwing anything out, the rubbish accumulated around him, piling higher and higher, making false walls within the room. These fabricated bulwarks created narrow walkways, a weird labyrinth that enabled Nigel to pass from room to room, a mad maze created from mounds of magazines and videos, but more recently, and all the more treasured, DVDs.

All the material had a common theme—pornography. Nigel Flett loved what he called his 'erotica' and what his mother had called his 'filth'. Pornography was the only thing he had left in his tawdry life, well, that and his volunteering at the heritage railway. Two loves, pornography and steam trains, completely different but both involving a lot of huffing and puffing, and pulling and pushing.

He sat in near darkness, the room illuminated only by the TV and the glowing embers of the coal fire—one of the perks of his volunteering: a free bucket of coal now and then, but only when no one was looking.

The flickering light from the television illuminated his flaccid, white body as he lay spread-eagled on a dog-eared old settee. He was dressed only in questionably stained vest and y-fronts, his hand stuffed determinedly down the latter. He watched the moving pictures and listened to the heavy breathing of the pathetic actors shagging each other stupid on the screen. The actors were a little old for Nigel's taste, but he couldn't risk buying any of the illegal DVDs that he lusted after. It was far too risky. As the on-screen fornicators' breathing increased so did Nigel's and his breath begin to burn at the back of his throat, drying out his mouth as it did. Strangely, even though Nigel was focusing on the naked and thrusting bodies, he was enthralled by what was in the background of the shots, the little things that made it all the more real. That's how he liked to see it, as real as possible, because Nigel hadn't had real sex for years. Years and years. Not since the incident at 'the Home.' The incident that had been quickly covered up and made to go away by the powers that be. They had all been lucky; very, very lucky. Now it was as if it never happened.

As he watched the television and thought of the Home he started counting, making the words by sucking deep gulps of air in out.

'One... two... three. One... two... three.'

He continually counted these days, whatever he was doing. Whether it be putting coal on the fire or opening a tin of beans, everything was accompanied by the spoken commentary of his counting.

'One... two... three. One... two... three. One... two... three.'

Knock... knock.

Nigel stopped counting; his head turned slowly to the door that led out on to the street. The door that no one knocked on; ever. The last time must have been years back when his mother and father were still alive, when the door belonged to them.

Another knock, louder this time.

Knock... knock.

'Hello?' Nigel's voice was weak and it wavered.

Knock... Knock.

'Who's there?'

Jesus! He thought, this was starting to sound like some sick joke, though he didn't think it was funny.

'Not today thank you.'

KNOCK... KNOCK!

The uninvited visitor had not only interrupted his pleasure but also threatened to disturb the feathered monsters in 'the lounge'. Nigel didn't want them dirty devils flying about. He paused the DVD, leaving the actors mid-thrust on a juddering screen, and he shuffled to the door, safe in the fact that though his orgasm was interrupted, he could savour it later, maybe even as he talked to whoever was standing on his doorstep. That would be almost like the real thing. Wouldn't it?

KNOCK.... KNOCK!

Nigel counted his steps out loud as he walked.

'One... two... three. One... two... three.'

He stood behind the door, the fire light flickering on his flabby, almost naked body.

'What?' he croaked at the door.

Knock... knock.

He unlatched and then opened the door slowly, an inch at a time, and peered through the gap, shielding his uncomely body behind it, hiding from the mysterious caller.

'What is it?'

'Trick or treat?' whispered a cloaked figure from the shadows.

'What do you want?'

'Trick or treat!?'

Nigel could just about make out a figure in the dark, a figure in a long, black, hooded cloak, a cloak which covered the caller from head to foot and threw their face into shadow.

'I don't buy at the doorstep,' he informed the stranger and started to push the door to again.

'Trick or treat.'

'I'm not interested, now go away.'

The cloak covering the figure fell open, revealing white flesh, flesh that gleamed in the moonlight. Sadly, Nigel couldn't quite work out what part of the body this particular bit of flesh belonged to, but it glistened invitingly.

'Trick or treat?'

Nigel sucked in air through his teeth.

'One… two… three. One… two… three.'

Nigel's nostrils were struck by a burst of muskiness wafting out from under the caller's cloak. He found the whole thing not just intoxicating but almost overpowering. He rubbed himself and allowed the door to swing open wider.

'It's your choice?' hissed the visitor.

Nigel hesitated. Who was this late-night caller? he thought. He pushed the door closed a little more. As he did the caller let the cloak fall fully open.

'Treat,' said Nigel. 'I'd like a treat.'

'I can't give you a treat from out here.'

'You'd better come in,' croaked Nigel, his voice husky and trembling.

The creature slunk passed him into the room and he pushed the door to. When he turned back around, his visitor had dropped their covering to the floor.

'God in heaven!'

The naked vision stepped closer, whispering.

'Far from it, Nigel, I can assure you.'

'You know my name.'

'Take off your pants.'

For a split-second Nigel hesitated. Who was this person that he'd let into his house? What did they want? What's in it for them.

'Bollox,' he said, more to himself than the stranger, and he dropped his pants to the floor. He looked pathetic, painting a ridiculous picture dressed only in his soiled vest and dirty white ankle socks.

He was magnetised by the visitor's nakedness, drawn like a moth to a flame. When the creature held out its hand to touch him, he gasped with pleasure and disbelief: all fear forgotten, overtaken by lust.

'One... two... three. One... two... three.'

The stranger's free hand came from behind their back, arching through the air, flashing in the firelight, a hypodermic needle clutched in white fingers. The needle plunged deep into Nigel's fat neck. Paralysed by shock and the contents of the syringe, causing his legs to buckle, he crumpled into a kneeling position before the naked stranger, his body paralysed but his mind and senses fully functional.

He watched the naked vision that he had personally invited into his own home drift calmly around the room as if they didn't have a care in the world, checking stuff out and being careful not to knock over the piles of rubbish. They showed particular interest in the items on the sideboard, taking up the carving set and standing over the debilitated railwayman, the large carving knife in one hand and in the other the evil looking two-pronged fork, both highlighted by the light from the fire and television.

'Trick or treat?'

Not only was Nigel unable to move, he couldn't speak either. It was impossible for him to respond.

'No? Can't decide?'

Nigel could only stare up at them.

'Let's say… trick.'

Nigel's eyes were screaming in terror, but no sound came from out of his mouth. The visitor plunged the carving fork deep into his neck, skewering him on the twin prongs and stopping him from tottering over on to the floor. He couldn't scream, but his eyes grew wider with horror as the blade of the silver carving knife flashed through the air.

'Vengeance and recompense are mine. The day of your calamity is here.'

With one swipe of the knife, Nigel Flett's penis was sliced clean from his body.

Nigel screamed silently inside his head and watched as blood spurted from his groin, splattering over his tattered vest and the immaculate white skin of the stranger. The naked, blood-soaked figure stood over Nigel's twitching body, the bloody knife and fork gripped firmly in their hands.

'You know what you did.'

The fork was pulled slowly out of Nigel's neck and his dying body was allowed to slump to the floor.

The starlings began to murmur.

***

While Nigel Flett bled out on to his soiled polyester carpet, Detective Inspector Charles Brontë rode his matt-black Ducati Monster far too fast across the Yorkshire Moors. Brontë loved his motorbike. His ex, Margaret, said this was one of his major problems; she was not going to live with a man who loved a pile of metal more than her.

He was eager to be back home and out of the torrential rain; as much as he loved them, motorbikes were not made for English winters. It was all a bit too much for him nowadays, so he had to get home before he seized up completely. But hey, even younger men would struggle in the same conditions. In Brontë's dreams he believed he looked younger than his fifty-plus years, but his body felt every one of them. He'd had a good weekend exploring the moors surrounding Whitby and running up and down the coast road between Scarborough and Staithes, but he had work in the morning which he couldn't miss; more's the pity. Whitby itself had been... entertaining. Brontë had not been prepared for Whitby Goth Weekend and the town had been crammed to the gunnels with alternative and mysterious humanoids. While there, he had sat outside a black and white fronted fish and chip restaurant, appropriately named *The Magpie*. He watched a myriad of weirdos passing by: goths, punks, steampunks, emos and even the occasional hippy caught in some sort of weird eternal time warp.

'What the chuff's an emo when it's at 'ome, anyway?' he asked his best buddy, a white mongrel dog called Obi-Wan Kenobi; Obi for short.

Obi understood every word the police officer said but he seldom responded. He mostly saw no need to do so. Obi stared silently back at his owner and tried to implant the image of a dog eating sausages into his head.

'They all look the bloody same to me.'

Brontë absently tossed a piece of battered sausage to his dog, he didn't know why he did this, he knew they were not good for the dog but sometimes he couldn't help himself. Brontë loved sausages almost as much as he loved his dog, his Monster and his wife, and not necessarily in that order obviously. He would happily have sausages for every meal and often did. Obi-Wan fixed his glare once again on his master, forcing him to unwittingly toss more sausage on the floor.

'Woof,' said the dog.

'Look at all that leather and naked flesh,' Brontë said through a mouthful of chips, 'and look at all them tattoos and piercings.'

Obi ignored him and chewed on his bit of sausage.

'High-heels, stockings, suspenders... and that's just the fellas,' he laughed at his own joke. Obi licked the last of the scraps from off the pavement.

The fish and chip restaurant overlooked the harbour and swing-bridge and an early evening sea-fret condensed on their respective beards. The two of them sat in silence watching the world go by and were as surprised as each other when they were harangued by two large women of an indeterminable age. Two big lasses, slarted in makeup, strapped into taught, creaking faux-leather basques which complimented skin-tight denim jeans that looked like they had been applied with a spray can. To be fair, 'compliment' is probably the wrong word, they didn't actually compliment anything.

'My God, look at them and the price of cod,' said Brontë, stuffing a slack handful of scraps into his mouth.

'Oi! What you gawkin at, grandad?'

'Don't know, love, label's dropped off,' laughed Brontë.

The semi-naked bachelorettes laughed out loud. The one Brontë thought looked truly terrifying, the one with an 'L' plate strapped to her ample backside, shouted back, 'Eh, come back with us, why don't ye, grandad? We've got a caravan up at Reighton Sands, we could really get it rockin'.' She shook her extensive bosoms at him.

'Eh! Don't shake your tic-tacs at me, you'll give yourself a black-eye.' He sounded confident with the women but he wasn't really; in fact they made him feel uneasy.

'I am not shaking 'em at you, granddad, it's your little mate with the white beard I fancy.' The two women screeched in delight at their wit.

Obi-Wan had always had been a babe magnet and normally Brontë would have been pleased with the attention, but not in this case. He was bloody horrified.

'Come on, Obi-Wan, let's hit the road.'

'What's wrong with ye, biker boy? You afraid of us little girls?'

'Too damn right, love,' he muttered under his breath.

Brontë opened his old wax duffle-bag and placed it on the quayside bench, Obi-Wan, jumped into the bag and curled up. Pulling the bag closed, Brontë threw it across his shoulders and Obi settled into the middle of his back.

'You all right back there, matey?'

'Woof,' said the bag.

He zipped up his knackered old leather Belstaff and kicked the Monster to life, pulled out into the traffic and disappeared down the road, waving to the women as he passed. They jeered at him and one waved an enormous inflatable penis in his general direction.

Now he was nearly home and looking forward to a hot bath and a cold beer.

***

The Worth Valley was stunningly beautiful in spring and summer but cold and wet in winter. Hewenden Bridge, on the wrong side of the valley, really took the biscuit, never having the benefit of sunshine; it was a dark, damp desolate hole, winter and summer. That night it was particularly dark, particularly damp and particularly cold. The village clung, by the skin of its teeth, to the leeward side of the Worth Valley, a mess of old stone cottages clutching to the hill for grim death, for all the world looking like an excavated skull poking out of an archaeological dig. The village's cobbled street glistened in its wetness like crooked teeth, the street lights glowing like satanic eyes in fleshless sockets.

Mickey Grimshaw skulked his way down the back ginnels and snickets of the village. He avoided the main street so that he couldn't be spotted in the orange street lighting.

As Micky snuck along the back alleys, he sensed the ghosts of the past around him, the phantoms of people who had wandered these cobbles down the centuries. Murderers and muggers as well as farmers and shepherds. Oh, and thieves, he thought to himself, don't forget the thieves. Mickey was in good company.

The idea of the ghosts would normally have driven Mickey scurrying back to his bedsit with his tail between his legs, but not tonight. It being Halloween the streets had been heaving with vampires, werewolves and the ubiquitous half-naked cats, but all the fancy-dressed revellers were long gone. Not back to crypts, coffins and tombs but to snug warm beds, wrapped up against the winter's chill. But not Mickey. Mickey Grimshaw was on a mission.

Making his way into the backyard he planned on, he avoided making any noise that would announce his arrival. He carefully tiptoed around a rusting coal scuttle and stepped gingerly over an old shovel. He stood and listened at the cottage's back door and was pleased he could hear no sound from within; the only things he could hear was his heart beating against his ribs and his breath rasping in his throat. He stood for a second to calm himself.

He knew the old guy that owned the house didn't lock doors and slept downstairs in the front room. He also knew the old guy drank on a night and would be asleep in front of the fire by now, but most of all Mickey knew the old guy had money. He knew about the money because the old paedo had offered him plenty for certain... favours. Mickey always refused to do what the man wanted. Always but once. That one lapse made Mickey sick with disgust; he'd sworn he would never do it again, ever. Never again anywhere, but particularly not in that smelly old house. Tonight, he was prepared to enter the house and appropriate more money without having to do anything in return. He felt he deserved it. Taking a deep breath, he pushed open the back door, which squeaked ever so slightly, and he crept into the darkness.

Once inside, the house was surprisingly darker and colder than the street and he waited to let his eyes get accustomed. There was no sound at all. The old pervert must have got himself off to sleep, he thought, which was exactly what Mickey had hoped and planned on. He made his way through a corridor of rubbish, being careful not to disturb anything as he went.

In the hall there was a large silver cross hanging on the wall, Mickey had seen this cross before and knew it was solid silver. Carefully he lifted it from its brass nail. It was so large he could only just manage to get it into the bag that he had brought to carry his swag.

He could see a light, probably from a TV, flickering under the door at the end of the hall that led into the living room. He stood behind it and listened, his heart going fifty to the dozen. He believed he could hear a gentle, hushed whispering, no more of a murmur. It must be the TV, he thought, or was it someone snoring? Slowly and quietly, he pushed open the door and entered the room, he sensed more than saw what seemed to be a dark figure kneeling in the corner by the settee. Kneeling over what looked like the naked body of the old pervert.

With a swoop of black cloak, the figure arose and swirled towards him. Black. Silent. Frightening. Mickey staggered backwards away from the horrifying scene and collided with a pile of videos and magazines, sending them crashing to the floor. The dark hooded monster reached out to grab Mickey with hands that were dripping with blood.

Mickey screamed.

He scrabbled and slid on the scattered video cases, frantically running for the door, crashing into and disturbing more towers of rubbish as he went. He was closely followed by the dark beast, its arms outstretched, grabbing at him with gory, clawed, red-dripping fingers.

'It's a fucking vampire!' he screamed, 'it's a fucking vampire!'

Mickey burst out into the backyard screaming with the full power of his lungs. He span around to see the nature of the devil on his tail. As the black shape crossed the threshold it burst into a hundred black, screeching banshees that flapped around Mickey, battering him with their wings and covering him with their guano.

The air was black with screaming creatures flapping around his head. He dropped his swag bag to the ground and in a mad panic fumbled around in it for the silver cross. The cross stuck in his bag and he screamed louder in fear and frustration; finally, he managed to wrench the cross from out of the bag and hold it up before him, batting the dark flying shapes as he shouted and screamed at them.

'Get thee behind me, Satan!'

Mickey turned tail and ran. He charged down the cobbles at full pelt and out on to the metalled road at the junction below, he was still screaming when he ran across the intersection, straight into the path of a taxi.

There was a squeal of breaks, the mad blaring of a horn, and the screeching of tyres. Mickey, struck by the car, was thrown ten feet on to the pavement when, finally and thankfully, there was silence. Mickey had, at long last, stopped screaming.

The cloaked figure dissolved into the dark.

Chapter Three

Haworth Village.
The first of November. All Saints' Day.

Obi-Wan woke early and the first thing he did, after saying 'white rabbits' that is, was struggle to make Brontë wake up. He had tried his old telepathy trick of influencing Brontë's thoughts with a mind meld, but it hadn't worked; Obi was an excellent transmitter but Brontë was a poor receptor. He tried placing the image of his master wetting the bed into Brontë's head but that hadn't worked either. In the end he had to resort to barking madly and running round in manic circles.

He was now having to force Brontë to take the walk from their Haworth cottage along Hewenden Viaduct. This was one of Obi's favourite walks. They didn't do it often, because it was quite a trek and Brontë had vertigo.

That morning the wind blew the rain horizontally across the top of the viaduct walls and blasted Brontë on the side of his head, filling his ear with water; Obi, however, being considerably shorter, was in the lee of the wall and was in complete comfort and had dry ears.

Brontë stopped at one point and looked out across the valley, but the swirling mist obliterated the view.

Usually, when the weather was clearer, the viaduct scared the living daylights out of him; being able to see the ground so far below made his head spin, his legs cramp up and his tummy turn to an anxious mush. In his youth Brontë had enjoyed potholing with his friends but avoided climbing like the plague. Brontë was afraid of nothing in his life other than heights, oh and women of course. He looked down at Obi, who was sitting impatiently, waiting for Brontë to get a move on.

'Come on then, mi old mucker, let's get back for breakfast.'

'Woof,' said the dog.

Brontë had got Obi from Bradford Rescue Centre sometime shortly after his wife left him and just after he realised she meant it, and wasn't coming back. It was at that point that Brontë realised he was no loner, and that he actually hated being alone. He found he needed a presence around him and Obi-Wan fitted the bill perfectly, but obviously not a patch on the wife. When he'd collected Obi from the rescue centre he was a six-month old mongrel who was a frightened little thing, wary of everybody and everything, but he soon took a shine to Brontë and Brontë to him.

'Come on then, ye' poor little bugger, let's get off 'ome.'

'You talking at yourself, funny man?' This voice took Brontë by surprise. He looked down at the dog.

'You said that without moving your lips.'

There was a laugh from behind him.

'Ha, ha, funny man.'

Brontë turned around. Behind him, running on the spot, was a diminutive, youngish woman of Japanese or Chinese descent. Well, she had a camera round her neck and olive eyes. She was wearing running gear and a weird bobble hat.

'I'm talking to the dog.'

'Does he answer?'

'No, but he's a good listener.'

'Ha, ha! What is way of Haworth, does he know this?'

'He does but he won't tell you unless you give him a treat.'

'I'm all out of treats.'

'Just keep running that way,' he pointed down the viaduct, 'you'll fall over it.'

'Woof.' Obi agreed.

She laughed and jogged off, waving and as she went. Brontë tried to tear his eyes from her bottom. Under her tight shorts it jiggled like two ferrets in a sack.

Dog and man returned to their small house, the small house that was decorated and furnished like an old ladies' cottage, which is exactly what it was: an old ladies' cottage, the old woman in this case being Brontë's mother, Irene. Irene had passed away, leaving the property to Brontë, her only son. She had died almost at the same time that Margaret left him; all in the space of one week, no wife and no mother. He had moved straight in, full kit and caboodle. He had nowhere else to go. The plan had been to do the house up, but he'd never got around to it, apart from buying some roles of woodchip and anaglypta wallpaper, which still resided, wrapped and untouched, in a corner of the lounge.

The main thing about the house for Brontë was that it had a reasonable garden and a fair-sized greenhouse: the garden for Obi to sit and think and the greenhouse for Brontë to sit and drink. The family home that Brontë and his wife had lived in prior to their separation was rented out as a holiday cottage.

On returning from the walk, Brontë and Obi-Wan made their way into the kitchen. Brontë stuck a pan of sausages over a low flame on the gas cooker and left them to slowly carbonise.

'Guard those sausages with your life, soldier.'

Obi sat to attention under the sausage pan.

With the sausages left in safe hands, Brontë took himself off upstairs for a shower and to get out of his dog-walking gear, which was exactly the same as his gardening gear, his sitting in the greenhouse drinking beer gear and his motorcycling gear. He was drying his hair when the smoke alarm went off.

Whar... whar! Whar... whar!

'Is that the sausages all done then?' Brontë shouted down the stairs.

'Woof.'

The smoke alarm wailed like a banshee.

Whar... whar! Whar... whar!

To add to the chaos, the front door flew open with a crash.

'Granddad! Granddad! We are on our way to school and Grandma's car's broke down.'

Whar... whar! Whar... whar!

Three kids, screaming their heads off with excitement, burst into the kitchen. Obi, barked loudly, spinning in circles, and ran amok among the children, trying to bite their heels and ankles as he did.

Margaret Brontë entered the kitchen, shouting with the full power of her lungs.

'Silence!'

Far from doing as instructed, the children started singing at the tops of their very impressive voices.

'Granddad's cooking. Granddad's cooking.

Call the engine. Call the engine.

Fire! Fire!

Fire! Fire!'

'Bloody hell, I'm living in a world ruled by chaos,' he called down the stairs, 'get Grandma to waft the bloody thing with a tea towel.'

The alarm screeched.

Whar... whar! Whar... whar!

The children sang.

'Fire! Fire! Fire! Fire!'

Brontë shouted. 'Waft the bloody thing, Margaret! Waft the thing!'

Margaret wafted the alarm franticly with a tea towel.

Obi ran around and barked along with the madness.

'Woof... woof.'

Whar... whar! Whar... whar!

'Fire! Fire... Fire! Fire!'

And then there was silence. As quick as it all had started it stopped. The dog, the children, the wife, but most of all the bloody smoke alarm. They all shut up.

'Thank the Lord,' said Brontë.

Margaret leant back against the Welsh dresser and wiped her brow with the tea towel.

'Granddad, can we take Obi down the garden?'

'You can if you can get him away from the sausages.'

The kids ran out into the back garden screaming and shouting, chased by Obi, who was trying to drown them out, and to be fair was succeeding.

'Do you want me to turn your sausage, Brontë?' Margaret shouted up the stairs.

'Well I thought we were divorced, but it seems rude to say no. You can come up and give it a quick twist before I get dressed.'

'Keep your voice down and don't be so rude.'

When Brontë was dressed and back downstairs, the kids and Obi were tucking into sausages.

'Hey, little dudes!'

'Hey, big dude!'

'Those are my sausages.'

'Grandma said you wouldn't mind.'

'Oh, did she?' he turned to Obi. 'Fine guard dog you turned out to be.'

Obi ignored him. He was too busy eating sausages.

'Granddad, Obi was licking my face, he's so cute.'

'You wouldn't say that if you'd just seen him eating his own puke.'

'Eeerrrgghhh! Granddad!'

'Don't say "eats puke" in front of the children, Charlie.'

'So that damn car's broken down again?' he said changing the subject.

'Yes, I need the other one to get the kids to school.'

'By the other one, you mean mine? Which means I'll have to go to work on the bike.'

'So?'

'So! I'll get piss wet through.'

'Don't swear, Charlie.'

'Grandma, Granddad said "piss".'

'You kids can go put your waterproofs on.'

'Why don't I take the kids?'

'Cos, I want you to drop some stuff off at the holiday cottage. Some flowers and a bottle of wine, and give it a quick once-over, see if the cleaner's done her job this week. There's a lady arriving tonight; I want everything to be spick and span.'

'And there's me thinking we're divorced.'

'You know very well we are separated, not divorced, so you still have obligations. Oh, and by the way I may need the car for the whole week depending on what mine needs doing to it.'

'It's not *the car*, like it's ours; it's *my car* like it's mine.'

'Your mother always said you were no good at sharing. It's cos you were an only child.'

'If we're sharing and you get the car, what do I get out of it?'

'You, Charlie boy, get the privilege of escorting me to the parsonage for a lecture on "the Personification of the Brontë Moorland".'

'Oh God, why me!?'

'Because no one else will come with me.'

'No one in their right mind would. I have things to do, anyway.'

'Like sit around in your greenhouse with your mangy pooch and drink yourself stupid?'

'Come on, you know I hate the Brontë sisters. Isn't there anyone else? What about one of the daughters?'

'It's Bonfire Night. They're taking the kids to a fire in the park. Speaking of which,' she stood, 'come on kids, it's time to get you in the car. You're going to be late.'

They went out to the car, the kids shouting, strangely dancing and pulling even stranger faces. Brontë ran after Margaret, beseeching her, and Obi ran from one to the other, barking happily. As they drove off, Margaret slowed and spoke through the open window.

'Here's the flowers and wine,' she handed the items over. 'Just make sure everything looks welcoming. Have you got your key?'

He held his keys up as evidence.

'Aye, aye, captain.'

'Granddad, does Obi really eat his own puke?'

'Sadly, he does, my love, yes.'

'Why?'

'I don't know. perhaps he needs at least one hot meal a day.'

'Eeerrrgghhh! Granddad!'

*

Further down the valley, in Keighley Royal Infirmary, Mickey Grimshaw had spent an uncomfortable night on the Medical Assessment Unit, but at last had dropped off into a restless sleep, his dreams filled with bats and hooded beasts. The taxi had caused very little damage, just a broken leg and a few broken ribs. He'd live. Mickey had been sedated on arrival at the hospital, not because he'd been in so much pain but because he was in such distress.

Sergeant Jennifer Pepper walked up to the nurses' station and flashed her ID.

'I believe you have one Michael Grimshaw here. You phoned us about him.'

'Thank God,' said a fat, blonde nurse, who was sitting drinking coffee and typing on her phone, 'I hope you've come to take him away?'

'Is he badly hurt?'

'Nah, 'e's getting better all the time. Trouble is, the better he gets, the louder he gets.'

'Aggressive?'

'No, he's just a right royal pain in the intergluteal cleft.'

Pepper raised her eyebrows at her.

'Arse, love. He's a pain in the bloody arse. Blathering on about vampire bats, bloodsuckers and the undead. He's like a stuck record. He's down there,' she gesticulated with her phone, 'second on the right.' She went straight back to her social media account.

The police officer turned and followed the instructions and soon fetched up at Mickey's bedside. Mickey lay there, his face to the wall and his back to the world. It seemed now he had decided that to keep schtum was his best course of action. He wasn't saying anything to anyone any more.

'Michael Grimshaw, isn't it?'

'Who wants to know?'

'Well, I do, Michael.'

'It's Mickey.'

'In that case, I do, Mickey.'

'And who are you, when you're at 'ome?'

'Me, Mickey? I'm Sergeant Pepper.'

'Where's your band, then?'

'Band?'

'You know, the Lonely-Hearts Club,' Mickey laughed at his own mesmerising wit.

'Sorry, don't get it.'

'You know... oh never mind.'

She sat on the edge of his bed. He still kept his back to her.

'I'm from the police, Mickey love. And I've come here to find out what happened to you last night?'

'I was mowed down by a chuffin' taxi that's what, and I want bloody compo.'

'You ran straight out in front of it, Mickey love.'

'Bollocks. He ran me over.'

'I have witnesses. Two ladies from the WI inside the taxi.'

He turned on the bed to look at her.

'The taxi mowed me down.'

Pepper started poking around his bedside locker.

'Bless you, love. You're not telling me the ladies of the Hewenden Bridge Women's Institute tell porky pies, are you?'

'You're calling me a liar?'

'Yes love, you wouldn't know the truth if it jumped up and bit you on your skinny behind.'

'You'll get nowt out of me.'

Pepper pulled the silver cross from his swag bag.

'Leave that stuff alone it's mine. You need a warrant for that, I know my rights.'

'Where'd you get it from, Mickey?' she inspected the cross. 'It's nice.'

'I found it.'

'Yeah, like I haven't heard that one before.'

'I didn't kill 'im.'

Sergeant Pepper turned and looked at him.

'What!?'

'He was already dead before I broke in, I found him like that.'

'I'm sorry, love, what the hell you on about?'

'It were the vampire what killed 'im.'

'Have they been giving you morphine, Micky love?'

'I'm tellin' ye, the old guy was dead on the floor, covered in blood, the vampire was crouching over 'im.'

'A vampire?'

'Aye, and it came after me. Big long black cloak, shiny white skin. Chased me out the bloody house, it did. Big black bugger, surrounded by 'undreds of flapping bats.'

'You said it was white.'

'White skin long black cape. It were terrifying.'

Pepper dialled a number into her phone.

'Rhiaz... get me a uniform down here as quick as you can. I want someone sitting with a certain Mickey Grimshaw until I get back, I don't want him sneaking off anywhere. When you've done that I want you to meet me up at...' turning to, Mickey, 'what's the address?'

'Railway Cottage, Main Street.'

Pepper spoke back into the phone. 'Rhiaz, get yourself to Hewenden Bridge, up the cobbles, Railway Cottage. Soon as the uniform gets here, I'll be on my way to join you.'

She turned back to Mickey.

'So, Mickey, about this... intruder?'

'Vampire!'

'Vampire, right...' She snapped her fingers. 'Hang on a minute, that's why you had the cross.'

'Nah, I wasn't expecting no vampire. You were right first off, I nicked the cross.'

*

Brontë parked the Monster by the holiday cottage on Moon Street, the house where he and Margaret had spent much of their married life and where they had, in Brontë's words, 'dragged the kids up'.

Margaret ran the cottage as a holiday home which just about paid for the apartment she rented in Wadsworth. Going to the back door, Brontë let himself into the kitchen. He swung his duffle-bag, which smelt strongly of dog, on to the kitchen top and produced a bottle of wine, which he placed in a basket on the table, and a bunch of flowers he stuck in a vase on the drainer. Most of the flower heads have been ripped off due to the blooms sticking out of the top of the bag as he rode there on the bike, mostly bare stalks stuck out of the top of the vase. He filled it with water anyway, the missus would never know, and carried it through the hall to the lounge.

At that precise moment a naked woman stepped out of the downstairs bathroom.

The woman clocked Brontë and Brontë clocked the woman. They froze. There was a brief shocked silence before all hell broke loose.

The naked lady screamed, threw her towel over her head and screamed some more. Brontë, completely flummoxed by the whole palaver and not being entirely sure what to do, screamed right back at her. This spurred the women into action, she took flight down the hall, screaming some more as she went. She slipped dramatically on the hall rug, causing her to perform the splits and almost straddle the hall table as she surfed passed. She only managed to save herself from falling by snatching hold of the banister rails and spinning herself back on to her feet and completing an almost perfect handspring on to the stairs.

Brontë, by what instinct he knew not, gave chase. This was probably, no definitely, the worst thing in the world he could have done. The woman screamed some more and regaining her balance after the rug slide and gymnastics, she picked up speed and hit the staircase at full tilt. Taking the steps three at a time, with her hand holding the towel tightly over her head, she disappeared up the stairs.

Even though Brontë was in severe shock, he realised somewhere deep inside that something was wrong. He wasn't complaining though, with the woman focused on keeping her face covered it left all the more interesting bits on view.

He ran after her shouting. 'It's all right! It's all right!'

Halfway up the stairs he thought better of chasing a naked woman while shouting at her at the top of his voice. He stopped.

'You from viaduct, you follow me. You go away. I call police.'

'It's OK, I am the police.'

'What the hecks?'

'I am the police.'

The woman crouched on the landing and hid her nakedness behind the balustrade. She was breathing heavily.

'What on earths police wants with me for?'

'Well I'm not really the police...'

She screamed again.

'No listen! I am the police but not right at this moment. At the moment I'm the owner of this house. I'm not on official police business. I came to sort the house out, look, I brought flowers.' He showed the flowers as evidence.

'I no want flowers.'

'No, I brought flowers for the house, for the next quests. For you, if that's who you are. You're early. You're not meant to be here until tonight.'

There was a pause.

'Show me IDs.'

After he'd fumbled through his pocket, Brontë threw his warrant card up the stairs.

'What police wanting with me?'

'The police want nothing with you. I just want you to come down.'

'No way I come down. Police or no police.'

'I want to explain... and apologise.'

'You wait there, Inspector Policeman.'

She tossed the warrant card back down the stairs.

'I put on clothes. You see too much already'

*

Brontë sat in the cottage kitchen, drinking coffee with the woman he had just chased bare-arsed naked down the hall. They were both embarrassed. He observed her as they talked. She was very slim, small and beautiful, and as it turned out she was indeed Japanese.

She spelt out her name to him.

'Y-U-M-I.'

'Yummy?'

'No,' she laughed, 'my name sound like "you-me". It means beautiful.'

Perfectly apt, thought Brontë.

'I from University Yokohama, studying lives and works of British writers.'

Her long black hair was now dry, and she was dressed in faded blue denim dungarees, a plain white t-shirt and flip-flops. Brontë struggled to keep the image of her naked body out of his mind but he knew the image would be tattooed there forever. They'd have to bleach his brain to remove it.

'You're here to study the Brontë sisters?'

'Yes, but I end up myself being studied by a Brontë, that very funny.'

Brontë actually blushed like a teenager. 'You weren't meant to be here till later.'

'I rigid bored in Stratford, I like be here, now. Forget about earlier please, I no care you see me. It all over now. How come you called Brontë? You descendants?'

'Not that anyone knows about.'

'You name Brontë and you live Haworth; very funny.'

'You want to hear the best of it, my first name's Charles, or Charlie. When I was a kid my mates called me Charlotte.'

She threw her head back and laughed. Brontë had once again to chase the thought of a few minutes ago from out of his head.

'I like that, I will too call you Charlotte.'

Brontë thought to himself, *my dear, if it keeps you smiling at me like that, you can call me what the chuff you want.*

'Charlotte it is, then.'

He saluted her with his coffee mug.

'Brontë very funny name, no sound English.'

'That's 'cos it's not, it's Irish.'

'You are Irish?'

'Not me. Family probably were,' he pointed behind him, 'way, way back.'

*

Detective Constable Mohammed Rhiaz Khan parked in the top car park and set off to meet his sergeant. Passing the post office, he read the Hewenden Echo billboard

'Allotment Holder Bit by Adder'. *They're weird up here in the outer villages*, he thought, he didn't get them at all. There was only himself and close family that were really all right, and sometimes he wasn't that sure about them either. He arrived at the address and stood on the worn stone doorstep of Nigel Flett's house and waited patiently for backup. He'd been told there was a possibility that there was a body in the house and not to enter; well, there was certainly no fear of that. Rhiaz had never seen a dead body before and he wasn't going to go in on his own. Some support would need to arrive before he would set foot in the property.

Backup, when it did arrive some minutes later, was in the form of Sergeant Pepper, and this pleased Rhiaz no end. He liked Pepper. She was good natured and wasn't racist, which was surprising in the police. He liked the way she treated him just like she treated everyone else, with complete and utter irreverence.

Pepper had called him from the hospital, told him to meet her at this address and had given him very little else, something about a traffic accident and a burglar. The burglar had claimed there had been a murder at the property. Pepper had laughed when she said it was some sort of an occult killing, a vampire she'd said. She had treated the story with complete contempt and told Rhiaz to secure the place, not to enter and wait for either her or the inspector. Too damn right.

With a name like Jennifer Pepper and being a sergeant in the police and all, Pepper's nickname should have been pretty well nailed on, and initially that had been the case. Colleagues tried to get a rise out of her with innuendos involving the Beatles and Lonely Hearts. After a bit they realised it was just like water off a duck's back to her so they gave up. Her colleagues abandoned all thoughts of nicknames, until that is some wit came up with, *Yorkshire Puddin'*! An ominous day in the annals of Yorkshire Police folklore.

A great big Liverpudlian rugger-bugger rather foolishly referred to her as the *Yorkshire Puddin'* when Pepper was within ear shot. The canteen had gone deadly silent. With one effortless karate kick to the back of his legs, Pepper had dropped the offender down on to his knees. Another to the chest sent him arse over elbows and flat on to his back.

'Stay there, mate,' she'd said. 'Stay exactly where you are until I leave the room.'

The felled officer looked like he was considering his options.

'Don't even think about, buddy. You try get up off that fat arse of yours before I walk out of that door and you'll receive the same but this time to your head.'

No one called Pepper *Yorkshire Puddin'* ever again, they just stuck to Pepper. But sometimes, when she wasn't around and were sure there was no chance she'd turn up, they rather affectionately referred to her as *The Karate Kid*.

It's a shame she would never know; she would have loved it.

*

DC Khan watched Pepper's battered Astra estate pull up on to the cobbles, hazard lights flashing.

'Morning.'

'Morning, Sarge.'

'You looked inside yet?'

'Hell no. I was waiting for you, Sarge.'

She climbed out of the car.

'Oh no my little dusky friend, after you,' she gestured to the door, 'I insist.'

Rhiaz, knocked on the peeling door but leapt back out of the way as if he expected Christopher Lee himself to come flapping out.

'Doesn't sound like there's anybody in,' he said to Pepper.

'Well, no one alive at any rate.'

'Do you think we really should go in?'

'Oh yes.'

'We can't just walk in. We don't have a warrant.'

Pepper cupped her ear with her hand.

'Hark, is that the call of distress, I hear?' She pushed the door handle down and the door swung open. 'See it's open already. After you, Constable.'

Rhiaz warily pushed the door a little further ajar and peered into the dark. He could see nothing, so he stuck his head into the room, his legs shaking, his feet ready to run at any sign of movement.

'My God, it pongs a bit.'

'What of?'

'A zoo?'

'Stop showing off, Rhiaz, you've never even been to a zoo,' she stepped forward. ''Ere let's 'ave a whiff.'

'What is it?'

'Ah ha, smell that sweet, metallic stench.'

'Yes, sort of underneath the animal smells.'

'That, my little friend, is the unmistakeable smell of blood. It smells like iron.'

As well as never having been to a zoo, Rhiaz had never smelled iron either, but he remembered the taste of blood from being a child. The thought made him gip.

'Tell me this is not happening.'

'Rhiaz, me old chum, this is not happening.'

'I don't believe you, Sarge.'

Pepper stepped past him and stood in the doorway.

'Jesus H Christ!'

They found Nigel lying in a pool of blood.

'Rhiaz, you call scene of crimes. It's time I called the Gaffa.'

She pulled her phone from her pocket and stabbed at the buttons with a stubby finger.

'He's not going to be happy. In fact, he's going to be very upset.'

'Why upset?'

'Detective Inspector Brontë is not overly fond of dead bodies.'

*

Brontë left the beautiful Yumi in the cottage and was just about to throw his leg over the Monster when his mobile phone rang. Brontë had a lifelong hatred of all things affectatious, until it came down to his much-loved mobile phone. Brontë loved his phone. He hated computers, thought they were at best a necessary evil, he hated games consoles and all that other irrelevant stuff people had, but he loved his phone. He couldn't believe someone had invented something so gob-smackingly perfect. As a child he was nuts about secret agents, he was mad about *The Man from U.N.C.L.E* and 'Double-Oh-Seven'. He envied them their gadgets: their radios, cameras and all the other spy paraphernalia.

Then, when he'd got to the ripe old age of fifty, the things he coveted and prayed for as a child he had all his very own. His phone was a walky-talky, a camera, a satnav, a TV and more, oh so much more. The only two things his phone could not do was open a tin of beans and remove boy scouts from horses' hoofs. This was fine by Brontë. He didn't have a horse and beans cans now opened with ring pulls. He had set a custom ringtone on this much prized possession; whenever anyone called it rang out with the James Bond theme tune, which is exactly what it did then.

Dum-Der-De-Dum-Dum-Dum...

The ringtone stopped as he thumbed the answer button and put the phone to his ear.

'Hello!' said the phone. 'Is that Brontë? Charles Brontë? Double-oh-five and a half; licenced to thrill?'

'You're not funny, Pepper'

'So, why's Rhiaz laughing?'

'Cos he's got some bizarre, Asian sense of humour thing going on that no one else understands. What's happened?'

'We've got us a weird one.'

'Yeah, I can hear him giggling.'

'Nope, a lot weirder than Rhiaz.'

'Where are you?'

'Hewenden Bridge'

'No wonder it's weird.'

'You need to come over.'

'Look, Margaret has stolen the car for the foreseeable future so I'm on the Monster, I'm dropping it off at KickStart Bobs. Pick me up there in about twenty minutes.'

'I'm not your bleedin' taxi.'

'No, you're my bleedin' sergeant, and a sergeant with wheels at that, so come and get me.'

The phone went dead.

*

Brontë roared over the moors and let the bike have her head as he hit the aptly named *Mad Mile*, a notorious mile of twisting road where drivers and riders alike went mad. A mile of winding road where people pushed themselves and their vehicles to their limits and risked life and limb trying to get a 'ton-up' on the snaking bit of highway. Brontë, screwed the throttle back and the Monster's speed gauge crept up. He had never managed the hundred miles per hour of his dreams, he was lucky to get it up towards the nineties before he hit the last bend and had to slow sharpish before he lost control on the negative camber. Today he got to eighty-five before he bottled it. He turned the bike into a stone courtyard under the arches of Hewenden Viaduct and pulled up under a big sign depicting a manically grinning leprechaun astride an extravagant chopper. Below the graphic a banner that proclaimed proudly, *KickStart Bob – Motorcycle Mechanic.*

Dexy's Midnight Runners' *Come on Eileen* belted out of a little garage where the manic leprechaun himself was franticly working on a chopped Harley Davison Fat Boy. Brontë had been seeing this Romany bike mechanic for years now but still rarely understood a word he said.

'You all right, Bob?'

'Feck yeh, you all righ yessen, 'Spector, wha's tha' feckin' crack wid ye en whey?'

The Irish sounding words shot out of the mechanic's mouth like bullets from a gatling gun. All blurring into one long stream of an unfathomable, unintelligible diatribe. Brontë assumed he'd asked him how the bike was.

'I've a slack clutch cable. Gears keep slipping?'

'Feck nell, Charlie, am snow dunder as tis an the feckin' wife jus gonnan pissed off wida scoota-boy wi-outa bloody tank you very much nor nuthin'. Won minit she wars ear, an' nexed, dare she feckin' was... gone! To be 'onest wids ye. Me 'ead's up me feckin' 'ars.'

Brontë just stared at Bob.

KickStart Bob pulled on the clutch lever two or three times and Brontë noticed the grease-covered tattoos running down his arms, one depicting a chimpanzee wielding a wrench, with the label *Grease Monkey*, and the other a fist seemingly punching its way out through the biker's skin, encircled with the words, *Irish Bare-Knuckle Boxing*. Yet the most disconcerting of all his tattoos were not on his arms at all. He sported a single tattooed tear dripping from the corner of his right eye, the eye that never stopped twitching.

'I doughnut half much time ye nose, 'Spector,' he rubbed his forehead leaving behind a generous smear of grease, 'hive sex bikes 'ear hall ready weighting four work.'

Brontë so completely flummoxed by the unintelligible language could do nothing but look back at the mechanic and smile.

'You're an 'ard man, 'Spector.' He sucked his teeth. 'Juice leaf eat 'ear, 'arm naught pro massing no tin mind ye an' hive naught four you to ride while it sits 'ear neaver.'

'My erm... my mate's picking me up anytime now.'

'Ham ate, eh!? Feck nell, I wish I had a feckin' mate. All I have is this dump of a garidge and a feckin' wife that's feckin' fecked off.'

Pepper pulled the Astra up beside the bikes and climbed out, reealing plenty of thigh, as she did. KickStart Bob was seriously impressed, which showed across his whiskered face.

'Sweet Mary mother of Jesus! Is that ye feckin' mate?

'I'm not his mate, I'm his colleague.'

'I wish the feck Ida colleague like you, love; you could help with greasing me nuts, any day.'

'You call me "love" again and I'll whip the buggers off for you. OK? It's Sergeant Pepper to you.'

'A Lonely Heart eh? I could keep you from being lonely, lo—' he managed to stop before he had repeated the offensive word.

'If I had a pound...' the rest of the sentence was lost as she followed Brontë back into the Astra, shaking her head.

She wound her window down and called after Bob.

'When will you have it ready?'

'Toddy... wither liddle help from me friends.'

'You're not funny.'

She drove off leaving KickStart singing 'With A Little Help From My Friends' at the top of his voice using his spanner as a microphone.

*

The battered Astra pulled up on to Cobbles. Brontë and Pepper climbed out and Pepper entered the dark, musty house through the back door into the kitchen.

Brontë took a deep breath and followed her in, looking around and taking in the surroundings.

'Makes Chez Brontë look like a palace.'

'The guy was a regular hoarder. There's piles of crap everywhere.'

'So, what we got? Young Mickey Grimshaw targets the house, thinks it's easy pickings, sneaks in and makes straight for the family silver.'

'Yup, he claims he'd just got started when he heard an unearthly scream from hell and he almost tripped over what he calls a "vampire", kneeling over the fat naked guy.'

'Vampire?'

'Blood-stained mouth, fangs, the works, and the victim with two bleeding puncture holes in the neck.'

'Ridiculous.'

'That's his story and 'e's sticking to it. A real live vampire.'

'If it were real and a vampire, it wouldn't be "live" now would it? It would be undead.'

'Smartarse.'

'Does Mr Grimshaw do drugs?'

'No hallucinogens that he admits to. He has a bit of previous for weed, but says he wasn't toasted last night.'

Brontë lifted an eyebrow.

'Inebriated,' she explained.

'So, according to Mickey, he was chased out of the house by the Prince of Darkness and followed by a cloud of bats.'

'Which turned out to be starlings... we think.'

'I'm sorry?'

'The house is a complete wreck, boss. For years it's been left to fall into rack and ruin. Look here, ivy's taken over half the ground floor and starlings have started to roost in it. Seems Mickey disturbed them, they took flight and chased him out the house when he fled.'

'Not bats?'

'No bats.'

They stepped through into the dining room.

'So maybe there's no vampire neither. Let's see, it could have been our victim who disturbed Mickey as he rifled through his drawers, so to speak, and so Mickey did him in to shut him up.'

A noise from the sofa distracted the officers and a great black shape loomed up out of the shadows. Brontë jumped back in horror.

'Sweaty Norrocks!'

'Morning, Brontë,' said the monstrous black shape.

'Bloody hell, you almost gave me a heart attack.'

'Well thanks for that, nice to see you too.'

'Sorry,' interrupted Pepper, 'I forgot to say the pathologists and scene of crimes had arrived.'

The heads of two masked SOCO officers appeared above the back of the sofa. They waved cheerily and called out in unison.

'Hiya!'

Carol Redman, the pathologist, had a bright, red lipsticked mouth, long black hair, black leather coat and red patent leather Dr Martens. She played lip service to protocol by wearing blue latex gloves, which only just covered glaringly red acrylic nails.

'I like the new barrier clothing.'

'You'll have to excuse my attire, I'm not meant to be working today. You don't normally catch me in my civies.'

'You got cause of death yet?'

'I'll know that when I have him back on the slab.'

'Anything to go on at all?'

'Just a general observation… It looks like he's had his penis cut off. I have done no real exploratory investigation; it looks rather unsavoury down there.'

'How long?'

'I can't say, like I said it's missing.'

'How long's he been dead, smart arse?'

'What is it about "when I have him back on the slab" that you find so difficult to comprehend?'

'So that's all you have? Well thanks a bunch for bloody nothing.'

She stood and looked at him for a while, her hands on her hips.

'There's two puncture marks,' she gestured to her neck, 'just here next to the jugular.'

Brontë and Pepper exchanged looks.

'Stupid question,' said Pepper, 'but the wounds to the neck…' She broke off unsure how to go on.

'Go on,' encouraged the pathologist.

'They're not a bite, are they?'

'A bite as in bloodsuckers, Sergeant? Tell me you don't believe in the…' she affected false fangs with her trigger fingers, 'undead?' She grinned at the police officer.

'No, but could it be an animal or something?'

'Can't say, sorry, not until he's back on the slab.'

Brontë stepped a little closer to the body and pointed down at the face and pushed a curl of greasy hair aside with his pen.

'What you playing at, Brontë?'

'Er, hello, I didn't touch anything, I'm keeping my dirty great mitts off your evidence, see, I'm using my pen.'

'He's seen it on the telly. Barnaby's always doing it,' explained Pepper.

'That's ok on the bloody telly, but here it's spreading crap all over my crime scene.'

'Look here.' He pointed with his pen.

The coroner and police officers gathered a little closer around the body.

'There's blood all around the mouth. Are we assuming they cut his tongue out too?'

'I opened his mouth, there are lose flaps of skin inside the cavity.'

'So, they've taken his tongue as well as his little fella.'

'You'll have to wait till—'

Brontë and Pepper spoke together. '...You've got him back on the slab?'

'Hey, you guys catch on quick. Right, Brontë, the body's ready to be shipped back to the lab and the SOCO guys are ready to start packing up the evidence. So, if you've finished with me, I'll be seeing you.'

'Yup, the sooner you're back the closer I'll be to getting some answers, oh and tell your team when they're bagging and tagging to keep a look out for this guy's dick.'

'Right, I shall be on my merry way,' she moved towards the door. 'By the way, have you noticed his socks.'

'His socks?'

'White ankle socks, the mark of a kiddy-fiddler if ever there was one. Take my word for it, Brontë. See you soon.'

'Soon?'

'Oh, this won't be the last, believe me. Not by a long chalk.'

And with a swish of black leather and a waft of patchouli oil, she was gone.

'Why is everyone in Hewenden Bridge so weird?'

'They migrate here from all over the country. They come for the magic mushrooms and never leave. But she's not your straightforward Hewenden Bridger.

'I'm lost'

'Hewenden Bridgers are marked on a scale of how weird they are, a bit like grading pencils. First there's HB, that's just your straightforward Hewenden Bridger, just your normal everyday hippy type. The next level of weirdness up are the VHB: Very Hewenden Bridge. Right up to UHB: Ultra Hewenden Bridge. Dr Carol is your proverbial UHB.'

'What does that make me then?'

'Out of your depth, Brontë. Always out of your bloody depth.'

*

Brontë, Pepper and Rhiaz, now dressed in appropriate barrier clothing, sifted through the piles of rubbish that the obsessive-compulsive victim had hoarded over the years.

'It's a thankless task,' moaned Rhiaz, 'we're going to be hours at this rate. It's a long enough job at the best of times but with the amount of stuff that's here it's going to take forever. Biggest problem is though, it's all pornography, it's disgusting...'

'My God! Look at the size of that thing and the price of haddock,' Pepper held up the centrefold of some magazine called *Stallion*.

Brontë and Rhiaz stared at her.

'Pepper! We have an impressionable young constable with us.' Admonished the Inspector as Rhiaz squinted at the mag over her shoulder.

'Nobody should be seen in that state by anyone other than their partner and even then, only with the lights out.'

'What's all the fuss about? Every bloke's got one; it's no big deal.'

Pepper was still holding the mag up and scrutinising it from different angles.

'I'll tell you what all the fuss is about, just look at the size of that bloody thing.'

'I'd rather not, thank you, and I don't think you should, Rhiaz, either, unless you are a lot better off in that department than the rest of us. It will only give you an inferiority complex.'

'This guy would give *Red Rum* an inferiority complex.'

'What would your boyfriend say, Pepper? If he knew you were looking at that with such a salacious grin on your face.'

'Say? He can say what the chuff he wants. He won't be my boyfriend much longer, I can tell you. Not now I know there's guys out there walking around with these bad boys nestled in their under-crackers. Have either of you...?'

'Don't even try to discuss with me what I may or may not have in my underwear'

Pepper began to study another mag. 'I was going to say have you ever tried anything like that?' Laughing, she showed them the picture.

'I never would try anything like that with Mrs Rhiaz, she'd have a dickey-fit.'

'And if I did, I wouldn't be able to swing my leg over my saddle for a month.'

They worked on through the pile of stuff, sneezing from the dust and sometimes retching from the smells.

'You know this is making me gip. It's disgusting,' Pepper protested.

'Shouldn't we have contamination suits on, or at the very least be wearing masks, boss?'

'Now what the bejesus is this?'

Brontë pulled a pile of letters from an old Jacobs Cream Crackers tin.

'If I know this guy,' moaned Rhiaz, 'they could only be French letters.'

'And probably used,' added Pepper.

'Now how weird is that?' said Brontë. 'How very bloody weird is that?'

'Well? Don't leave us in suspenders. What is it?'

'Letters, letters addressed to this house.'

Brontë sat on the floor and leafed his way through them. 'All from the same place, all with the same frank from the same institution.'

'Where?'

'You wouldn't believe it.'

'Try me.'

'They're all from America. All from a certain North Carolina Institution.'

'What institution?'

'The Raleigh Corrective Institute for Women.'

'An American prison?'

'Not just from an American prison, Rhiaz me old chum, these have all come from death row.'

The officers looked from one to another for a couple of seconds.

'Bloody hell!' said Pepper. 'You couldn't make this shit up.'

'What do they say?'

'We won't start going through stuff now, bag it, tag it and move on.'

They worked for a considerable time bagging very few items and discarding the majority. This was usually a job for scene of crimes officers, but these were unprecedented circumstances. Never had so much to be done by so few.

'OK, you guys, that's enough. We'll get a squad-car to cart this back to the incident room.'

Constable Rhiaz made his way across the room and stopped at the door.

'Sir!' Rhiaz gestured to a silver buttoned uniform hung from the back of the door that led to the upstairs. 'What's this, did he work on the buses?'

'What is it?' asked Brontë. 'A bus conductor's?'

'For God's sake, people don't wear uniforms like that anymore,' exclaimed Pepper. 'When was the last time you were on a bus?'

'I hate buses, you have to mix with other people,' confessed Rhiaz.

'What is it then?'

'Is it a railway man's uniform.'

'Well, I have been on a train recently and they don't dress a bit like that, either.'

'They did in the 1930s.'

Brontë snapped his fingers. 'The Hewenden Valley Heritage Steam Railway.'

The penny dropped for Rhiaz too.

'He's a volunteer at the steam railway.'

'Looks like it.'

'I think we should take a trip down memory lane and have a chat with them big boys down there playing at trains.'

*

As the officers left the cottage, Brontë flung open the cottage's front door and knocked a figure off the step, sending it staggering on to the cobbles.

'What the fuck!' said Brontë.

Pepper leapt out on to the stone sets and grabbed the figure by the scruff of the neck.

'Ok, fella! What you doin' skulking around on bloody doorsteps, eh?' She immediately realised who and what she was manhandling. She let go of the collar and stepped back. 'Forgive me, Father.'

'Why's that, young lady, have you sinned?' said the man fully attired in priest's robes, dog collar and all.

'No, no. Just nearly knocked you flat on your ar— well anyway. Can we help you, Father?'

'I shouldn't really be here. I mean, I should really come back at a more appropriate time.'

'Don't worry yourself, Father. What can we do for you?'

The priest turned to walk away but stopped and hesitated.

'I didn't know Nigel had family.'

'We're not family, Father. We're police?'

'The police… well, well! My goodness… just imagine…'

'Yes, just imagine.'

'No, no, you see. Well, I heard that there had been some trouble and wondered… well, if I could be of any help to Nigel.'

He's prattling, thought Brontë.

'Nigel what Father? Nigel... erm?'

'Oh, Flett, Nigel Flett.'

'And did you have the honour of knowing Nigel Flett, Father?'

'Did I know him?

'Yes, Father, did you know Nigel Flett?'

'Oh dear, has something terrible happened?'

Pepper stood forward.

'I'm sorry, why should something have happened?' she asked.

'Your... erm... your colleague, he said "did" I know him, not "do" I know him.'

'Well, did you, Father?'

'I wouldn't say I knew him... he was just one of my flock. Ha, ha, yes, one of my recalcitrant flock.'

'Like the starlings eh, Father?'

'Ah, yes. Very funny. See what you mean... very funny yes. The poor creatures in the ivy. Well, time I was off. No rest for the wicked, eh? Not that I am wicked. Ha, ha. Well goodbye now.'

Pepper followed him a few steps up the road.

'Father, where can we get in touch with you? If we need to talk again.'

'I can't see that being necessary, erm... Constable?'

'Sergeant, Sergeant Pepper. Your local knowledge might be invaluable.'

'St Michael the Martyr's, up at the top of the cobbles.'

'And your name?'

'Father Patrick. Patrick Murphy.' He laughed. 'And I'm not even Irish. Well, I'll be seeing you.'

'Oh, you will, Father.' Brontë smiled. 'I am sure you will.'

*

The three police officers crossed the coal yard of Hewenden Bridge Railway Station and wended their way through piles of coal, coke and random engine parts. They made their way towards an old, Pullman railway carriage, which had been unsympathetically converted into an office cum shed.

'Isn't this where they filmed that Jenny Agutter film?' asked Rhiaz.

'*The Railway Children*? Yeah, some of it, mostly in Haworth, though just up the track.'

'I was in that film.'

The two officers looked at Brontë.

'Bollocks!' they said in unison.

'I can tell you I was.'

'You were in a film with Jenny Agutter?'

'I was, yes.'

'What the hell were you? The station master's cat?'

They laughed at Brontë.

'I'll have you know I was one of the lads playing hare and hounds.'

'Playing what!?'

'Christ, you kids. If you can't play it on a screen you're not interested. Hare and hounds, it's a paper chase. The hare runs off leaving a trail of paper and the hounds have to catch him before he reaches his destination. It's a running game.'

'Well,' said Pepper, 'there you are then.'

'There you are then,' echoed Brontë, 'me and the other runners were a bit disappointed cos she never got her tits out.'

Pepper choked.

'For Christ's sake, Brontë, she was only about eleven.'

'Ah well that's where you are wrong, smarty pants. I was a teenager and she was older than me. I remember quite well the films she's made where she did flash her boobs about, but not *The Railway Children* I'm afraid.'

'Do you know, that's the problem with you fellas, you can never remember important stuff like wedding anniversaries but never forget the first time you got an eye full of some women's breasts.'

They walked on in silence.

'Ok, that's enough; I know exactly what you're thinking. Just stop it, OK?'

'Actually,' said Brontë, 'you accuse me falsely. I was thinking of nothing other than Bernard Cribbins.'

'You're a weird old bugger, Brontë.'

'You got me bang to rights, Pepper,' admitted Rhiaz. 'I have to be honest, I was thinking of boobies.'

They entered the carriage through an open door, above which swung a sign, declaring it to be the *Coal Yard Office*. In the corner of the carriage glowed a pot-bellied stove. It threw out an unbearable amount of heat as well as clouds of smoke that leaked from the joints on the door and chimney pipe. The air was so thick with smoke that you could not only smell it, you could taste it. Everything within the place was completely black, the whole kit and caboodle covered in layer upon layer of coal dust and soot, making each item blur into the next. Just one big mass of varying shades of black.

From the gloom, a disembodied voice, came from out of that blackness.

'I'm over here, lads.'

'And lass,' corrected Pepper.

The officers still couldn't make anything out in the blackness until from out of the dark emerged a white toothy grin. Like the Cheshire Cat, a huge white grin, floating body-less above a desk. The teeth moved of their own accord.

'Aye, sorry, and a lass.'

'Can you put a light on or draw the curtains back or something,' asked Brontë. 'I can't see a bloody thing.'

'I like to blend in with my background,' said the teeth.

As the police officers' eyes became accustomed to the dark and the sooty environment, they could just about make out a pot-bellied figure sat at a desk next to the pot-bellied stove. Sooty hair, black all over his face, black soot-smudged clothes, nothing but black. They could only really see him when he moved. When he stopped moving they lost sight of him again. The teeth were his only real giveaway, oh and occasionally the whites of his eyes could be seen, levitating above the teeth.

'What you honkies wanting with me? Not coal I think.'

'Are you Black?' asked Rhiaz.

'Aye I'm black and proud,' claimed the teeth, 'but I want born black, oh no. Even Snow White'd turn black if she 'ad my bloody job. The wife loves it though, always said she fancied running off wi' a Black man. But I was born as white as you lot.'

He waved his sooty paw towards Brontë and Pepper.

'Well, you two, any road, not the coconut.'

'What?'

Pepper was horrified, and ready to drag the coalman over his desk to beat him to a pulp.

'Leave it, Pepper, he means I'm not a proper Black, it's been said before.'

'Black on the outside but white in the middle, just like me. If you spit on your hanky and give that Black skin a rub it won't be long before you get through to the white, always the same with Black coppers'

'What makes you think he's police?'

'Cos he's with you, Brontë. I've watched you around this village ever since your mother struggled pushing you up them cobbles in yer pram. I know every bugger in this village and I've sold coal to every Tom, Dick an' 'Arry. I've delivered to every school, hospital, shop and factory. I've sold coil to all your family an' all, and I remember thinking how strange it was when you became a copper; particularly after knowing what your granddad wa' like.' One of the white eyes above the teeth disappeared as the coalman winked.

'You have been around for a while if you know my granddad.'

'The names Albert Ackroyd, I've worked 'ere for a while, that's true, ever since yard belonged t' corporation, and even though it now belongs to me, when I go 'ome on a night, I still aren't worth robbin'. I may as well give the bloody stuff away, the profit I make on it.' One eye momentarily disappeared again. 'Now, what can I be doin' ye for, Ossifers?'

'Big chap. Lives up Hewenden Bridge Main Street. Volunteers down here. Goes by the name of Nigel Flett, you know him?'

'Comes in 'ere from time to time to get coil fo' waiting room stoves.'

'What's he like?'

'He's a volunteer at a steam railway, what the chuff do you think he's like?'

'What do you mean by that?' asked Rhiaz

'They're alright most of 'em, anoraks and train spotters, which is fine. Some in fact are pretty cool lads. A few 'ave never grown up, still playing with their train sets.'

'Was he seeing anyone in particular down here.'

'Do you mean did he 'ave a girlfriend?'

'Did 'e?'

'I don't really think 'e was much of a ladies' man. They're bloody weird some of 'em 'ere, shuntin' each other all over t' shop. Side to side and top t' bloody bottom.'

Brontë wasn't sure what *top t' bloody bottom* meant; he wasn't sure if the coalman was speaking geographically, sociologically or anatomically, so he kept shtum.

'It's amazing what you get to see, when you're out and about delivering.'

'Seen any strangers hanging about the place?'

'Aye, there's a lot of *off-come'd-'uns* up 'ere nowadays and not just tourists neither, all the houses are being taken up by foreigners, like this lass 'ere.'

'Foreigner! I'm from just over the hill I'll have you know, and I've lived in the village for eight years.'

'Aye, well you might 'ave lass but you're still *from off* to me, after forty years you can class yourself as being proper Hewenden Bridge. Any road up, I can't 'ang around here all-day chatting t' likes a you lot, I've got to be getting' on. What you need is someone who knows them volunteers better than me. Tha's best asking in t' café, down in the station itself. You can ask Fanny.'

'Fanny?'

'Fanny Funnel.'

'Bloody 'ell,' snorted Pepper, 'that's an unfortunate name for a lady, whoever she is.'

Albert Ackroyd laughed.

'I'm telling you, Sergeant, that woman aint no lady. That's for sure.'

'Well, I think we'll go find out for ourselves. Thank you, Mr Ackroyd.'

'Aye, tarrar, call again sometime, why don't ye?'

'We might just take you up on that, Mr Ackroyd,' said Brontë. 'You never know your luck.'

The police officers walked back across the yard.

'What an existence. Poor old bugger,' said Pepper

'Eh! Less of the poor, if you don't mind,' Brontë admonished her.

'You think 'e's got money?'

'He's rollin' in it; money to burn, that lad. It's like they say, where there's muck there's brass, and they don't come much muckier than Mr Albert Ackroyd. Right, you two start house-to-house inquiries. I'll go search out Mrs Funnel.'

'You watch yourself, Brontë. Remember, she aint no lady and that's for sure.'

*

The platform smelt of oil and was full of smoke. The engines hissed and bellowed like steampunk dragons.

Hushhh... shwushhh... chuff...

Every so often great clouds of steam and smoke swooshed across the wet stone flags.

A uniformed guard stood in the billowing steam, his uniform strange even for Hewenden. He wore salwar kameez, a Jinnah hat and brown brogue shoes, all of which complimented nicely the brass buttoned uniform jacket of the railway. Brontë nodded at the man as he passed by.

'Assalam walaikum,' said Brontë.

'Walaikum assalam,' replied the man.

Brontë gestured to the man's uniform. 'You from Pakistan?

'Nah mate, I'm from Bradford.'

The café doorbell rang once as Brontë pushed it open.

Ding!

Things were not that much different inside the café as they were on the platform. The tea geyser hissed like the engines as it jetted gusts of steam across the room.

Hushhh... shwushhh... chuff!

The cooking bacon spewed out the smell of hot oil. Adding to the smog was an old woman who sucked on a cigarette and puffed out clouds of smoke.

As Brontë approached she spat on her t-towel and rubbed a grease stain off a plastic gingham tablecloth. This was a roly-poly of a woman, almost as wide as she was tall, and to be honest, there no way she could have been accused of being tall. She had very little going for her aesthetically. She was ugly, had warts on her face, was slightly bald and hadn't a tooth in her head. It slowly become clear to Brontë that she was as thick as two short planks too.

Brontë, flashed his ID at her.

'Fanny Funnel?'

'Aye love,' she replied with a nasal moan, 'and don't bother with any jokes, I've 'eard 'em all before. Now, what would Detective Inspector Brontë be wanting with me?'

'Does every bugger know me round 'ere?'

'You're famous, Brontë. Must be your good looks,' and she laughed like a drain.

'OK, very funny.'

The woman curtsied.

'I'm 'ere all week, folks.'

'Do you know a Nigel Flett, volunteer here on the railway, lives up the Cobbles?

'I do know him, love, I went to school with 'im and so did you... But you'll not remember that, Brontë; we was in a few classes below you. You wouldn't 'ave hung about with likes of us, back then.' She winked. 'In fact, I once got Sarah Umpleby to ask you to go out with me.' She laughed at the memory.

'And did I?'

'Did you buggery; you went out with Sarah-bloody-Umpleby.' She laughed louder.

'I hope it wasn't too disappointing for you.'

'Aye, it were that, Brontë, it were guttering.'

She winked at him, stuffed a ginger biscuit into her mouth and gnawed on it with her gums. A little saliva ran down the wrinkles around her hairy chin, carrying crumbs of the biscuit with it.

'You wanna cuppa tea, love?'

Brontë could think of nothing worse than taking anything edible from this woman. The smell of her, the size of her and the dribbling biscuit crumbs were really making him off.

'No, I'm good, thanks. Now, how well did you know him?'

'Nigel?' She sucked on the biscuit a little. 'As well as most and less than others. I knew his kids more than him, when they was younger they used to hang about wi' mine.'

'Where can I find his kids, are they local?'

'Why, what's the dirty old bugger been up to now?'

'What could he have been up to?'

'Bloody owt! There's nowt I wunt put past that lad.'

'You were telling me about his family.'

'Was I now... Well, there's a lad and a lass. That's as much as I can tell... The lad was bit of a rum bugger, a bit shot at, if you ask me, but the lass was all right as I remember.'

'Names?

'Can't remember what they were called. Flett was obviously their last name back then, but don't know now. No... can't remember. Maybe 'Arry? That's it, yes, 'Arry.'

'Addresses?'

'Haven't the foggiest, love. I think there may have been an aunty too. Lived on the road up towards falls, still there last I 'eard. What was she called, now? Wyck! That's it, Cicely Wyck, if I remember rightly when. Now she were a rum old bugger, I can tell you that.'

'According to you, Fanny, every bugger's strange.'

'Well, ain't that the truth. There's nowt so queer as folk, eh Brontë? There's only me an' you that's all right... An' I'm not so sure about you.'

Fanny Funnel laughed and spat soggy ginger biscuit crumbs all over the horrified detective.

*

Later, Brontë stood outside a shamble of cottages up by the falls and scanned the moor, the heather and grasses, brown and ginger. He tried to keep the mental image of Fanny's biscuit out of his head; it wasn't working.

Pepper knocked on one of the cottage doors. It was the third time she had knocked and she realised that it was likely there was no one at home. She was hoping to find The Wycks' cottage.

''E's not in, missus!'

Two boys, both about ten years old, were lounging across the handlebars of their bikes and stared at Pepper and Brontë with undisguised fascination.

'He? Who's he when's he's at home? We thought the Wycks lived here.'

'Nah, it's their weird old slave that's who…'

'…but 'e's not in.'

'How do you know he's not in?'

'Cos he never is, that's why.'

'You'll never find 'im in, missus.'

'He's never in his own house, just slaves for them vampires.'

'Vampires?' Pepper looked at Brontë.

'Yep, real proper bloodsuckers.'

''R Mum says 'e's always up there shagging the Brides of Dracula.'

The boys laughed.

'Your mum says that does she?'

'That's right, missus. They never come out during the day…'

'…Only as dogs'

'Dogs?'

''S right. They're big fuck-off dogs through the day when 'e walks them…'

'...and they turn into the undead on a night. Woo...'

'...woooohhh!'

'And 'e does the shoppin' for 'em.'

'Yeah, whatever... what does he buy for them, garlic and blood?' Brontë laughed at his own wit.

'That's stupid, Mr Smartarse, vampires hate garlic.'

'They wouldn't 'ave it in the house, would they, eh?'

'Everyone knows that.'

'We'd better go take a look at this for ourselves,' said Brontë.

'They live at number ten.'

'We better get over there, Sergeant.'

'You got a silver bullet, mister?'

'Vampires is crosses, silver bullets is werewolves.' Brontë winked at the boys. 'Everyone knows that.'

The boys burst into laughter and rode off, howling like werewolves.

'Aaaaaahooooo!'

*

At number ten, Brontë read a sign on the gate.

'"Judecca"! Christ, people call their houses strange things.'

'Why anyone would want to call a house anything is beyond me'

'It'll be a mixture of two people's names, like Jude and Rebecca, "Judecca". You see our house would be,' he thought for a moment, 'Brontëpper or Pepponte.'

'In what parallel universe would we ever have a house together, Brontë?'

'Fair point.'

'You don't know what Judecca is, do you, Brontë? Wow! I know something you don't know,' she took a deep breath and smelled the air, 'oh my God, this feels good.'

'Pepper...'

'No, no, wait a minute, let me savour the moment. I know something you don't.'

'Pepper!?'

'Judecca's not a made-up name, it's from Dante's Inferno. It's where Lucifer burns in hell's inner circle.'

She turned and looked at him and then whispered.

'We are about to enter... the inner circle of hell.'

'In that case,' he opened the gate for her, 'after you.'

She walked through the gate and laughed. Brontë followed but was not laughing. He pointed out a red Porsche on the drive.

'Look, there's a bunny motif on the number plate,' he gesticulated to the car and grinned inanely.

'Classy.'

'Looks promising.'

'You're so shallow. Girls in basques, with their busters sticking out all over the place, do not drive around in cars with bunny motifs. This will belong to some old slapper; I'll put a tenner on it.'

They rounded the corner of the house where they were leapt on by three humongous Alsatians.

'GRAAR!!'

The dogs barked ferociously, snarling, salivating, straining at leads, trying to break loose. The two officers jumped near clean out of their skins.

The only thing keeping the beasts from ripping their throats out were three strong chains. Well, they hoped they were strong. All Brontë could see before him were the snapping teeth and spraying saliva of the barking dogs that raged and bawled into his face.

One grey, one black, one white.

A man was struggling to hold the huge dogs back. He was grappling with the big chains fighting for control of them. He was only just winning the battle.

Brontë snarled back, his anger brought on by his fear.

'You get them bastards out of my face or I'll call the dangerous dog squad and they'll shoot the bastards sooner than you can say heel.'

The man with the dogs didn't appear to be fully persuaded and looked like he was considering his options. Keep holding tight or let them go.

He was tall and sinewy with stubble on his face and head. He was wearing old jeans, boots and a t-shirt emblazoned with the big lips and licking tongue of the Rolling Stones.

'Says who?'

'The police, love,' Pepper flashed her ID at him, 'so get them under control now or we will have the buggers shot.'

The man hollered at the dogs and pulled on their chains and they dropped back on to all fours, panting and dripping drool. But they still eyed up Brontë and Pepper hungrily.

Pepper took control.

'Right, we'll start with a name.'

'What, the dogs?'

'Don't be a smartarse, it doesn't suit you, mate.'

The man reconsidered. 'Caleb.'

'Caleb, what?'

'Smith.'

'Yeah, like we're gonna believe that, right.'

'Ye can believe what the 'eck you want, copper. Without a warrant I don't give a flying fuck.'

'Does a Cicely Wyck live here?'

'She'll be inside. Though I doubt she's up. They don't get up till it's got dark.'

Brontë smiled in memory of what the boys had said of their mother's theory.

'You'd best wait here,' advised Caleb Smith. 'I'll go tell her highness you're here.'

Caleb walked off down the garden with the dogs in tow. All four disappeared into the house.

'Christ!' moaned Brontë. 'I almost shit myself.'

'Only almost, you were lucky.'

'What sort of dogs were they?'

'Big bloody frightening ones. Do you think they really are the Brides of Dracula?

'That would make him Eyesore.'

'That's Frankenstein you idiot, and even then, it's Igor.'

'I'll stick with Eyesore thank you very much.'

Seconds later, the door reopened and a woman's head popped around it and looked them both up and down.

'You'd best come in,' said the head to Pepper, 'and bring lover boy in with you.'

The head disappeared back into the house.

'Told you,' said Pepper. 'No bunny girl that one, that's a tenner you owe me.'

'We never shook on it.'

'Cheapskate.'

*

In the small front room, the curtains were closed and a flame-effect electric fire glimmered in a brown-tiled fireplace. The bars on the fire were not lit and so gave off no heat, but the flickering light bulb dappled the walls and ceiling with a circling warm glow.

There was no sign of Caleb and the only evidence of the three dogs was the smell, or was it cat? Looking around, Pepper could see numerous cats lurking in dark corners and everything was covered in cat hair. The evil canines may have been missing, but they had been replaced by three strange-looking women: one blonde, one grey, one brunette. Two were sitting side by side on a threadbare velvet settee, the third stood behind it. The two on the settee were the blonde that had stuck her head around the door and a grey-haired woman who could have been her mother. Each of the women had a cat curled in their laps. A black-haired girl behind the settee who could easily have been the blonde's daughter was catless. They may all have had different hair colouring and different ages but other than that they were like peas in a pod. They were certainly not creatures of beauty. All three were overweight and chinless. They had hooked noses, hanging jowls and crooked teeth, and as if to compensate each face had been slarted with makeup.

The women wore stained, dirty dresses which were short enough to reveal a discomforting amount of thigh, and low enough to revel a disconcerting amount of cleavage, cleavages on which silver pentagrams bounced, suspended on silver chains that hung around their fat, freckled necks.

Pepper smiled at the idea of them being vampires. She couldn't imagine these three flapping their arms and flying around in the moonlight. She whispered under her breath into Brontë's ear, in a croaky, witchy voice.

'When will we three meet again?'

Brontë kicked her.

Apart from the doggy-catty odour the room also had a sickly musky smell, and Pepper was not sure if this came from the lack of ventilation in the room or from the women themselves. The bottled blonde studied Brontë like he was prey. Pepper could see from the woman's eyes that she was impressed with what she saw and she looked hungrily at him. Oh my God, Pepper thought, she's going to eat him alive.

'And whose little boy are you?' said the woman.

Brontë hesitated, embarrassed. The young brunette giggled. Strangely these three women, who really were nothing to write home about, acted like they thought they were God's gift. They didn't impress Pepper one bit. Pepper addressed the grey-haired woman.

'We're from the police. You must be,' she considered her notebook, 'Cicely Wyck?'

'Must I indeed?'

'Well are you, or aren't you?'

'I might be. Depends what you want?'

'There's been an incident…' stammered Brontë.

'Pooh! Hark at that, mother, it talks,' said the blonde, and the grey-haired old hag cackled. For a moment there was an embarrassing silence, all eyes on Brontë. The blonde ate him up with her eyes and to Pepper's disgust she actually licked her lips.

'I'm Carrie Wyck,' said the blonde.

'And the others?'

'This is, as you so rightly surmised, is Cecily…' the grey-haired hag ignored the police officers, '… and my daughter, Elspeth.'

The daughter smiled at Brontë and wriggled a little, she was fat and could possibly have been pregnant as well, but it was hard to tell for sure. She had her hand cupped under her enormous tummy like she was cradling her baby, but she could just as easily have been cupping a more intimate part of her body. Among all the fat it was hard to tell. But the expression on her face as she ogled Brontë inferred it was the latter. Pepper looked at the girl and wondered if she was actually salivating. Surely not. Pepper turned and looked at Brontë, who looked like a rabbit in headlights. Bloody men.

'Do any of you know a man called Nigel Flett? Volunteers down at the railway.'

The three-woman looked from one to the other.

'What's the old reprobate been up to now?' asked the grey-haired old woman.

'That's interesting, why "reprobate"?'

'Have you met him, love?'

'Sort of.'

'Then you know exactly why I call him that. What's he done?'

'We're trying to trace his family.'

'The old bugger's dead then, is he?'

'I'm sorry, what makes you think he's dead?'

'You'd hardly be tracing us if he hadn't returned his library books.'

'Do you know of anyone who would like to harm him?'

'Like him dead you mean, other than us?'

They smirked, giggled and laughed.

'Well?'

'Well his kids, a boy and a girl, Harry and Lesley, would do for a start.'

'Why his kids?'

'Because… well let's just say he was not a particularly nice daddy.'

'Where can we find the kids?'

'Harry workth in one of them fanthy cafes up the cobbleth,' lisped the black-haired girl. 'You know, one of them that thell coffee by the thot and not by the thpoonful.'

'And where can we find Lesley?'

'Haven't a bloody clue, and the door's that way.' Said the grey-haired Cicely.

*

Outside the house, Brontë sucked in great lungfuls of fresh air.

'Well that was a big waste of time,' moaned Pepper.

'Rubbish, we found out where the son works.'

'We found out you're a complete and useless tosser.'

'Bollocks,' he said as he climbed into the car, 'we knew that all along.'

Chapter Four

Haworth Moors. Top Withens.
The evening of All Hallows.
The first of November.

The wind blew like a bugger up at Top Withens. It blew on the old house, it blew on the dead heather and it blew on the old stone walls, but most of all it blew on Father Patrick Murphy. The priest skulked about in the darkness and pulled his scarf tight around his neck, not as much to keep the wind off his neck but more in an effort to camouflage his dog collar. Other than the collar, he was dressed completely in black; black trousers and black shirt all covered by a long black cassock. A long black cassock that swirled around him in the wind like a cloak; with the collar covered he was invisible in the dark, which was just how the father liked it.

Concealed in the darkness the father peeped through the open shutters of Withens Riding Stables, he watched the young girls brushing their horses. Even though it was not yet tea time it was dark enough to sneak about unobserved, and the bushes in which he stood helped to conceal him too. The priest liked to watch and not be observed; he didn't like being seen.

The girls were young and wore tight jodhpurs with short t-shirts, which made them look quite fit for human consumption. However, it was really boys that were the reverend's dish of choice. But there were no boys here. That was the way of the world: boys don't ride horses. He could hear the laughter of the girls over the sound of the beck as it cascaded over the waterfall close by. In the summer the waterfall was a good place for spying too, holiday makers would strip down to their next to nothings and splash around in the pool and in the fall itself. Occasionally, the father was lucky enough to catch some of the locals skinny-dipping in the pool below the fall. Most were too old for his own particular tastes but there was the thrill of stalking and the added excitement that they didn't know he was there. They didn't know he was sneaking around in the bracken and heather watching their nakedness. Hey, any port in a storm.

The father's own first sexual experiences had been with a man far older than himself, someone old enough to be his father, or even grandfather. He had been groomed by his local priest, coaxed into doing things he liked and yet did not like, things that he hated but that also gave him pleasure, things that pleased him but disgusted him. Love and hate; hate and love. After that he couldn't manage to hold down any normal relationships. He couldn't have normal sex, with men or women. That's why he had become what he had become: a priest.

Now he had to make do with creeping around in the dark and stealing sneaky looks at people, and tonight it was stable girls. He knew he was wrong. He knew his church disapproved, but he wasn't the only one. The church would cover; they had in the past. He knew he would one day have to answer to his maker and he prayed nightly for leniency, after all he did worship a merciful God.

What was that?

He was distracted by a noise in the darkness. He was sure he had heard a sound over the noise of the giggling girls and the babbling beck. He caught his breath and froze as he heard the noise again, his heart thumping with the fear and excitement.

What was there?

He thought he could make out an extra dark bit in in the surrounding blackness. A more solid bit of black than the dark of the night about him. Yes, there it was, a shape in the night. Should he hide and slither away or introduce himself and bluff it out. He uncovered the dog collar, he would bluff it out. People did not suspect priests of irregularities.

'Hello?' he said.

Nothing. No reply, and it seemed the movement had stopped too.

No, there it was again, going down towards the water's edge.

'Is there anybody there?' he whispered into the night air and followed the figure towards the water. 'There's no need to be afraid,' he told the darkness. He was afraid and he was getting more afraid by the minute. Shit, what was out there?

The dark shadow became a white, almost silver figure in the dark, and with a little splash it disappeared into the pool of water.

Were they naked? he thought. Were they swimming in the nude? He crept forward to the water's edge and watched the silver shape gliding through the water, beautiful and ethereal. The person in the water, he could see it was a person now, swam towards him and held out a hand to him.

You've got to be joking, he thought, *I'm not going in there. Not on your life.*

The hand waved at him and came closer.

'Help me,' hissed the swimmer, 'help me.'

The father crept a little closer. What a chance, to help this naked swimmer, to touch their flesh. To be so close to a naked body.

'Wait,' he said, 'I'm coming.'

He reached out to the swimmer and took their hand.

And the trap snapped shut.

The swimmer grabbed his hand in a vice-like death grip and hauled him into the water. He'd heard of this before, where drowning swimmers could grab their saviours and drown them in their panic. He fought to get away but he was smothered by the arms and legs of his assailant, because assailant it was. Their arms upon him, pulling at him, grabbing at his neck. He lashed out in self-defence but he was no fighter and his struggling was pointless. Amid the chaos and panic he saw a flash of silver above his head and felt a sharp pain in his neck.

Everything went black.

As Father Patrick regained consciousness, he found himself to be completely immobile. He was struggling to breath, freezing cold and deafened by the torrent of water that was cascading over him. He gasped for air but couldn't work out when the water was covering his face and when it was not. Sometimes he managed to gulp in air but most times he choked on water. He couldn't scream because when he tried the water filled his mouth and nose. He gulped for air again but a great spout of water filled his mouth.

Each wrist was tied with rope, his arms outstretched, wide apart, spread-eagled across the waterfall, a torrent of water gushing over his head and his naked body. He desperately tied to catch mouthfuls of air between coughing out spurts of partially inhaled water and wriggled on the ropes like a fish on a line. Whenever he did succeed in gasping a mouthful of air he managed a stifled scream to attract attention.

There was no one there to hear his cries.

No one, that is, other than the dark cloaked creature standing on the rocks at the top of the falls, a creature that listened until the priest's floundering and screaming stopped and everything fell silent. Everything, that is, other than the splashing of the water flowing over the fall.

When the priest was silent and still, the dark shape turned and disappeared into the night, leaving the priest dead, crucified across the falls. Crucified like his lord but for one difference: blood did not run from a wound on his side. It ran down from his groin, down his leg to be washed away by the waterfall.

Chapter Five

Waterfall car park.
The second of November. Early morning.

Jeanne Hepworth's pretty face, agility and fashionable clothing, added to her trendy hairstyle made a full package that belied her eighty-seven years, and she was as fit as the proverbial butcher's dog.

She parked her car early each morning at the waterfall car park and walked down the short path to the falls where she swam naked in the pool; wild swimming she called it, and she loved it. It was the cold water on her body that Jeanne liked. It made her feel so very alive. When you are eighty-seven it is so good to feel alive.

The car park owners were pretty handy with their clamps and fines. If anyone outstayed their ticket for more than one minute the car would be clamped. No excuses, no messing, no mercy. Each morning Jeanne paid for an hour and was always back within forty-five minutes; once bitten twice shy.

There was never anyone around the falls at that time in the morning. The place was always deserted so she felt quite safe. Who would want to look at an old woman in the buff? Nobody. Nobody that is, except that dirty old priest from St Michaels and the Whatsits. *Bloody priests, who'd have 'em?* she thought.

Some mornings she saw him hanging about in a furtive sort of way, pretending he wasn't trying to get an eyeful. He was harmless though, just a dirty old peeping tom.

As Jeanne approached the waterfall she noticed a dark shape in the water that ran over the top of the stone outcrop. As young as she looked, her eyes were not what they used to be and she struggled to identify what the shape was. It looked to her like something had been swept down the beck and stuck on a branch in the water.

She got right up to of the fall before she could make out that the dark shape in the water was a figure of some sort; it took a little longer for it to sink in that the shape was a body, and a little longer still to realise it was dead. A dead body in the fall.

'Fucking hell,' she said. The first time in her eighty-seven years that Jeanne Hepworth had used the 'f' word.

Jeanne was shocked. Who wouldn't be? Shocked but not afraid. She had buried both her husband and her son, so she wasn't afraid of death. She studied the crucified form in the water and worked out it was the pervy priest. She didn't know his name. She was no church goer. She had not been in a church since she'd buried her son; she did not, could not, believe in a God that allowed the killing of children.

She took her phone and with her wrinkled finger jabbed at one large numbered button three times.

Nine. Nine. Nine.

'Police!' she said into the phone.

It is a shame, she thought, *there'll be no swim today.*

'Oh hello. I've just found a dead cleric.'

*

Jeanne gave the nice police sergeant with the funny name her details and told her all that she knew, and all that she had seen, which was nothing really.

'I'd come down for a swim...'

'You came for a swim in the beck!?' As Pepper noted this down in her little black notebook she couldn't hide the surprise from her face.

'I'm old, love, not dead.'

'Hey, I'm not judging.'

'I swim every morning, dear. I skinny dip in the waterfall pool.'

'Skinny dip!?'

'Oh, I'm sorry. I have shocked you now, dear.'

'Impressed me, more like. So, did you notice anything different this morning, apart from the priest that is.'

'Oh, it wasn't any different this morning than any other, dear. He was down here most mornings; mind you...usually he wasn't dead and crucified I suppose.'

Brontë climbed down the side of waterfall and joined the two women.

'Jeanne, this is the boss, Inspector Brontë. Brontë, this is Mrs Hepworth. She found the dead priest.'

Brontë nodded at the old lady.

'You OK, Mrs Hepworth? Can we help at all?'

'No, love, I'm fine, you and the sergeant get on with your job. She has my details if she needs me later.'

Brontë turned to Pepper.

'What on earth was a priest doing up here, any road?'

'How disappointing. You don't look naïve, dear.'

They turned to the old woman and Pepper raised her eyebrows.

'He often came up here to google my titties.'

Pepper laughed.

'Ogle,' she corrected her. 'Ogle!'

*

Jeanne made her way back to the car park. It wasn't until she arrived back at the car that she saw the stupid little man fixing the clamp to her wheel.

'Oh, come on,' she said. 'I can't be more than two minutes over.'

'You've got eyes love, read the sign,' said the clamper.

'I've read the sign, I come here every morning, I know what the sign says.'

'Then you should 'ave been back on time shunt ye', love?'

'I'm sorry. Look... I've just been with the police. They held me up. I found a body.'

'Look, love, I really don't give a flyin' monkeys if you saw the second coming. It'll be seventy-five quid to take it off.'

'You have to be joking.'

'No, I'm Frank Gommersal. The boss is called Councillor Swaine. If you've got a problem with the quality of my work, take it up with 'im. 'E's in the hut.' He gestured towards said hut with his head.

Councillor Anthony Swaine was indeed in the hut and he was doing his job, counting money. The man had no soul and no heart. Even his wife called him a 'right tight bastard'. He stopped his counting to explain his business ethos to Jeanne.

'If I let everybody off, I'd have no business, now would I? I have to earn a living somehow. Have to keep the wolves from the door, haven't I?'

'I was helping the police.'

'Then you've got more to worry your pretty little head about than a meagre seventy-five quid. Pay the nice man your fine and he'll whip off your clamp and you can be on your way.'

'I was held up by the police.'

'Then get the money back from them. Leave me in peace.'

Jeanne had to stop herself from screaming into his face. The man was odious. She fought back tears of frustration. She refused to give him the pleasure of seeing her cry.

'You...' she hated profanities of any description '... shit!'

This only seemed to entertain the councillor more and he laughed. Jeanne stormed out of the hut. She wondered what her late husband would have done. Don't get mad, get even was his mantra. She could hear him now.

'Bide your time, girl. Bide your time.'

Jeanne Hepworth gritted her teeth, set her chin and paid her money to the gorilla in the high viz jacket. In return he released the clamp with a smile and he winked at her as he hoisted the clamp up on to his shoulder.

'This isn't over yet,' she said, 'not by a long chalk.'

As she drove away she leant out of the car window and called out at her tormentor.

'By the way, you odious little man, your breath stinks.'

She gained some satisfaction from the hurt look on his face, and him standing there speechless, breathing into his cupped hand.'

In the hut, the councillor smiled to himself as he observed the interaction. He smiled because he had noticed her holding back her tears. It was turning into quite a good day.

Jeanne drove off and for the second time in her life she used the 'F' word.

*

Brontë and Pepper drank tea in the makeshift police incident room which they had set up in Haworth Church Hall. There was nothing big enough in Hewenden Bridge, so it had to be Haworth. This pleased Brontë no end. Haworth was far pleasanter than Hewenden Bridge.

The tables and chairs had been folded flat and pushed back up against walls that were covered in children's colourful drawings that depicted the story of Joseph and his multicoloured coat.

'So, what have we got from the autopsy?' asked Brontë.

'Nothing as yet. Body's hardly got back to the morgue. I don't think it's even on the slab yet.'

'What about the first chap, Nigel Flett. They done him yet?'

'Morticia says we'll have the report by close of play today.'

'Close of play? Bloody ridiculous. When will I get the priest's report, a week next Pancake Tuesday?'

'You connecting the two, boss?'

'God only knows. Yesterday a guy's killed by a huge vampire bat and shortly after a Catholic priest turns up on his doorstep; that hits about nine-point-five on my weird-shit-ometer. And to top it off, said priest is crucified across the bloody waterfall; that's another nine-point-fiver. You have to admit the cases are at least united in weirdness. What was the priests name, Father Patrick, wasn't it?'

'Father Patrick Murphy.'

'Did she say if the priest was... complete?'

'Do you mean did he still have possession of his todger?'

'I could have put it better, but yes.'

'Morticia says we'll have to wait for the report, she was getting a bit touchy.'

'Bloody woman.'

'I could get the divers out, search the beck?'

'Nah! We'll wait for the report, let's see if it's missing before we start throwing money around looking for it. What about the letter we found at Flett's house, anything interesting there?'

'More weird shit.'

'What score?'

'Oh, I'd say...' she sucked her teeth '...a nine-point-niner.'

Brontë lifted his eyebrows. 'Go on, you've got my attention.'

Pepper held up a SOCO bag which contained the letter.

'This is a reply seemingly to a letter sent by our friend Nigel Flett to an inmate on death row, in a prison... sorry, corrective institute, in North Carolina.'

'Loads of weirdos write to prisoners on death row.'

Pepper pulled on a pair of blue latex gloves, snapping them seductively in Brontë's general direction as she did so. She carefully took the letter out of the bag and read aloud.

'Dear Nigel, I hope this letter finds you in rude health. Thank you for your correspondence. I was interested to hear how things are back in Brontë land.'

Pepper lifted an eyebrow at Brontë, he waved at her to carry on.

'Thank you for your concern around my health. I can assure you I am quite fine, considering the circumstance. I have come to terms with my fate and I expected no different from the beginning. I accept my comeuppance, as I am sure you will accept yours when the time comes.'

'Bloody hell!' exclaimed Brontë.

'Yours sincerely, Currer.'

'Contact the prison...'

'Corrective institute.'

'Whatever. Find out who this Currer is and what we're dealing with. I want to know if they've been fried or not. Maybe the damn yanks have released some nutjob who's just come a calling over here. Get on to the States and find out what you can.'

'Rhiaz is already all over it.'

'And?'

'And we'll have to wait a bit. He says they'll all be in bed.'

'What do you mean, they'll all be in bleedin' bed?'

'Time difference, Inspector.'

'Time difference my arse. Get him to get 'em out of bloody bed.'

Brontë got to his feet and made for the door.

'And while he's waiting for the whole of the American continent to wake up, tell him to see what he can drag up on that bizarre bloke with the mad dogs. He's about as bent as five bob note.'

'What about the Witches of Eastwick?'

'Aye, and them too.'

'Where you off to?'

'Me!? I'm off back to Hewenden Bridge. I'm going to have a word with Nigel's son, if I can find the bugger, see what he can tell us. I'll meet you up at the café.'

'Which café?'

'Up the Cobbles, the one where you 'ave to throw and paint your own mug before you can drink.'

Brontë stopped on his way out.

'You can take your time. I'll call in at the church and see what dirt I can dig up on our crucified vicar.'

'Priest.'

'Whatever!'

He slammed the door behind him.

'A "please" wouldn't go amiss,' said Pepper to the empty room.

*

It was strange coincidence that Brontë had wanted to 'dig up dirt' on the priest, because when he arrived at St Michael the Martyr's that is exactly what he found. In the corner of the graveyard, under the old yew tree, there was a priest digging up dirt.

'Having to burry 'em yourself nowadays, Father?'

'Sorry?'

Brontë pointed to the priest's bucket and trowel.

'Ha! No, it's the molehills I'm after.'

'I see,' said Brontë, but he didn't.

'They do make a right old mess, them moles.'

'You need a mole-catcher.'

'Heavens no, we don't want to be rid of them. It's God's work they'll be doing.'

'You've lost me.'

'When we burry the bodies, we throw a handful of soil on top of the coffin.'

The priest demonstrates by scattering a handful of soil on the grass, and recited scripture in a holier-than-thou voice, 'You return to the ground, since from the ground you were taken, for dust you are, and to dust you will return.'

'Like, *Ilkla Moor Baht 'at*?'

'I'm afraid I'm probably not as au-fait with your Yorkshire anthem as I should be, particularly for one who lives and works in the county.'

'When you're dead and buried the worms will come and eat thee up, ducks'll come and eat up worms, we'll eat the ducks and so we shall all have eaten thee.'

'I'll probably just stick to what I know,' said the priest.

'But where do your moles come into it?'

'You can't go throwing great clods of earth on top of coffins, now can you? It's not dignified and it upsets the relatives. When the mole does his excavations, he creates a lovely fine loam. I collect his little hills to gracefully scatter on the coffins in a dignified manner. It's an old trick.'

'God moves in mysterious ways.'

'I'm thinking you're not here to learn about the ways of my God.'

'No, you're right, Father, I'm not. I'm here to learn about the ways of priests.'

Brontë flashed his ID.

'Ah! The Garda no less. And what would you be wanting with me,' he peered at the warrant card, 'Inspector Brontë?'

'What can you tell me about Father Patrick Murphy?'

The priest looked away, gathering a little more soil while he gathered his thoughts. The soil he scooped into his bucket, his thoughts he mulled around in his head for a bit before turning back to the policeman.

'I think a very shocking thing has happened up at the waterfall. I think least said best mended.'

'That's not how it works, you know that very well. What can you tell me about Father Patrick Murphy?'

'Nothing, I'm afraid, other than he was a troubled soul.'

'And what was his soul troubled with, Father?'

'I've only been in the parish a little while. I really don't know anything. He did take advantage of the confessional with the bishop on a number of occasions.'

'So, I'll need to speak to the bishop.'

'I don't think the bishop will be able to help, not in relation to a man's confessions.'

'The church likes to cover things up.'

The priest paused as he formed a response in his head.

'Let us say the church likes to look after its own problems.'

'Some would say not well enough.'

'Let he who has not sinned cast the first stone, Inspector.'

'That doesn't put you in a good light, Father. When it comes to what I imagine are Father Patricks particular sins, I could easily pick up a stone and throw it. Are you telling me you could not?'

'I am telling you I would not, not that I could not.'

Brontë shook his head at the priest and made his way back down the cobbled street.

The father came across and leant against the stone wall.

'The fact of the matter is we have to protect the church.'

'The fact of the matter is the church should protect the children. Suffer the little children to come unto me, remember.'

*

Brontë made his way down Hewenden Bridge High Street towards the café where Harry Flett was rumoured to work, or at least had worked. He glanced through the shops' windows and shook his head at the piles of tat that were sold as souvenirs to tourists. Who on earth wanted or needed an Emily Brontë paper weight? Not him, that's for sure. He was stopped in his tracks by the billboard outside the post office. 'Vampire Bites Burglar'. Looked like someone had got to Micky Grimshaw. He smiled and continued down the street.

Pepper was waiting outside the cafe smoking a roll-up, which she extinguished when he arrived by grinding it into a cobble-set with her boot.

Brontë wafted the smoke away in irritation.

'Disgusting habit.'

'Ha, I've seen you smoke, Brontë.'

'I have never claimed to be anything other than a hypocrite.'

He stuck out his hand.

''Ere, givus one.'

She offered him her tobacco tin and papers.

'They're rollies.'

'Forget it, then.'

'You're in a good mood.'

He ignored her.

'What happened with America?'

'God knows. It all seemed to go tits up after the Kennedy Assassination.'

'You're so not funny, Pepper.'

'I think I am. When I left Rhiaz said America was still fast asleep, so he hasn't spoken to their cops. He did get a bit of a lead from the internet, to a newspaper covering some related story. He left them a message and he's hoping some reporter's gonna get back to him. Did you find out anything on the priest?'

'Yep, he's a right, dodgy bastard.'

'What makes you say that?'

'Cos he's a fuckin' priest and they're all right dodgy bastards, the bloody lot of 'em. Come on, let's go in and get a brew.'

The pair turned to enter the café. The sign over the door proclaiming its name, which Brontë read in complete disbelief.

'Gobble on the Cobble!? Give me strength.'

'It's not strength you lack, Brontë, it's tolerance.'

'My God, who the hell do you think you are, bloody Yoda?'

The bell on the café door announced their presence.

DING!

They found themselves standing in what looked like an art studio and gallery rather than a café. People sat around painting ceramic pots as they ate, drank and chatted. They were a mixed bunch but mainly UHBs.

Sitting astride a potter's wheel, an attractive middle-aged woman was spinning a pot. She had long red hair, a freckled complexion, a denim apron, Crocs and the biggest and brightest home-knit jumper the world had ever seen. The parts of this woman that weren't covered in clay were covered in paint. The bell had attracted her attention. She stopped what she was doing and stood to great them as they entered.

'Ah, here you are at last?'

'Sorry!?'

'No, no, don't apologise. I'm just glad you could get here at all.'

The two officers exchanged glances.

'You are here about the door?'

The police officers looked at her askance. The potter sensed things were not as she thought, or indeed hoped.

'I'm hoping to hell you're the joiners here to fix the door.'

'Were not, no, love, we're the police. This here's Inspector Brontë and I'm Sergeant Pepper.'

The potter nodded at them individually. 'Good Morning.'

'Good Morning.' Her eyes possibly lingered on Pepper slightly longer than Brontë.

'OK, you're not here about the door per se but you are here about the break in. The two are connected.'

'Sorry?' replied the officers in unison. 'You probably won't get a visit from the police, they'll probably just give you a crime number.'

'Great. Well, in that case you must be here for a caffeine fix and to spin some clay?'

'Christ almighty,' said Brontë, only just under his breath.

Pepper knew this was going to be one of those situations where she should take charge. She could almost see Brontë floundering out of his depth.

'We're the police, love. We're looking for a man...'

'It looks like you've already got yourself one. Bit old, but he looks like he might scrub up ok.'

'The man we're after goes by the name of Harry Flett?'

The woman hesitated but only slightly before she replied.

'Look, you two grab that table in the corner, I'll bring you both a coffee over. I'll tell you my problems, you tell me yours. Americanos ok?

'You got any good old-fashioned Yorkshire tea?' asked Brontë.

The potter affected a broad Yorkshire accent. 'An' where'd they grow that then, lad? Up on them famous Yorkshire tea groin' terraces round Bingley? Eh by gum!'

'Harrogate, I believe,' retorted Brontë.

'I like him, he's a keeper,' said the potter to Pepper. 'So why don't you just pop him over there whilst I get you some clay to throw.'

'Pepper dragged Brontë off to a table.'

'Clay to throw?' said Brontë, this time definitely not under his breath.

Pepper kicked him under the table.

'Shush! Leave this to me.'

The potter soon returned to the table carrying hand-painted mugs of coffee and a jug of warm milk.

'So, some fella name of Barry Plett, you said?'

'No, we said, Harry Flett. You know any man of that name?'

The potter bit her finger and exaggerated a long drawn-out ponder.

'No, can't say as I do.'

She turned around to shout at the barista, another UHB middle-aged woman.

'Roz, you heard of some fella called Harry Flett?'

The barista shook her head.

'Nope, what's he meant to have done?'

The potter looked right back at them and waited.

'We heard he worked here,' said Pepper.

'Well you heard wrong, love, cos no man of any description works here. They're unreliable and afraid of hard work and just clutter up the place. So, sorry about that, but I can't help you.' She smiled at the officers, placed her hands flat on the table and pushed herself up. 'But this won't get the baby a new frock. I've got work to do, can't sit around here chatting to you two little charmers all day.'

She moved off, back to her wheel.

'Coffees are on the house.'

Pepper and Brontë sat and sipped coffee for a little while.

'And just for the record, what would your name be, love?' asked Pepper.

The potter crinkled her eyes.

'Do I need a solicitor?'

'I don't know, do you?'

'Oooh. I do like you. Not only clever but witty with it. How's your coffee doing?'

'We're still waiting for a name.'

The potter returned to the table and sat. She gave a long sigh and looked at Pepper for a while as she sipped her coffee. Slowly she placed her mug on the table.

'I am Harry Flett.'

'You're a he!?' squeaked Brontë.

'For God's sake, man, of course not.' She looked at Pepper and raised her eyebrows.

'What is your name then?' asked Pepper. 'Harriette?'

'Nearly. It's Angharad. Angharad Flett. Harry, for short.'

The three of them sat watching the condensation running down the inside of the café windows. They were drinking more coffee and looking out at the rain on the cobbles.

'We're sorry about your father.'

'It is sad, I suppose. But what's worse is he lived so close by and I haven't spoken to him in years. Years and years.'

'You didn't speak to your father.'

'Never liked him. Was always frightened of him if truth be known. He was a bully. When I left home that was that. Went down to live in Liverpool and never really thought of family. I've only been back up here a couple of years and never saw the need to make contact again. It's not a crime, you know. You can't bang me up for it.'

'We're trying to find out what happened to him. Did he have family or friends in America?'

'God no! He hated anyone who wasn't from Yorkshire.' She sipped her drink. 'In fact, he hated anyone who wasn't from Hewenden Bridge.'

'What about holidays or anything. Did he travel to America?'

'No way, he never went out of the village as far as I know.'

'Is there anyone who might have had a grudge against him?'

She went silent for a moment.

'Well… there's always 'r lad.'

''R lad?'

'My brother, Lesley.'

Brontë laughed.

'We got it back to front. We had Harry down as the boy and Lesley the girl.'

'Typical bloody police, all arse about tit.'

'Where is your brother? Have you seen him?'

'It's like I said, I haven't made contact with any of my family, and that means my brother too. So, I'm afraid I can't help you. So, if you've finished your coffees, I really have to get back to my wheel.'

Harry escorted the pair of them to the door. On the step Pepper stopped.

'I really am sorry about your father, Harry.'

'I just want to forget everything.'

Brontë and Pepper left. As they did, the door closed behind them and the little bell rang.

DING!

They were walking down the cobbles when the little bell rang again.

DING!

Angharad, stood on the steps.

'It's true,' said the potter, 'I haven't seen my brother for an age. He doesn't want to see me because he tries to forget the past. I don't know where he is. He doesn't have a permanent address. Just rides around on his flaming motorbike with his so-called mates. They sort of live nowhere and everywhere. Now he really did hate father, blamed him for what he put us through.'

'What about your, mother?'

'She's dead.'

'Suspicious?'

'As suspicious as sclerosis of the liver can get.'

'Thanks,' they walked off down the cobbles.

'Hey,' Angharad called after them, 'if ever you fancy going out for a night that ends in a drunken brawl and a mad shag in front of the fire, hey I'm your gal.'

Brontë turned. 'Fortunately, I'm a married man.'

'I wasn't talking to you, Inspector.' She went back into the café.

DING!

Brontë laughed out loud.

When they climbed into Pepper's Astra, he was still smiling.

'Right, it's time to go home. There's no more we can do today. Obi-Wan needs his supper and I need my beer.'

He fastened his seat belt.

'Take me back to KickStart Bob's, if you would.'

'Picking up the bike?'

'Hopefully, but mainly I'm sure old KickStart could tell us quite a bit about who rides what bike where and when.'

*

Back at the KickStart Bob's, Brontë paid Bob from a wad of notes.

'That's jus fifty-squid, 'Spector.'

'It's always fifty-quid. Why is it always fifty-quid?'

'Keeps tings simple,' he winks, 'ye know what I mean?'

Brontë counted five tenners into KickStart Bob's grubby hand and was holding a sixth tenner just above the small pile he had created.

'By the way, Bob, you ever come across anyone called Lesley Flett?'

'Never heard of him.'

Brontë fixed KickStart with a look.

'What makes you think it was a *him*? Lesley is usually a girl's name.'

'That'll be darn tummy being psychic, 'Spector.'

'Lesley's a biker from round here, rides with a group of his mates?'

'Lucky bar-steward, eh? But like I told you, 'Spector, I don ave anny mates.'

Brontë held three notes within KickStart's easy reach.

'Just give us a little nod in the right direction.'

'C'mon, 'Spector, ya can't spect me t'grass?'

Brontë added another note to those already on offer.

'Hive told ye, 'Spector, I know no Fletts. I don't know Lesley Flett foreshore.'

KickStart pocketed the money, bribe and all, turned and walked back towards his garage.

'And I sirtenly don' know no Flett called Angharad.'

Brontë wasn't sure if his eye twitched or if he winked as he disappeared into his garage.

Chapter Six

Tomato Dip.
The morning of the third of November.

The following morning, after a drive down the Keighley bypass in the battered blue Astra, Brontë, Pepper and Rhiaz pulled into the 'Tomato Dip', a greasy spoon frequented mainly by bikers.

Many years ago it might have been called a bistro, but now it was just a cafe, a place where bikers ate spam or bacon sandwiches and drank instant coffee from mismatched mugs. Most of the bikers hailed from Yorkshire and Lancashire, congregating at the café before making their way up to the Dales for a 'bit of a burn'. The bikers sat in groups of varying sizes and discussed where they could go flat out, get their knees down, and where there were or weren't speed cameras.

Rhiaz sat forward in the back of Pepper's car resting his arms on the two front seats, which were occupied by Pepper and Brontë.

'Boys and their bloody toys,' said Pepper as she span the Astra into a parking bay, next to a line of brightly coloured motorcycles. She lifted an eyebrow and looked at Brontë.

'So, are these guys dangerous?'

'Ha! These guys are as dangerous as bread and butter pudding. They'll all be bankers, and insurance salesmen; over fifty and overweight.'

'Like you, Brontë.'

Brontë ignored her.

'Are they in gangs?' asked Rhiaz.

'See their jackets, their club names are on the back. Those lads over there by the canal side, they're the Wycoller Crew MCC and the gang over there on those choppers, they're Harrogate Harley Owners MCC.'

'What's an MCC when it's at home?'

'An MCC's a group of friends who go out for fun runs. MCs are as far away from these guys here that you can get; MCs are gangs whose members are really, really bad boys, what you might call Hells Angels. Only one C in it but a whole world of difference.'

'So, these guys here like to dress up, ride their bikes and pretend they're something they're not?' said Pepper.

'Well, pretending to be what they are, a rotary club on wheels and completely harmless bikers. Well completely harmless that is until they kill themselves wrapped around a lamp post.'

The police officers looked around the groups of men of a certain age, the men wore garishly coloured leathers and stood around in groups, talking and smoking. Most had beards and shaven heads and some even had coloured Mohicans which were stuck across the top of their helmets.

'My God, look at this lot. Granddads breaking bad,' laughed Pepper, 'or more like breaking sad.'

'Nice bikes though,' said Rhiaz.

'Oh my God, look at that pillock. He has fluffy tiger ears stuck on his helmet. I thought bikers were meant to be hard bastards, really bad boys?'

'Remember, these guys are not Hells Angels.'

Pepper got out of the Astra and looked around.

'I'm gonna have to get you a set of bunny ears for your helmet, Brontë.'

'Now then, Pepper, play nicely.'

'They all look like their mums have washed and pressed their clothes before they've come out.'

She called to a group of bikers.

'Excuse me, love, I hope you've got your vest on. It could get nippy later.'

'All right, don't antagonise the natives, we want information remember. Split-up and see if you can get anything on Lesley Flett.'

'Do you ride with anybody, Brontë?'

'I'm an unsociable bastard, Rhiaz. I don't mix with anyone, I only hang around with you two cos I have to.'

While the other two police officers went off to speak to bikers, Brontë had a look around at the bikes. Most of them were boys' toys. Bikes that would spend most of the year in heated garages behind automatic doors, covered up against the cold winter weather.

'You got a bike?' said a voice.

Brontë turned to see a man in black leathers drinking from a steaming mug and leaning against a Kawasaki Z1000.

'Ducati Monster.'

'Nice. You ride with anyone?'

'Nah, I use it for going to work and back and the odd spin to the coast. You heard of any clubs around about lately?'

'MCs?'

'Yeah.'

'You don't want to be messing with them, mate.'

Brontë showed him his ID.

'It's business I'm afraid.'

'Funny, you don't look like a pig.'

'What's funny is my boss says I don't act like one either.'

The biker looked Brontë over.

'You know any biker that goes by the name of Lesley Flett?' asked Brontë.

'I don't know any names and I don't want to neither,' he placed his empty mug on a low wall and threw his leg over the Kawi. 'There used to be a group that hung out up at the Withering.'

'My God, so they did.'

The biker gunned up his bike.

'You watch it, mate, those guys don't like folks messing in their affairs and particularly not your sort of folks.'

The biker rode off and Brontë high fived him as he past and then called out to his colleagues.

*

Back on the ring road, Rhiaz took a call on his mobile.

'Hello? Yeah, speaking. Who? Capability what? Goldman?' He covered his phone with his hand.

'It's the guy from the newspaper in the States'

'Put him on speakerphone.'

'You're on speakerphone,' said Rhiaz into the phone. 'My sergeant and inspector are here, so no swearing.'

'So, my little English cousins, Capability Goldman at your service, what can I do you for, sirs?'

'The Inspector needs your help, Mr Goldman.'

'You're inquiring about one of our condemned.'

'That's right, sir, someone called "Currer" but that's all we have, other than they're on death row in Carolina.'

'Ah, a certain little lady known as the Ice Maiden.'

'Ask him if she was actually executed,' said Brontë.

'The boss wants to know if she fried or not?'

Brontë mouthed the word 'fried?' to Pepper who lifted her eyes to the Astra's roof.

'Nope, she didn't fry, buddy.'

Brontë and Pepper shouted together, 'She didn't?' They looked at each other.

'What happened to her, was there a stay of execution?' asked Pepper.

'Never mind that, was she released?' asked Brontë.

'Not fry, mis amigos, lethal injection.'

'Shit!' said Brontë.

'So, she is dead? She was executed?' asked Pepper.

'Oh yes, sir, dead and buried.'

'That's it then,' said Brontë, 'she's not involved in any of this shit over here, she's dead.'

'Sorry guys,' said the phone.

'No worries, thanks for your help…'

'Hang on, Rhiaz, before he goes, ask him if anyone came to the execution.'

'Capability, did—'

'Yeah, yeah I heard the guy. Funny he should say that, someone came to the execution, just the one guy.'

'Only one. Is that normal?'

'Nothing's "normal" when it comes to executions, but no it wasn't normal. Only one visitor came to the execution and the Ice Maiden gave a little speech.'

'Who?' shouted Brontë and Pepper together.

'Just some random Asian bloke'

'An Asian?'

'That's right, sir, never did find out who he was. God knows I've tried. He just disappeared into the crowd. It was obvious he wanted to remain... anonymous.'

'Can you find out who he was?' asked Brontë.

'Can't promise anything, but I'll have another go. I'll call you back if I come up with anything. Take it easy, guys'

'Ok,' said Rhiaz, 'catch you later.'

As he clicked the phone off, Brontë looked round at him.

'Catch you bloody later?'

'It's the only American I know.'

'What now?' asked Pepper. 'Shoot up to the Withering, confront the guys up there, see if they know of a Lesley Flett?'

'For Christ's sake, Pepper, you don't just rock up to a MCs pub with the blues a-flashing and siren a-blaring. You'll achieve naff all like that, everybody'll curl up like hedgehogs. I'll pop up to the pub and talk to the bad boys tomorrow. You and Laughing Boy here can get off to the station...'

'The nick?'

'The train station. There's an Asian guard that volunteers there, bit of a coincidence don't you think? I want him questioned. Find out how long he's been in the country, if he's ever been to America. Yada, yada, yada.'

*

At home, sat in his greenhouse with a few bottles of Timmy Taylor's Landlord, Brontë, was talking things through with Obi-Wan.

'Tomorrow, I've gotta speak to a group of really naughty boys.'

The dog ignored him.

'I really could do with some backup,' he slugged back some beer straight from the bottle. 'You wanna come?'

Obi ignored him some more.

'Rhiaz, is a little on the wet side.'

Obi-wan rolled his eyes.

'I could call firearms, but they're probably a bit overkill.'

Obi turned his gaze on to Brontë and projected an image into his brain.

'I don't suppose I should take Pepper, she's too antagonistic.'

Obi continued to stare at him.

'I suppose I might take her.'

Obi placed his head between his paws and fell to sleep, his job done.

*

Sat in Hewenden Bridge Railway Station, Rhiaz questioned Mr Mohammed Mirza, who looked magnificent in his railway regalia.

'I don't even know why you are questioning me. What could you possibly think I could have done?'

'Well, I'm questioning you because... well, because...'

Rhiaz struggled to put into words what he meant.

'Because what?'

'I'm questioning you because you are Asian.'

'Is that a crime nowadays, because if it is you need questioning too.'

'This isn't going as well as I thought.'

'You're not wrong, there.'

'The police are...' he thought '...interviewing?'

'Good, "interviewing" sounds much better.'

'The police are interviewing every Asian male that has connections to this station or this area.'

'In relation to what?'

'Murder.'

'Ha, you think I'm the Moors Vampire,' he laughed, 'and yet I am walking about in broad daylight. You are so funny.'

'What do you know about the Moors Vampire?'

'Just what I hear on the jungle drums, it's all over the village. Nigel Flett is dead, by the hands of a strange, cloaked creature of the night.'

'You knew Nigel Flett?'

'Of course I know him, we volunteer at the same railway, don't we?'

'And?'

'And, what?'

'And what did you think of him.'

'He was strange. I didn't like him. That is about all.'

'What do you know about Carolina?'

'Nothing could be finer than to be there in the morning.'

'We could continue this down the station if you wish.'

'I apologise, young man, please continue.'

'Have you ever been to America?'

'Though I have travelled extensively in the east, I have never been further west than Morecombe.'

'And do you know of a Currer Bell?'

'Of course.'

'Whoa! Hold your horses. What do you mean, of course?'

'I mean, Constable, I know who Currer Bell is... or should I say... was.'

Rhiaz flicked open his notebook and began to scribble notes.

'How on earth do you know of Currer Bell?'

'Because I live in Haworth and I'm well read.'

'Which is relevant why?'

'Currer Bell was the nom-de-plume...'

A look of confusion flickered across the constable's face.

'You know, non-de-plume... Pseudonym...?'

'Oh, right, yeah.'

'Currer Bell was the pen name of Charlotte Brontë.'

Rhiaz was somewhat confused, his mind racing, a look of complete confusion spread across his face.

'But Currer Bell was executed by lethal injection in a South Carolinian Prison.'

Now it was the turn of the railwayman to look nonplussed.

'Well they never mentioned that at the Parsonage Museum.'

*

Brontë and Pepper pulled up into the car park of the Withering or t'Withering, as it had been known locally for many a year.

The pub was one of the highest in the country and was a windswept and desolate old hole high on the moor. It had initially served the sheepherders, farmers, wool-packers and coiners who eked a lousy living on the satanic moors. These trades were all but lost now and since the drink-driving regulations the only clientele the pub attracted were biker gangs and crooks who trafficked anything from sheep to people in the back of white vans.

There was no protection from the wind so when Brontë and Pepper climbed out of the car, the doors were nearly blown off their hinges and down into the valley below.

'Sweet Mary, mother of Joseph! This is a miserable, godforsaken hole,' Brontë moaned as he pulled his Belstaff tight around himself. Pepper ignored him. She was more interested in holding on to the bottom of her skirt.

They staggered and stumbled across the car park past a number of bikes, bikes that were not the brightly coloured posing machines of the peacocks at the Tomato Dip. These were serious bikes, all of them black and chrome. They were mainly Harley Davidsons and Indians, and a couple of long-forked Triumph Bonnevilles. In pride of place by the pub door sat a fat 1100cc chopped Yamaha and despite the fact that the wind tried to blow Brontë off his feet and the bike off its stand, he stopped and admired this brute of a bike. As Brontë looked over the bike he noticed the registration plate, or more to the point, the hand-written plaque where the plate should have been, it read *Fuck the World*.

'Nice,' remarked Pepper.

'Very nice,' said Brontë.

'I was being sarcastic, I meant the registration plate.'

'Sorry, I thought you meant the bike.'

They heard loud music and laughter coming from out of the pub.

Pepper giggled and pretended to look frightened.

'Christ! It's like something out of *Dusk till Dawn*. Surely we'll find our vampire here.'

Brontë grabbed her arm and held her back at the pub door. He stopped and looked at her for a moment.

'This really is not a laughing matter, Pepper. Remember what I said about MCs. These lads really are proper gangsters. They do live outside the law.'

'They're outlaws?'

'They seriously are outlaws. So, with that in mind, perhaps you could work on not upsetting anybody.'

'What, little old me?'

She grinned at him and pushed her way into the pub.

The room went completely silent.

Stood in the doorway and taking everything in, she could see instantly that these guys really were not just trying to look bad, they didn't need to. These were the real article.

Standing in the smoke-filled bar Pepper was overcome by the smell of smoke, sweat and skunk. There was something else in the mix too, something heady, and then it came to her: it was the stink of testosterone.

Brontë entered the bar just behind her and stopped in the doorway as the door swung shut behind him. Every face in the pub was turned towards them.

The drinking, smoking men wore a uniform consisting of greasy stained jeans and old worn leather jackets. Each jacket bore a number of patches. The patches on the back depicted the skull of a wolf with glowing red eyes. Above the skull was a flier that read

The Pagan Wolves and underneath another that simply read *Fuck the World*. There was plenty of flesh on show too but most of it was coloured blue with tattoo ink.

A large man with a shaved head, a greyish to black beard and three tattooed tears dripping from his right eye stepped forward. He had rings in his nose and ears and a dotted line with scissors tattooed around his neck alongside the logo *Cut here*.

He raised his head a little and looked at Brontë and then spoke in a quiet, slow voice.

'Are you fuckin' mad? Comin' in 'ere? Can't you see who and what the fuck we are? Eh?'

The bikers put down their glasses.

'You must be off your 'ead, Mate. An' bringin' your fuckin' bitch in too? Now turn around and get the fuck out of my fuckin' pub.'

Brontë had never in his life been closer to just turning and running. The only thing that stopped him was that he had Pepper with him and didn't want to leave her.

And it was then that Pepper spoke up.

'Oi! Shit for brains. I shall explain in words of one syllable or less, cos you don't look very bright. I – Am – No – Fuck – Er's – Bitch. Got it?'

'Oh shit!' exhaled Brontë.

There was a moment's silence when you could have heard a cotter-pin drop.

'You don't want to fuck with me, love,' said the biker, 'I really am one bad mother.'

'You're a bad mother are you! Well I'm a single mother, and according to my daughter I'm the worst mother in the world. So, *love*, there's nothing you can say that's gonna shock or scare me. So, you might as well cut the crap from the very off.'

The big biker slowly turned his gaze back on to, Brontë.

'Is she with you?'

'She is, yes.'

'I'm really sorry for you, mate. Really, really, sorry.'

He turned his attention back to Pepper.

'And, if you are, as you say, *no fucker's bitch*, then you might buy us a drink,' he gestured to the bar.

Pepper looked at him and then at Brontë. 'Ok. I'll have a pint with ye,' she said, 'but I think my boss needs one more than me.'

'Then the boss can pay,' he turned to the bar. 'Pints for us all.'

This elicited jeers and laughter from the throng that were now standing down from high alert.

Brontë placed fifty quid on the bar. What with this and bloody KickStart it was turning out to be an expensive week.

The bar staff, who were also dressed in leather and denim, pulled drinks for Brontë, Pepper and the large biker, and they went and sat at a small, round table in a window alcove. The bar staff carried on pulling pints for the rest of the room.

The biker glanced at Brontë's Belstaff jacket.

'You some sort of poser or 'ave you got a bike? You wearing biker gear but arrived in a clapped-out old Astra.'

'I've got a bike, I've had a bike since before you were born.'

'Good, I don't like people pretending to be what they're not.'

'Then you're not gonna like this... we're the police.'

'I know you're pigs, I smelt it when you came in. She's all right though,' he gestured to Pepper, 'as long as you're with her, you're safe.... ish.'

He swigged ale from his pint.

'What do you want with me, anyroad? No tax? No insurance? I'm also riding without a number plate?'

'We'd noticed.'

'What can I say? I don't like authority.'

The biker sparked up a hand rolled cigarette, the smoke of which reeked of cannabis. He offered the joint to Brontë.

'Two's up?' he offered.

Brontë didn't react in any shape or form. The biker inhaled deeply.

'So, go on then, what you after? It must be big stuff if you've risked coming in 'ere.'

He exhaled the smoke all over Brontë.

'I want to find Lesley Flett.'

Brontë noticed a slight hesitation and maybe the tear drop tattoos twitched a little. The biker took a swig from his glass and placed his hands down on the table. Each finger of each hand was tattooed with a letter. On the right hand the letters spelt H-A-T-E, and on the left they spelt exactly the same: H-A-T-E.

HATE and HATE.

'He's not 'ere,' said the biker.

'Where do I find him?'

'You won't find 'im. If he wanted to speak to you, he'd find you, but 'e don't, so 'e won't.'

'Are you his official spokesman?'

'I really don't think you know who I am. Not really. You think you do, mate. You think you know us guys, but really you don't know the 'alf of it. I can speak for any or all of these guys.'

'And are any of these guys Lesley Flett.'

'You should quit while you're ahead, fella. I haven't bashed your brains in cos I quite like your plucky little mucker 'ere,'

He leant forward and rubbed Pepper's shoulder.

'But you're on borrowed time. You'd best drink up and get yourselves off if you have any sense.'

Brontë could never take a hint.

'I need to ask him a couple of questions is all.'

'Like did he kill his old man?'

Brontë and Pepper did a double take.

'How the hell did you know that?'

'Like you... officer, I know a lot of shit that I shouldn't.'

'Where is he?'

'Did you not 'ear me? It's time to go.'

'I could come back with a warrant and a Black-Maria full of bobbies.'

The biker laughed; proper guffawed.

'Do you really think us lot would give a shit about that?'

He smiled at Brontë.

'I'll not say it a third time... I'll walk you to the door.'

Brontë and Pepper left their drinks and were escorted off the premises by the big bald biker and a little group of the gang.

'Good night, officers... oh and please don't call again.'

Brontë and Pepper stood outside on the pub step for a while and Pepper linked her arm into Brontë's.

'That was nice, Brontë, you'll have to take me out again sometime. You really know how to treat a girl. Come on. Let's get in the car, it's brass monkeys up here.'

Driving the car back over the dark and windy moors the police officers chatted.

'Would I be right in thinking they were Hells Angels?'

'You would. *The Pagan Wolves*, a seriously unpleasant gang of thugs.'

'We've worked with many seriously unpleasant thugs before.'

'I don't think you've come across such an unpleasant bunch of vicious bastards as the Wolves before, and to top it off there was a hell of a lot of 'em.'

'They might be bad boys, but their mums stitched nice patches on their jackets.'

'That's their *colours,* earned and not bought. Earned by being loyal to the gang and doing unthinkably bad things.'

'And the patch that said "one per cent", is that the average amount of brain power they have?'

'Ah, one per center patches used to instil fear and earn respect from the general public and other motorcyclists.'

'It's all a bit complicated isn't it?'

'OK, look! Here's a crash course on Hells Angels. In America in the sixties the American Motorcycle Association...'

'Like the guys down at the Tomato Dip.'

'Exactly, just regular guys who enjoyed riding around on motorbikes. Well they were fed up with always having they're reputation tarnished by the *outlaw motorcycle groups*.'

'Who were like the Wolves.'

'Right again! So, the American Motorcycle Association put out a statement: ninety-nine per cent of motorcyclists were just ordinary Joes and were law-abiding citizens. This obviously implied that the last one percent were bastards and outlaws. The outlaws were delighted with this, they were happy to be the other one per cent, hence the patch.'

They drove in silence through the dark for a little while. The rain blown by the wind so hard now that the windscreen wipers hardly stood a chance.

'So, Brontë, that's gotta mean you're a ninety-nine per center.'

'Yep, sadly I am.'

'You know what, let's call the station and organise some back up. Let's show these guys they're not as badass as they think they are.'

'Sadly, Pepper love, they could probably get more backup than us, and it will be a lot more organised. They would certainly be more frightening than our lot could ever be.'

There was silence again as Pepper thought things over.

'What's with the face tattoos, anyway? I mean the whole world and its aunty has a tatt nowadays. They're not really the sign of a gangster any more are they, but what's with the tears?'

'Prison tats or homemade tattoos, the tear at the corner of the eye represents shedding a tear for someone you have killed. The more tears you have the more people you have killed.'

'Is that true?'

'God only knows, but I wasn't about to ask him.'

Pepper went silent again for a while and then from out of the blue she spoke up.

'I have a tat!'

'Go bollocks!' snorted Brontë, 'I've never seen it.'

'No, and you never will, neither.'

Brontë and Pepper drove on in deep thought. Pepper could almost hear Brontë's brain turning over.

'OK, come on, where is it?'

Pepper was all modesty and eighteenth-century coyness. 'I'm sorry, Detective. I don't know to what you appertain'

'I appertain to what and where your fictitious tattoo is.'

'There's some things in life that you just don't want in your head, Brontë; the mental imagery could drive you insane.'

*

Jeanne Hepworth made her way through the door of the police station and went up to the reception window.

'Excuse me.'

She waited patiently for the desk sergeant to finish on the phone. He winked at Jeanne to let her know she has been acknowledged but he continued talking into the phone.

Sergeant William Cartwright was a fat, bald copper with red cheeks and a large sweat patch under each armpit. Jeanne could almost smell him through the glass. When he did eventually complete his conversation, he replaced the handset on its cradle and turned his attention to her.

'So, me old love, what can I be doing you for?' he asked quite cheerily in a loud voice.

'What you can be doing me for, young man, is to stop calling me, your *old love*. I may be old but I am most certainly not your love. I am neither stupid nor deaf, so please do not address me as if I were.'

The sergeant stood agog and blinked at her.

'My name is Jeanne Hepworth, so you, Constable, can call me Mrs Hepworth. I am here to report a crime.'

The desk sergeant gathered his pad and pen and looked directly at her.

'Right!' he paused as he gathered himself. 'What exactly is this crime, Mrs Hepworth?'

'Robbery. Daylight bloody robbery.'

The sergeant scratched away on his pad with his Bic.

'And just where did this robbery take place?'

'The robbery took place up at Hewenden Bridge car park, the one by the waterfall, where that so-called... *councillor...*' she emphasised the word with some distain, 'Anthony Swaine, clamped my car and charged me seventy-five pound to have it taken off. It's like a protection racket he's running up there. He needs a right good bonking.'

The constable hesitated. This was sticky ground and he did not want to upset the lady any more than necessary.

'Bonking?'

'You know,' she mimed punching someone, 'on the nose. A right good bonk.'

'Mrs Hepworth, the whole of West Yorkshire Police Force thinks he's a right b—' he reconsidered, '...bully, but sadly there's very little we can do about it.'

'But I was on official police business. Ask that man there,' she pointed at, Brontë who had just entered through the swing doors. 'I was helping him and his sergeant with their inquiries.'

Brontë walked across the foyer past the reception window with a random roll of woodchip wallpaper, which he'd scavenged from his cottage, stuck under one arm. The sergeant called to him and waved him over, happy to pass the book on this one.

'Inspector, you're wanted.'

Brontë crossed over to the reception window.

'Hello, Mrs Hepworth isn't it? Found our dead priest in the waterfall?'

'That's right, Detective. I was interviewed by your sergeant, nice lady with a funny name. Now, Detective, when I went back to my car, I found I had been clamped by that highwayman at the car park.'

'Councillor Swain basically does what he wants with his own land, there's very little we can do. He shouldn't but he does. What can I say, he's a complete cock, but hey, aren't they all?'

Jeanne was frustrated but refused to let it show.

'There is no sense in this world any more, no common decency. When a fat, arrogant landowner can hide behind the law to bully old ladies it is shocking. There's no honour or chivalry left. Are they just old-fashioned principals that have no place for you lot nowadays?'

'Look, I can't promise anything, but I'll go have a chat with him.'

'I don't want promises, I'm not even all that bothered about the money, I just want someone to go up and give him a right good bonking.'

Brontë raised his eyebrows and looked enquiringly at the sergeant on the desk.

'Thumping,' explained the sergeant.

*

Up in the incident room, with the assistance of Rhiaz, Brontë rolled out the wallpaper.

'Boss?'

'Yes, Rhiaz.'

'You know the Asian guard down at the steam railway?'

'Not personally but I do remember I asked you to interview him.'

'Yes, that's right, well I did that, ok? And he knew the victim and didn't really like him, but he had alibis which check, right?'

'I'm sure this is leading somewhere, Rhiaz.'

'Right yeah well, he said... he said Currer Bell was Charlotte Brontë's pen name.'

Brontë stopped in his task of unrolling the wood chip.

'And!?'

'And... well it is, sir, I looked it up. It is!'

'Well, Christ knows what that means. You better follow it up, Rhiaz. Here, grab this,' he handed him the end of a long piece of woodchip.

They stuck the long piece of wallpaper horizontally across the wall with drawing-pins.

'What exactly are you doing, boss? Shouldn't it be the other way round, running up and down the wall?'

'We're not decorating, you wassock. Even I wouldn't hang wallpaper with drawing-pins. Right, go and get your little black marker.'

At this point Pepper entered with three mugs of coffee.

'His little black what, sir!?'

Brontë threatened her with a look. 'Right, Rhiaz, now write "Nigel Flett" on the paper, we're making a timeline.'

Rhiaz moved to the left-hand side of the wallpaper and was about to do as he was bid when Brontë stopped him.

'No, not there, write it halfway along the length of the roll, right over there.'

'Doesn't the timeline start with the murder of Nigel Flett?'

'Maybe, maybe not. The murder of our Nigel might or might not have been the start of all this. As yet we don't know, do we?'

Sitting on her desk, Pepper threw in her two-penneth.

'What's all this in aid of?'

'It's going to be a timeline of events. Well, it is when Rhiaz gets his finger out.'

'Very high tech. Can I borrow your abacas?' said Pepper.

'The chief super's gonna be so not impressed,' added Rhiaz.

'Like I give a flying monkey's what that bent bugger thinks.'

The room fell silent. Rhiaz, who had a clear view over Brontë's shoulder, was silently trying to warn Brontë of impending danger. He stared intently at Brontë, a look of warning spread across his face, and winked rather unsubtly.

'You got something in your eye, Rhiaz?'

Rhiaz's silence spoke volumes, far more than a thousand words or a picture could have. Brontë could sense eyes burning into his back.

'Very appropriate, Brontë, you make a far better decorator than you do, Detective. Maybe a change of career is in order.'

Brontë turned to discover Chief Superintendent Crupper standing over him. Crupper was, in Brontë's words, an unpleasant, bald slap-head, with a huge beer gut that hung over his belt quite dramatically. Brontë had often mused that it must have been years since the superintendent had last seen his feet. Crupper also had a gap between large protruding incisors which stuck out over his bottom lip when he sneered, which was often. This gave him the look of some sort of ridiculous imp. By some inexplicable and deluded reasoning, the chief superintendent believed this made him God's gift to women.

'The desk sergeant tells me you're looking into a complaint about Councillor Swain, Brontë.'

'Well that's pretty close to the truth, yes... sir'

'I don't want any nonsense, Brontë; the councillor is a bona-fide businessman.'

'He's a right, robbing bastard... sir.'

'If people don't obey the rules they should face the consequences.'

'Maybe the councillor should be made to face a few consequences of his own.'

'If I hear you've been making a nuisance of yourself with the councillor... well just don't, that's all.'

The superintendent lifted his hand and waved one finger in Brontë's face.

'Just give me one reason, Brontë, one good reason and I'll banjo you back into uniform as quick as... you won't know what hit you, lad.'

'Lad!? It's a long time since anyone called me lad. I think I could easy give you a couple years... sir'

'Then act like an adult and dress like it. You look like a bloody yob.'

With that Crupper walked away. He completely ignored Rhiaz as he passed him but stopped in front of Pepper.

'How's it going, Sergeant?'

'Very well, sir, thank you.'

'Your ears must have been burning yesterday, Sergeant.'

'Really, sir.'

'You could a go a long way, Sergeant, "with a little help from your friends".'

'Very funny, sir, I've not heard that one before.'

'I've been telling the board all about our lovely Sergeant Pepper, I have.'

He stuck his tongue between his lips and the gap in his teeth and made a salacious, sucking sound.

'Pepper! Always makes me think of something hot and spicy.'

He winked at her and he walked towards the door, giving his imp smile with his wonky teeth. Behind his back Pepper mimed sticking her finger down her throat and throwing up. She had luckily stopped when Crupper turned in the doorway and threw Brontë a parting shot.

'I got a message earlier they were waiting for you down at the morgue, Brontë. I must admit it raised my hopes when I thought they awaited your body. Sadly, they meant they wanted you to attend the post-mortem. You're holding things up.'

*

Down at the morgue, Brontë leant against the wall as far away from the slab as possible. He hated post-mortems and the trouble was everyone around him knew it and enjoyed watching him suffer.

'You ok, Brontë?'

'I'd rather stick rusty pins in my eyes, Pepper, you know that.'

'It's just another part of the job, boss, not pleasant but necessary.'

'I know my job, Sergeant, I just don't like this part of it. I can deal with dead bodies when they're lying on some floor or even crucified across some waterfall, but not when they are cold, white and laid out on that slab.'

Dr Carol Redman was presiding over proceedings, her mouth still strikingly red, her long black hair swooshing around all over the shop. She still wore the red Dr Martens but she'd lost the black leather coat, which she had traded for forensic pathology gear: goggles, mask, gloves and a lab coat, the latter was splattered in blood and God knows what else. She had taken great pleasure in watching Brontë's displeasure.

'You might need to get over here and take a closer look, Inspector.'

'Just get on with it, Morticia.'

Brontë had been calling her this for so long it had stuck and now everybody used it. She didn't mind too much. She had a sense of humour and she felt it was pretty perfect for an ex-goth with her hair. She nodded to her aid, who Brontë called Pugsley, but never to his face, who uncovered the body and then took his camera and hovered in the background. Brontë stayed back against the wall, looking anywhere but at the body. That was Brontë's major stumbling block with post-mortems: he never knew where to look. Not just because of the horror of it all but also the undignified nakedness of it all. It felt wrong, looking without consent. He would never normally look at person so intently, because he would be aware that they were looking right back at him. There's some sort of contract; you look at me, I look at you. There was an equality about it all. But not here. Here there was no equality. The body is looked at but cannot look back in return. It made Brontë very sorry for the victim. Christ, he would hate it himself. Not being able to cover himself up. The final indignity. Just imagine lying there.

'Are you with us, Inspector?'

'Yeah, Morticia, get cracking will you? The sooner this is over the better.'

'Then please step forward and join us at the table.'

The pathologist hid the little smile on her face by pulling the surgical mask up to cover it.

Brontë took one step forward and tried to look anywhere but at the cadaver. The rest of them stood around the slab and looked at the pale, fat, body of the railwayman.

'I think we can all agree that Mr Flett is dead,' said the pathologist. 'The next step is to determine the manner of that death. Is it: A. Natural, B. Accidental, C. Suicide or M. Murder?'

'I'm no pathologist,' commented Pepper, 'but I think we can rule out the first three.'

'As hard as it is to say, I think your sergeant's right. It's hardly likely to be natural. I don't think it could be accidental or self-inflicted, so that does leave us with good old-fashioned murder.'

'Mmmm, my favourite,' said Brontë.

The pathologist stopped and looked at him.

'Sorry, bad joke,' said Brontë, 'it's how I get by when I have to deal with this kind of shit.'

'Oh, I'm sorry, Detective, that's what counts for humour in your world, does it?' Morticia leant over the body. 'We start with an external examination, looking for wounds and first impressions. Microphone please, Gary.'

The aid held the requested piece of equipment up so it could capture her words of wisdom.

'White... male...'

'Difficult to check without the important bit being there,' said Pepper.

Morticia continued speaking into the mic as if Pepper did not exist.

'...approximately sixty... hair colour black turning grey, not much to the front and nearly to the shoulder at the back.... unshaven... eye colour... grey... scar on the chin... presently no visible moles... no tattoos that can be seen and... Aha!'

Brontë took a step forward. 'What do you mean, aha?'

'Our victim has a little prick...'

'We thought that had gone,' said Pepper.

Morticia silenced her with a glare and waited a second. 'Thank you, Sergeant I'll just wait for the laughter and applause to die down a little before I continue.'

'I'm sorry,' said Pepper, who wasn't at all, 'it's a syndrome I have, a bit like Tourette's but less sweary.'

Morticia returned her attention back to the body.

'What he has is a puncture mark here on his neck. It was almost obscured by two larger puncture holes.'

'What sort of punctures?' Brontë moved next to her, looking at the neck. 'Could it be a bite?'

'Could be a bite?'

Pepper joined in. 'Oh my God, we are looking for a vampire.'

Morticia ignored her.

'The smaller could be an insect bite. It's very small.' She looked over her mask at Pepper. 'The larger punctures... not so sure.'

'Could they be a bite from a set of fangs, maybe?'

'Sergeant, there is no such thing as the living dead.'

'You don't work with Brontë.'

'So,' the pathologist continued her inspection, 'the smaller wound could be a needle... an injection... there's no other signs of IV drug use, though.'

The pathologist gestured to the technologist, who stepped forward and took photographs.

'The larger holes look like he was stabbed with a fork,' she acted out her commentary, 'maybe to hold him still while slicing off his penis with the carving knife.'

'Do you really need to enjoy this so much?'

'There's nothing like getting pleasure from your work.' She turned her attention to the technologist. 'Gary, can you prop the body up for me please?'

The technologist placed a rubber brick under the body.

'This support under the top of the back enables the neck and head to fall back and pushes the chest up, like so.'

Morticia, gestured to the cadaver.

'This makes it easier for me to start the cutting.'

With the head pulled back, Nigel Flett's mouth had fallen wide open.

'Hello, hello,' she looked into the mouth, 'and what have we here?'

'Has the tongue been removed?' asked Brontë.

'Let's have a little look-see, shall we?' She held out her hand. 'Forceps.'

The required tool was placed into her waiting hand. She firked about for a bit with them in the victim's mouth.

'Voila!' she declared triumphantly.

Brontë and Pepper stepped forward, eager to see what had been discovered.

Fishing down between the cadaver's teeth with her tongs Morticia retrieved a mess of bloody tissue from out of the victim's mouth. They stared at the bloody mess.

'Well, well, it seems we were mistaken about the tongue, Brontë.'

Studying closely Pepper asked. 'What the hell is it?'

'Well, Pepper, my dear,' said the pathologist. 'We have just found the missing penis.'

'Christ almighty! It was there the whole time.'

'Yep,' she dropped the penis into a specimen bottle, 'seems like I mistook the penis for a tongue.'

'I suppose its easily done,' Pepper said, her eyes shining with mischief.

Brontë impaled her with a look.

'Don't, Pepper.' He returned his attention to Morticia. 'I need to know what killed him.'

'For that I need to go inside.'

With a few deft strokes of the scalpel the pathologist cut a huge 'y' incision across the railway guard's chest.

'Come on,' said Brontë, looking rather green around the gills, 'let's leave 'er to it.'

*

In the Cock and Bottle public house, Brontë sat in the bay window seat, way over in the corner and well out of the way of other patrons. He had purposefully sat himself out of the way. He wasn't in the mood for people, but was enjoying being warmed by the fire blazing in the inglenook fireplace, completely lost in a world of his own.

Brontë loved a good old Yorkshire pub, but since the smoking ban in the early part of the second millennium they had really come into their own. Without the smell of tobacco smoke these ale houses smelt of burning logs, beer and roast beef. If Brontë could bottle the scent he believed he'd make a fortune.

The wind and rain thrashed the window and blurred the view across the moors. The sienna bracken and green heather merged seamlessly into a Payne's grey sky making a Turneresque masterpiece of the double window.

The glass panes rattled in their frames and the frames trembled in their mullions. The wind threatened to push the whole lot in, throw it across the tap room and smash it into the inglenook.

Pepper returned from the bar with two pints of Old Peculiar, one of which she plonked in font of Brontë. The other she took a deep swig from herself.

'Penny for 'em,' she said.

'Just appreciating God's own county. Where's the grub?'

'Won't be long.'

Brontë sucked a large slug of amber beer from his pint, smacked his lips and sat back to look out of the window. He was soon lost in his own world again, or somebody's world anyway.

'I 've got to admit, Pepper, I'm at a complete loss.' He drank more beer. 'What the hell is going on?'

'It's got to be about sex.'

'I'm not so sure.'

'Freud says everything is about sex.'

'I think, Pepper, it might have been Freud that had the problem with sex, not everybody else.'

'It might be about sex, but it's not sexual.'

'What's the difference?'

'Well it's doesn't look like the murderer is looking for sexual gratification, does it? There's no evidence of sex.'

'What about the whole penis thing. That has to be about sex hasn't it?'

'The injuries have emasculated the victim, that's sort of the opposite of sex.'

'So, you think it's about gender?'

'God knows what it's all about.'

'This just doesn't feel like the usual sort of serial killings.'

'OK Colombo, how many serial killings have you actually been involved with?'

'I'll have you know, young lady, I was one of the team on the Ripper case.'

'Bleadin' 'ell, Brontë, in the eighteen hundreds? You're even older than I thought.'

'The Yorkshire Ripper, smart arse, one of my first postings.'

'Peter Sutcliffe?'

'That's the guy. This doesn't have that feel. It's nothing like anything I've ever known of, or heard of before. This is something else, but I don't know what.'

'Like what?'

'I don't know, this feels targeted, calculated, more reasoned somehow.'

'What do you mean, reasoned? How can it be reasoned?'

'I don't know, but I'll tell you when I do.'

'And in the meantime.'

'In the meantime, Pepper, in the absence of a profiler, what would you say we've got here?'

'Well I've never come across one myself, but in all the books I've read about psychopaths...'

'Books? As in books related to your continued professional development?'

'No, books as in related to crime novels. You know Val McDermid and Kathy Reichs? Well, according to them, psychopaths are generally white, middle-aged, male, with big egos... Bit like your average police officer.'

A waitress waddled over to their table. She was dressed in a tight white shirt and black skirt. The buttons of both were straining on their threads. What with the buttons and the shuddering window panes Brontë did not feel safe at all.

'Bowl of chips?' announced the girl.

Pepper put up her hand.

'Mine, please.'

The bowl was all but thrown down in front of her.

'Bangers and mash?' The waitress looked at Brontë. 'Must be you, love.'

The plate was thrown down in front of him, slopping onion gravy on to the table top. She waited and looked at them.

'What's wrong?' asked Pepper as she picked up a chip.

'No tip!?'

'Aye love, I'll give you a tip,' said Pepper, 'get a bigger blouse.'

The woman snarled and left.

*

The two officers sat and ate in silence for a little while, with Pepper dipping her chips in Brontë's gravy.

'Funny name for a pub, *Cock and Bottle*. Sort of reminds you of this morning, when Morticia stuck Nigel's little fella in that sample jar.'

Brontë froze, a sausage on his fork halfway to his mouth. He stopped before he took a bite.

'Fancy that, Brontë. The murder sticking the todger in the victim's mouth.'

Brontë, looked in distaste at the sausage and tossed it back on to his plate.

'Thanks a million, Pepper.'

'What?' replied Pepper in all innocence. 'Don't you want it?'

'I'll never be able to eat another sausage again.' He stood and downed his pint. 'OK you go back to the incident room. You can drop me off at the station to get my bike.'

Pepper picked up the discarded sausage and, with a twinkle in her eye, she took the sausage in her mouth and bit off the end and winked at Brontë as she did.

'Pepper, you are one sick bitch. Why I hang around with you God only knows'

'Well I quite like you too, Brontë. If you were two inches taller and twenty years younger I could quite go for you.'

'If I was two inches taller and twenty years younger I wouldn't look twice at you.'

'Ouch! Touché, Brontë. Touché.'

'Come on. I need to see a man about a clamp.'

*

Brontë rode his bike into the waterfall's car park.

Frank Gommersal was busy fastening a clamp to the front nearside wheel of a Skoda Octavia with a Blue Badge on the windscreen. He was smirking to himself.

Brontë flashed his ID at the grinning oaf.

'I'm on official police business, you interfere with that bike in anyway and I'll do you for obstructing a murder investigation.'

The oaf pretty much ignored him.

'Where's your boss. Is he in his hut?'

'Check for ye'self.'

Brontë knocked on the door of the hut and entered. The interior was hot and stank of paraffin, all down to the heater in the corner. A man, whom Brontë assumed was councillor Anthony Swaine, was stuffing an envelope full of fivers into an old safe. The man turned round, looking worried.

'What do you want?' he asked sharply.

Brontë flashed him his ID.

'Anthony Swaine?'

'Councillor Swaine to you, Inspector'

'Detective Inspector to you, *Councillor*.' He exaggerated the word 'councillor'.

'So, what can I do for you *Detective* Inspector?' Repaying the compliment on the word 'detective'.

'I'm looking for a highwayman, Councillor. Some thieving scumbag that steals from old ladies.'

'Careful now, Officer, I know the chief superintendent very well, we are members of the same club.'

'Ah, that'll be the obnoxious twats club, would it?'

'You don't want to be blotting your copy book with your superiors do you, Brontë? Don't want to be making false accusations?'

'I can see it in the press. Local councillor, chair of the Conservative Club, all round top dog in these 'ere parts, clamped an old age pensioner, a grandma at that.'

'The signs are very clear. If she can still drive her car around at her age, she must be able to read the signs. You outstay your ticket; you pay the fine. It's quite simple.'

'For God's sake man, she's over eighty, and your hoodlum made her cry.'

'She shouldn't be out in the big wide word if she can't deal with it without crying, now should she?'

'Won't be good for votes, Councillor, will it?'

'There's no elections for months and months. Everything will have blown over by then. The electorate has a short memory.'

'I told her I would have a word with you man to man, get her money back.'

'If you promised her money back then you better give it her, Detective Inspector. I don't run this car park as a charity. It's a business, a legitimate business. It's how I make my money. If people go over the time limit, then that is their lookout.'

Brontë stepped right up to the councillor. 'I will get you back for this, don't think I won't... *Councillor.*'

'Many a man has thrown down that gauntlet over the years, very few ever succeeded... *Officer*'

Brontë exited the hut.

'I don't like bullies, Councillor, you've not heard the last of this.'

'I think you'll find that it is you that has not heard the last of this. I play golf with your boss. He won't think too kindly to you threatening his partner. He won't like that at all.

'Yeah, well I've made some new friends today, Councillor and I don't think you'll like them at all.'

*

Back at the police station, Brontë entered the investigation room and went straight to update his timeline. He whipped the marker pen from Rhiaz's hand and a mug of coffee from Pepper's.

Pepper was flicking through mugshots of local ne're-do-wells on her computer. Brontë looked over her shoulder.

'I've told you before, Pepper. No computer dating on company time.'

'Ha, see how I laugh.' She stood. 'Well I'd best go make a coffee. You want one? Oh no you've got mine.'

She got up and left.

'So, my fine little Islamic friend, what you come up with?'

'I've come up with the gen on Caleb Smith…'

'Bloody hell, that is his name?'

'Yep, and he does have a shady past.'

'How shady?'

'Assault with a deadly weapon.'

'Jees-us, what'd he do?'

'He beat his games teacher round the head fifty-five times with a cricket stump.'

'Jesus Christ. How old was he?'

Rhiaz panicked and frantically flicked through his file.

'I don't think it said. He must have at least been to teacher training collage for a few years and...'

'Bloody Smith, not the teacher, you prat.'

'Oh! Thirteen.'

'Shit, what brought it on?'

'The young Caleb said the teacher was cheating.'

'What, like with is mother?'

'He claimed at the trial that the teacher was fixing scores and unfairly promoting some boys above others, so he had punished him.'

'Well that's bloody weird.'

'There's an unofficial note at the back of the file.

'Unofficial?'

'A hand-written sheet stuck in the back after the case was closed. Written by the investigating officer.'

'That was helpful of him.'

'He felt Caleb might have been trying to save face, with the lame cheating story.'

'Go, Rhiaz lad, spit it out.'

'Seems that the gym teacher in question had a predilection towards prepubescent boys.'

'Any evidence?'

'No sir, all rumours. No boys came forward to speak, and like I said, if it was true, Caleb was keeping shtum.'

'What happened to Caleb?'

'He served nearly thirteen years.'

'That's a lot.'

'Apparently he was not a model prisoner.'

The doors swung open and Pepper re-entered with a large mug in her fist.

'Has Rhiaz told you about our vampire's dog walker?'

'He has that. We need to pull our friend Caleb in for questioning.'

'What for?' said Pepper. 'We've got nowt on him.'

'He has a record for violence. He apparently nearly killed a man for abusing him. He could have killed these two for the same reason. The two victims were right pervy bastards and had their little fellas cut off. Could have easily been revenge killings, right?'

'He was thirteen for God's sake, and it was at least twenty years ago. He's been clean ever since.'

'Pepper, you of all people know that just because someone hasn't been collared, doesn't mean to say they're innocent.'

'And just because someone was bad once, doesn't mean they'll stay bad.'

'And just because...'

There was a cough from the corner of the room and the two officers stopped and looked round.

'Morticia called,' Rhiaz chipped in.

'What she have to say for herself?'

'She's done the autopsy on the priest.'

'And?'

'She discovered that—'

'Rhiaz you've got exactly one second to—'

'There was river water in his lungs,' spat out Rhiaz quickly.

'He drowned?'

'Probably.'

'Probably?'

'More than probably.'

'And?'

'And he was suspended across the waterfalls with something called a...' he checked his PACE notebook '...a martingale?'

'What the heck's a bloody martingale?' asked Pepper.

'It's an item of horse tack. There is a stable up there I suppose.'

'One of you best get up there and have a word. You, Pepper, I don't want Rhiaz up there around all those jodhpurs.'

'You're going to love this, boss'

Brontë raised his eyebrows in response.

'Guess.'

'Just get on with it, Rhiaz.'

'Guess, Pepper.'

'Ah, let me see... erm... post-mortem shows a puncture in his neck.'

'Kerching! Back of the net! Give the lady a cigar. We got us a vampire.'

'There's no such thing as vampires, Rhiaz.'

'Maybe not, Pepper, but it does prove the cases are definitely linked.'

'Seems like it, boss.'

'We've got us a serial killer.'

Brontë took a swig of Pepper's cold coffee and was deep in thought.

'What did she say about his penis?'

'His penis had been removed, but we already knew that, right?'

'But did she find it? During the autopsy, was it in his mouth?'

'She said,' he read from his notebook, '"penis cut off with a sharp implement, not found".'

'Could have fallen out of his mouth as he drowned.'

'If it fell out, where is it?'

Rhiaz, jumped up, 'I'll get the scuba guys out, have a bit of a look about.'

'Scuba guys?"

'Underwater search team, they may find something.'

Pepper laughed, 'God knows. It could be in Hull by now or gobbled up by some halibut or heron.'

'I'll get on to it right now.'

Rhiaz grabbed his phone and started banging numbers into it.

Pepper looked across at Brontë quizzically.

'Our guy's not your usual sort of serial killer though, is he? Takes no trophies, leaves no messages, no toying with the police. Just weird random deaths.'

'These killings are connected and not just cos they're the same architect. Something's linking them.'

'I suppose them having their cocks cut off could be some sort of weird message to us.'

'This is not about showing off or challenging us; the murder's just getting the job done, and seems to be making a bloody good job of it too. From what I'm thinking the mutilation of the body is all about the victim, it's a punishment.'

Rhiaz thought for a moment.

'What about crucifixion across a waterfall? That's hardly a crime of passion, a spur of the moment murder, is it?

'Exactly, Rhiaz,' she turned back to Brontë, 'that's not a message at all, then?'

'I'm just saying this guy's not your usual serial killer, that's all.'

'Guy?!'

'Well he's gotta be a "he" surely? Had to be big enough to overpower his victims. He seemed to find that pretty easy.'

'So, only men are strong, is that it, Brontë?'

'You know what I mean.'

'Right, Rhiaz, if one of us two were going to overpower you, me or Brontë, who'd have the best chance?'

'Well you, Sarge.'

'Exactly.'

Brontë looked shocked. 'Bloody charming!'

Before Pepper had a chance to prove her point they were disturbed by the chief super bursting in. Crupper was bright red and blowing steam out of his ears.

'Brontë! My room! Now!'

When Brontë entered, Crupper was standing in his office behind a huge mahogany desk.

'You wanted to speak to me?' Brontë did his three-beat pause '...Sir.'

'Sit!' the superintendent spat in his face.

'It's not the nineteen-seventies, sir. We are now meant to show a modicum of mutual respect.'

'I said bloody sit,' Crupper almost exploded with anger.

Brontë held his ground and stood and looked at the irate chief.

'You went against my expressed orders, Brontë.'

'Which were what exactly, sir?'

'I ordered you not to go and bother Councillor Swain.'

'I thought that was more of a guideline than an order, sir.'

'I told you not to speak to him.'

'We just had a little friendly chat.'

'He says you threatened him. How dare you threaten a man of such... well... how dare you?'

'How dare I threaten a man of such what, sir?'

'How dare you threaten any man?'

'It was hardly a threat. More just a few words of helpful advice.'

'I'll give you a few words of helpful advice, Brontë. Stay well away from the councillor and his bloody car park.'

'Will that be all, sir?' Brontë turned to walk out of the room.

'Brontë, hear me now. You go against my expressed orders one more time and I'll banjo you, lad. I'll banjo you back into uniform quicker than... well... bloody quick that's for sure.'

'And I thought you didn't like threats...sir.'

'This is no threat Brontë, it's a fucking promise.'

*

It was drizzling up at Withins Riding Stables. Verity Toop, covered from head to toe by a hooded long black outback coat, was out in the exercise yard lunging Polly, her rowan stallion. The horse was on a long line and Verity encouraged him to circle with a lunge whip. Both horse and human were at peace with the world and with each other. Their peace was interrupted by a girl in jodhpurs, hoody and riding hat.

'Wilshy!' shouted the girl.

Verity looked over but the horse continued to trot on.

'What is it, Abby?

'There's a woman here to talk to someone about that chap that was found in the waterfall, wanted to know who was in charge so I've brought her here.'

And indeed, there was a woman standing behind the young rider. Verity waved her over. As Pepper walked across the yard the young rider called again.

'Wilshy, do you want me to take Polly in?'

'If you would, love.' She handed the equestrian equipment to the girl, who led the rowan away.

'Sorry to bother you, madam.' Pepper flashed her ID. 'I'm Sergeant Pepper…' she awaited the inevitable joke and was pleasantly surprised when none came.

'Please to meet you, Sergeant.' She extended her hand. 'Verity Toop.'

Pepper shook the woman's hand.

'I'm sorry, the girl, Aby, said something about "Wilshy"?'

'Ah, that's a rather unfortunate nickname that I acquired many moons ago. It's a long story.'

'I've got plenty of time.'

The woman laughed and threw back her hood, revealing hair the colour of her horse. She sat on a pile of hay bales and Pepper joined her.

'Well you see, Sergeant, when I was in my pomp I was a bit of a name in the riding fraternity. Winning acclaim and ribbons and trophies all over the shop. I was quite a bit of a looker back then if I do say so myself. Well I was infatuated with a young a stable lad and we hit it off pretty well, if you get my drift. Anyway, one thing led to another and I ended up letting him photograph me.'

'Comprising?'

'Oh yes, V compromising, clad only in unbuttoned jodhpurs and holding a riding crop.'

'And?'

'And the bastard sold them to a certain man's magazine and they posted them in the Readers Wives section under the glorious title of "Wilshy Whipham?" And that, dear Sergeant, is how I got my nickname, and it has stuck for all these years. I don't mind, it's a good reminder. And a good lesson for all these girls in this world of mobile phones.'

'My God, I bet you could have killed him.'

'Sergeant, if I could have got hold of him I would have more than killed him, I'd have cut his ruddy tackle off. Never mind that, what was it I can help you with. It must be to do with the incident over at the falls.'

Pepper looked at her for a while, a little lost for words.

'Sergeant?'

'Sorry. Yes, the incident. We are asking if people have noticed anyone hanging about?'

'The girls reckon they're always seeing things up on the moors, strange people walking about, but no one's mentioned anything about vampires.'

'Vampires?'

'That's the story in the local press.'

'Bloody hell, I could strangle that Micky Grimshaw.' She took out her notebook. 'And have you had any thefts, anything going missing?'

'Funny you should say that. We have, just one item.'

'Not a martingale by any chance?'

'It was. how the hell did you know that?'

'I think, Mrs Toop—'

'Miss.'

'Miss Toop, you're going to need to come into the station and make a written statement.'

'I don't understand.'

'The man who was murdered down at the fall was suspended on a martingale and also had his privates removed. That's two coincidences too many for my boss.'

'For God's sake, Sergeant, you just claimed that you would strangle someone called Mickey something or other. What was that, a proposal for premeditated murder?'

Chapter Seven

The night of Samhain.
The third of November.

Though Hewenden Bridge graveyard was spot lit by the moon's silvery light, there was a large shadow cast by the church tower, which was thrown across the old stones like a blanket.

Cicely Wyck snuck silently across the yard. She crept from headstone to headstone and kept to the darkness of the church's shadow, her silver hair shining bright when she occasionally drifted out into the light of the moon. The silver hair matched perfectly with her long white robes. In one hand she held a heavy hessian sack and in the other a curved, silver blade flashed in the moonlight.

Cecily was there for one reason and one reason alone. Tonight was a special night, a night of celebration. Tonight, it was Samhain, the pre-Christian moon festival with roots older than the Celts themselves, older than any records of man. Tonight was the one night of the year when the doors to the other world were opened, the night when creatures crossed over from the other side to this side, when the souls of the dead cross to mix with the souls of the living. Unhuman creatures known as the Sidhe were let loose on the world of men.

This was the time of year when the beasts were brought down from the summer pastures and slaughtered for the winter. Slaughtered under the flickering light of bone-fires that were lit to protect and to cleanse.

Blood and fire.

The old gods resurrected to ensure that the tribe and its livestock survived the winter, the souls of the dead encouraged to visit the homes of their ancestors. A time when places were set at dinner tables for the dead, when offerings of food and drink were left out for those that had passed.

The veneration of the dead.

The love and respect of the deceased is in the belief that the dead have a continued existence, and possess the ability to influence the fortunes of the living. People would dress up as the dead, going door to door in disguise causing mayhem and mischief, the chaos they caused for one night of madness, bringing balance and order to life for the rest of the year. Cicely was all set to execute her yearly ritual, to incite the souls of the dead to rise up, leave their graves and run amok.

When she arrived at the yew tree in the far corner of the yard, she paused a little and listened. She had thought she had been alone as she had made her way up the cobbled snickets and ginnels that led up to the church, but now and again she was sure she had heard rustlings from behind her. She thought she heard footsteps, but when she had looked back she could see nothing but shadows. She entered the cemetery by way of the old resurrection gate, which squeaked loudly as she passed through it.

Squeak!

She stopped for a while and listened. Nothing.

Crossing to the top corner she shook the hessian sack over the only grave stone in the shade of the old yew tree. The contents emptied out on to the lichened top: hazelnuts, mushrooms, apples, holly and mistletoe berries rolled out on to the stone. She used the side of the long, curved silver blade to stop an apple from rolling off the edge and on to the floor.

Squeak!

Cicely froze where she was and listened. Nothing.

She began to arrange the offerings on her improvised altar, when…

Squeak!

She heard the noise again. It was the gate. Someone was following her. Someone was coming up the path.

Crack!

What was that? A broken twig? Someone, or something, was stalking her up through the headstones?

Crack!

There it was again.

Cecily stepped backwards into the shadow of a large headstone that was toppled over at a crazy angle. She hunkered down as close as she could get against the cold hard stone and held her breath, unsure if she was frightened or excited. She was certainly exhilarated by the cold on her skin, the moonlight and the fear.

She could just about make out a figure as it stepped out of the shadows into a patch of moonlight. A figure in a long, black, hooded cloak, a cloak that covered the figure from head to foot and a hood that threw their face into shadow.

Cecily could hear the figure breathing heavily.

'What do you want?' hissed Cecily.

There was a short pause.

'What do you want?' hissed the hooded figure right back at her.

Cecily threw herself out from the cover of the headstone and grabbed the stranger from behind. The two hooded figures struggled in the moonlight. One silvery white; the other crow black. They tussled for a second and the crow black creature screeched and screamed like a wailing banshee.

Cecily halted the onslaught and stood and stared at the figure before her: a figure wrapped in what was now a ripped, dishevelled cloak which hung open, revealing the naked body beneath.

'For God'th thake, Grandma, chill the fuck out, will you?'

*

Not far away, back on the Mad Mile, Brontë rode the Monster towards home. He was completely pissed off with everything, but riding the motorcycle improved his mood somewhat. He was not riding particularly hard. He was on autopilot and he sang 'Born to be Wild' inside his helmet as loud as he could.

On the last 'Born to be Wild' Brontë screamed out at the top of his voice right into his helmet, steaming up the visor as he did, when a bike zoomed out of the mist and braked hard right in front of him.

'Jesus Christ!!'

Brontë slammed on the anchors and the bike fishtailed on the wet tarmac, the back-wheel flapping from side to side like a salmon. He automatically turned into the skid and heaved the heavy machine to one side to avoid a collision. The biker in front accelerated away from him and held a position of about three feet in front.

Brontë, blasted on his horn.

Parp!

He never really found this very satisfying on the bike. In the car you can hit the horn with your fist and scream and shout, which he found very therapeutic. On the bike it was just a matter of pressing a little button with your thumb. All right, you could still scream and shout, but it was not half as rewarding. He did his best to try and vent his spleen on the little button.

Parp!

Parp!

He kept pressing until he noticed the colours of the biker in front. The sawn-off denim jacket and a patch with a wolf's skull; a skull with red burning eyes.

'Fuck!!' he said to the inside of his helmet.

He immediately stopped 'parping' on the horn and he wasn't singing any more either.

A quick glance in his mirror and he saw the whole horrific truth of the matter, the entire gang of Wolves were riding with him. Gradually, the pack crept nearer and nearer and a number pulled level into an outriding position, outflanking him. He was surrounded and being escorted by a gang of wolves.

The speed of the convoy slowly increased.

'Double-triple-fuck!!' he spat into his helmet, speckling spittle on to the inside of his visor.

He was trapped in the middle of a thirty-plus biker convoy that snaked along the moor road like a black and chrome python. The bikers in black leather and denim with not a helmet in sight.

Being within the middle of the pack, Brontë could neither stop nor accelerate; he could turn neither left nor right. He just had to go with the flow. Just go with the flow and concentrate on the important things like staying on his bike. Like staying alive.

The group of bikers moved forward as one. They leant into corners and accelerated out of bends as they flowed along the road.

Brontë had ridden with groups of riders before, so he had no problem with keeping pace and time, but the closeness of each bike did worry him; one mistake from anyone and they were all stuffed.

The bikes were big, fat and low to the ground, all noise and exhaust. The bikers were not looking one way or the other, just looking straight ahead, riding forward like a big brooding mass, too cool for school and full to the brim of attitude. These guys were not flash, they didn't perform, they didn't need to. They were the main guys and they knew it, and when they were out and about, they made sure everyone else knew it too.

Brontë, could not only hear, but he could also feel the throbbing of the thirty-odd engines around him. There was no whining and screeching, no over revving, just one big throb of power and momentum. The smell of petrol and exhaust fumes was quite intoxicating, fuelling his already heightened adrenalin buzz.

Just as he thought it couldn't get much worse, the rain started.

Torrential rain.

Brontë's visor was made opaque by the water on the outside and was exacerbated from the fogging up on the inside. He was basically riding blind. The blindness acting as a catalyst for heightened anxiety, he threw the visor back and though the wind and rain stung his eyes and surface water from those in front was thrown into his face, he could see slightly better. The road, now shiny with rainwater, reflected the bright red and white lights.

Spray and fumes, light and noise, and ever-increasing speed.

Brontë was now frightened and yet invigorated all at the same time. He was like some adrenalin junkie, he wanted it all to stop but to carry on at the same time. The speed of the cavalcade increased some more. Brontë's speedo now pushed seventy.

This really is not safe, he thought.

The bikers filled the whole road from kerb to kerb, and Brontë wondered about oncoming traffic. He could feel his panic building. If anyone came the other way they were all dead, but he hadn't seen a car or anything since they started their ride. It was unusual for no traffic to be on the road at all but he knew that that this would soon change as they approached the Keighley bypass. Here five roads met like spaghetti junction.

As they passed side roads and crossroads Brontë noticed that they were all blocked off. There was a Wolf and his bike blocking all joining roads. Each entry road to the roundabout was also blocked by a Wolf. No one was going anywhere and the cars were backing up. None of the car drivers were complaining about being held up. Well, to be honest, you wouldn't, would you?

With roads thus blocked, the way ahead was left clear for the bikers to really get a shift on; so that's exactly what they did.

'Shiiiit!!!' shouted Brontë.

The cavalcade hit the bypass roundabout, at a hundred miles per hour and swooped round and along the road up towards Haworth and the moors.

More than thirty bikes at a hundred miles per hour.

The bikers' backs and arms were straight and relaxed, as they leant into each bend, their faces not exactly grinning but definitely portraying some pagan, carnal pleasure. Brontë's face showed no pleasure at all. He was terrified and was hanging on to his bike for grim death.

It was then that the Wolves began to howl.

'Arh-woooooooooooooooh!'

A howling biker, level with Brontë, turned and grinned at him.

It's KickStart-bloody-Bob, thought Brontë.

KickStart gave Brontë a cheeky wink with his teardrop-tattooed eye and Brontë remembered the biker's other tat.

'Speed Kills.'

Too bloody right, thought Brontë.

*

It was also raining back at the graveyard. It was raining on the graves and it was raining on the naked witches, making cold rivulets of water run down their goose-pimpled flesh.

The older woman standing over the table top gravestone was scattering holly and mistletoe berries over her younger doppelganger, who was spread-eagled across the stone.

'Holly berry red, menstrual blood of the goddess,' chanted the old witch, 'mistletoe white, semen of the god.'

The two women were hardly visible in the dark. Only occasionally did a flash of moonlight, breaking through the clouds, light up their white skin and sparkle on the silver pentagrams that dangled on their voluminous naked breasts.

The girl watched her grandmother cut an apple in quarters.

'It'th alwayth appleth, Grandma. Why ith it alwayth appleth?'

'It's always apples,' said the old woman, 'cos it's always apples.'

Though Cecily was too impatient to go into long explanations with her daughter, she did understand why apples were traditional in the ancient Samhain ceremony she was about to perform. Apples had even passed over into the more modern-day celebrations of Halloween. Using only their teeth, children tried catching apples floating in a bowl of water or swinging from a line, their hands tied behind their backs, a ritual known as apple-bobbing. The apples were the embodiment of human flesh drowning and hanging. The celebration she was about to perform was in honour of the already dead, offering them food to mark the continued turning of the Celtic year.

Cutting the apple in half she placed each half on the girl's naked thighs and then scattered the hazelnuts around them.

The girl laughed out loud.

'Oh Granny, what beautiful white thkin you have.'

The rain drops fell onto and glistened on the old women's translucent skin, her white, flaccid, fat body luminous under the moon.

The one who was both mother-to-be and a daughter herself laid naked on the cold gravestone. She held an apple in one hand and nuts in the other, forbidden fruit and gifts of nature. She closed her eyes and began a very low chant.

The grandmother placed the blade of her knife across her palm and pressed down, causing blood to run from her hand. It ran down the blade and dripped onto the white flesh of the apple.

'Oh my God, thith ith tho Thnow White,' screeched the girl into the dark and rain, 'the white, white flesh of the apple, and the deep, deep red of the blood. Have you got a tall, dark, handsome printh for me, Grandma, or theven little funny men?'

The grandmother laughed. 'The dwarfs of the old tales were not cute Disney characters. They were a gang of rough thugs, and the handsome prince a fool whose only desire was to steal the maiden's honour.'

'Thteal it!?' laughed the girl. 'The way I feel right now, I'd bloody give it to him.'

*

Brontë's cavalcade had reduced its speed now to a more sedate pace of around sixty-miles-an-hour as it ran up over Haworth cobbles and out up across the moors. The pack steered Brontë off the metalled road and on to a desolate moor top track, the rain still driving down. They forced Brontë onto the deserted Penistone Hill car park and gathered in a circle around him.

Brontë was shaking from fear and an overdose of adrenalin; in thirty years of biking, he had never been so exhilarated. As more bikers gathered around him, he was sensible enough to be just frightened, and the excitement ebbed away.

There was no excessive revving from the bikers, they just pulled up and left their engines ticking over and their headlights floodlighting Brontë. This calm, controlled gathering, in its way, was more threatening than the previous noise and chaos.

'Hallow dare', 'Spector Brontë sir,' KickStart Bob saluted, 'hand wares your feckin' girlfriend ton height, den?'

Brontë saluted KickStart right back.

'She's hopefully sitting at home, drinking a bottle of wine. It's where I should be, KickStart.'

''Tis ware you should be, 'Spector. You should antbee outear riding wid meander mates, so you shouldn't.'

'I thought you didn't have any mates, KickStart?'

'Well is ant dart the truth, 'Spector. Dees ear r not me mates atoll. Dees ears my brothers, is ant dart so, lads.'

As one the pack revved their engines in agreement.

''Spector! One of my brothers wood like a four mal intro duck shone.'

'Suits me, KickStart.'

KickStart Bob raised a hand in the air and, two-by-two, the Wolves, peeled off until there was just one biker left with KickStart.

'This ears hour press hid ant, 'Spector. I tink you met before butter nut prop hourly introduced.'

KirkStart nodded to the big biker beside him and rode off, leaving Brontë alone with the president.

The big, chopped Yami rolled forward till it was face to face with Brontë, front wheels touching and handle bars parallel to each other. It was the big chopped Yami Brontë had come across at the *Withins* and it was the big bald-headed biker that was sat astride it, his hands gripping the handlebars showing off the *HATE/HATE* tattoos to perfection.

The biker had no helmet and his shaved head was dripping with rain.

'The name's, Bonehead.'

'Suits you,' said Brontë.

'Friends call me Bone.'

'So, what should I call you?'

'You can call me Mr President. What do they call you?'

'Charles Brontë, friends call me Charlotte.'

'Suits you too'

'Thanks.'

'What shall I call you?'

'You can call me Inspector.'

The big biker laughed. 'KickStart told me you were a rum 'un.'

'I'm looking for a Lesley Wyck.'

'What's he done?'

'You know he's a he then?'

'What?'

'Lesley? It's not usually a boy's name, is it?'

'You grow up big and strong in these 'ere parts with a name like Lesley. What is it you want with him?'

Brontë looked Bonehead straight in the eyes.

'You Lesley Wyck?'

'And if I was?'

'Well, if you were, Mr President, then I'd have to tell you that your dad was dead.'

The two men looked at each other.

'I know.'

'You know?'

''E's been dead to me a long time has that man.'

'You don't seem too bothered.'

'Well, I am bothered actually, I'm bloody ecstatic.'

'Strange you being happy about your father's death... you and your big sister, both.'

'So, you've been speaking to 'r lass, Chief Inspector? She all right?'

'Seems fine.'

Bonehead laughed. 'She's a Flett, Inspector. She'll never be "fine". We're all fucked up, us Fletts. What she have to say for herself?'

'Nothing much.'

'She kill him then?'

'What the hell made you think that?'

'He wasn't a nice daddy, did things to her when we she was young. Things 'e shunt 'ave.'

'Did you kill him?'

'Should 'ave done it when I was young and I'd be out by now, well out, but I didn't have the balls back then.'

'Is that a yes or a no?'

'You decide, I don't really give a shit. He got what was coming to him.'

'You should have told someone when you were younger.'

'We did. We told mother dearest, but she was next to useless. She was always pissed and he beat seven shades of crap out of her all the time, anyway. Next thing I knew she was dead and we was in care, 'r lass with a foster family and me with the council.'

'How was that?'

'She had it all right, I suppose. As good as it gets.'

Brontë looked around, thinking. 'So, you think she could have killed him?'

'Could 'ave. Her or one of the others.'

'Others!? What others?'

'I don't know, there has to be others. If that's what 'e liked, I can't imagine him just stopping cos we was removed. 'E must 'ave 'ad a go at others,' he kicked the bike into life. 'So that's it, Detective Inspector. It's been nice talkin'.'

'Where can I get in touch with you?'

The big biker laughed. 'You can't. That's it, all over. And by the way, any of this gets out you're a dead man, and that's no false threat, Charlotte. Anyone hears about this and you... disappear.' He pointed at Brontë, 'We've done it before, Inspector, and we're not afraid to do it again.'

'You could help the others; the others you mentioned. Others that this may have happened to.'

Bonehead's voice became angry and he spat as he talked.

'Do we look like a fuckin' charity? We don't do good works, you prat. You're lucky you got what you did.'

Bone rode the Yamaha past Brontë but stopped for a parting shot.

'Your chain needs greasing, Charlotte. You should look after your bike. We don't want you coming off and getting hurt now, do we?'

He rode off to join his pack.

*

Grandmother and granddaughter had donned their robes, the ritual complete. The dead had been honoured for another year and were free once more to wander among the living. Job done.

In the dark of the church steps, a black cloaked figure watched the two women as they crossed the graveyard and exited back through the squeaky iron gate to be engulfed by the night.

The cloaked watcher made its way after them, slipping silently across the grass towards where the two witches had exited. On arrival at the iron gate the figure heard the gate squeak again and it quickly stepped into deeper shadow to disappear once more.

From their dark hiding place, the stranger watched the older witch return, wending her way back through the gravestones to the makeshift altar. The creature drew a shiny silver hypodermic from under its black cloak and flitted silently up behind her. The old woman turned to face her assailant.

'What do you want?' she said. 'I have nothing for you.'

'Oh, but I have something for you,' croaked a disembodied voice from under the hood of the cloak, 'I have retribution.'

Raising its arm above the old witch's head, the cloaked stranger plunged a hypodermic needle deep into the hag's scraggy, old neck. The old witch's eyes opened wide in shock and she looked for the face under the dark hood but saw nothing. The scream on her lips was silenced before it could leave her mouth and she passed into unconsciousness and collapsed to the ground.

'Vengeance is mine,' said the dark figure, 'the day of their calamity is near.'

*

The hooded figure pushed a wooden wheelbarrow through the old lychgate, the wheel rusty and unoiled so it squeaked rhythmically as it trundled along.

Squeak… squeak…

Inside the wheelbarrow, covered by a couple of empty coal bags, lay the unconscious body of Cicely Wyck.

Squeak… squeak…

The wheelbarrow pusher walked out of the churchyard at a steady pace and lumbered along the cobbled snicket. They knew that the old woman wouldn't stay unconscious for a lot longer and they needed her away from prying eyes when she started to come round.

Squeak… squeak…

Chapter Eight

The fifth of November. The day time before Bonfire Night.

Brontë had ridden home slowly from Penistone Hill trying to calm himself down. Back at home he sat in the greenhouse with Obi-Wan and he drank can after can of Boddingtons as the dog scoffed Bonio after Bonio. What with the manic bike ride and the meeting with the Wolves, all mixed up with two much beer, Brontë retired and slept like a baby.

After a good night's sleep Brontë fancied a good breakfast, so he had taken Obi on the usual viaduct walk, dropped him off back at home and then gone in search of a good fry up.

He rode to Hewenden Bridge, parked up, and walked up the main street towards *The Gobble on the Cobble* where he hoped he could kill two birds with one stone, a hearty-ish breakfast and re-questioning the buxom potter.

Two scruffy kids with dirty faces were hunched on the steps that led up to the café door. On the cobbles beside them, sat in a rusty old pram, was a poorly constructed Guy Fawkes. It was debatable who was the scruffiest: the two kids or the Guy. The Guy just won, thought Brontë.

The boys were chanting. *'Remember, remember the fifth of November. Gunpowder treason and plot. We see no reason why gunpowder treason should ever be forgot.'*

The boys verbally accosted Brontë as he approached.

'Eh-up mister, penny for the Guy?'

'Which of you wants the penny, and which one of you is the Guy?'

'This is the Guy, smart arse,' said one boy, and he pointed at the rough pile of clothes adorned with a skeleton mask for a face, 'and we want the penny.'

'A penny!?' teased Brontë. 'A penny's not going to get you very far.'

'Give us a quid then,' said the other boy, but it was both boys that laughed.

'What do I get for a quid? Just a look at your cruddy old Guy?'

'No, we know a poem.'

'A poem, eh? Well, for a poem, you just might deserve a quid.'

The boys recited their poem to Brontë.

'Penny for the Guy,
Penny for the Guy,
a big umbrella and a flashy tie,
Penny for the Guy,
Penny for the Guy,
Stick him on a lamp post,
Leave there to die.
If you 'aven't a got a penny
An 'apenny will do,
If you 'aven't got an 'apenny
Good luck to you.'

At the end of the so-called poem the boys screamed with delight and laughed like drains, while pointing at Brontë.

'Come on, mister, give us some brass.'

'Though your poem is hardly PC,' he delved deep into his pocket, 'for your cheek you can have fifty-pence.'

He tossed the coin into the Guy's lap. One boy grabbed the money and leaving their Guy where he was they ran off up the cobbles, cheering as they went. Hopefully they were bound for the nearest sweet shop, thought Brontë, but more than likely to the nearest off-licence.

Brontë pushed open the café door and his arrival was announced by the loud bell.

Ding!

At the counter there was a weird little man with long grey hair tied in a ponytail, which was pulled tight back so that it emphasised his widow's peak. He wore a long, hand-knitted Aran jumper that hung down below his knees. The sleeves were rolled up in thick wads around his elbows. Sticking out from the bottom of the jumper were two denim-clad legs that finished in a pair of flower-patterned Crocs. Over the lot was thrown a pinny, on the front of which was emblazoned the words 'You are what you eat' and under that 'Oh my God! I don't remember eating a legend'.

A VHB if ever there was one, thought Brontë.

'Now then, love, what can we be doing you for?'

'The lady, who I presume is your boss, told me she didn't employ men,' said Brontë, somewhat confused.

'She doesn't,' said the VHB. She winked at Brontë.

'I'll just have a breakfast and a coffee.'

'Would that be a Little Gobble or a Full Gobble?'

Brontë turned and looked at the VHB in total disbelieve, but the aproned barista looked back at him in complete innocence.

'We have two breakfasts, a *Little Gobble on the Cobble Breakfast* or a *Full Gobble on the Cobble Breakfast*.'

Brontë couldn't bring himself to say that he wanted a Gobble of any description.

'I'll just have a sausage sarnie, thank you... oh and a coffee.'

'Sausage sandwich and an Americano for Mr-Fair-Short-And-Average-Stranger,' said the waitress to herself as she started her barista-ing.

Brontë sat in a window seat waiting for his breakfast and mulled over the details of the case. As he did he had second thoughts about his breakfast. He'd gone off sausage.

'Excuse me.'

'Yes, love, what can we do you for now?'

'Make it a bacon butty, will you?'

'No bacon, love... I could crush you an avocado.'

'Never mind, just the coffee will do.'

'Banana quinoa and honey?'

'Coffee will be great thank you.'

'Double shot Americano coming right up.'

Brontë peered through the condensation running down the café window. The street was almost empty apart from the two lads who were now haranguing a Japanese tourist. She was taking photos of their Guy while handing over pound coins. The boys were lapping it up. Brontë was distracted by the waitress.

'Americano for sir.' The drink was placed in front of him.

'Thanks.'

'No problemo, mon amigo.'

The bell behind Brontë rang as the door swung open and then closed. A cold draft made him pull his collar tighter around his neck.

'Hello, Mr Charlotte Brontë!'

Brontë span around and standing directly behind him was the tourist with camera, fully dolled up in boots, puffa coat, scarf, mittens and a woolly hat with an embarrassing pom-pom swinging around on top.

'Ha! You no recognise me with my clothes on, Charlotte Brontë.'

Brontë scrambled to his feet and pulled back a chair for her.

'Yumi! Yumi! Sit down. Sit down.' He almost forced her into a chair. 'What can I get you? Tea? Coffee? Sandwich?'

He skilfully avoided offering her a *Gobble*.

'I will take tea, please and some toast, if I may.'

Brontë ordered the food and drink and was back with her almost before she had planted her bum in her seat.

'So! What are you up to today?' he inquired.

'What is "up-two"?'

'Sorry, what are you doing? What are your plans for the day?'

'I am getting *up to* nothing. You have spoiled my today plans, Charlotte Brontë.'

'How on earth could I spoil your plans?'

'Today I planned to visit with the... Brontë Waterfalls? But the road is all off-taped and the jolly policeman there said you had closed the falls.'

'Ahh! He would be quite right, yes. The falls are closed to the public. There's been a... well, an accident up there.'

'An accident? No one is hurt, I hope for them.'

'Well...' he wondered what to say, could think of nothing, so changed the subject instead. 'Anyway, you need another plan.'

'Ha, Mr Policeman,' she pointed at Brontë, 'you are changing your subjects. I think someone has been hurt.'

'A priest has been killed, I'm afraid.'

'And you think I am a sensitive little woman and you protect me from bad news.'

'Something like that.'

She sat and watched him for a second.

'What can be my other plan?'

'What were you planning to do tomorrow?'

'You asking me to date, Charlotte?'

'I'm asking what your plans were for tomorrow.'

'Walking in the invisible footsteps of sisters, over moors and back along viaduct, take photos of beautiful countryside.'

'Then why don't you do that today and go to the waterfalls tomorrow?'

She looked at him and smiled.

'This why you big clever policeman and me only naive student.'

'It's a gift,' he said, and hid his pleasure by taking a slug of his coffee.

They were interrupted by the James Bond theme emanating from Brontë's pocket.

'Welcome to Japan, Mr Bond.'

Brontë looked at her with undisguised admiration.

'I'm impressed, Yumi, you know James Bond movies?'

'I'm from Japan, Inspector Charlotte Brontë, not blardy Mars.'

Brontë laughed. He stuck the phone to his ear, listened to it for a second.

'Yep... yep... yep... yep.'

He stuck the phone back in his pocket.

'Big fan of Bond movies, Yumi?'

'I like Piers Brosnan, he could have my babies any day.'

'It has been said I bear more than passing resemblance.'

'Ha, you at least be funnier than Piers Brosnan, but you still changing subjects, has body been found by river?'

'Not by it, in it.'

She looked at him for a minute before she spoke again.

'We believe that when die, we must cross Sanzu river. The better your life, the easier cross. The good cross river by bridge, the evil are cast into dragon-invested rapids. Demons on bank measure karma.'

'What goes around comes around.'

'Sorry?'

'You get what's coming to you.'

'Was person who was found in river a good person, or was they bad person?'

'The jury's still out.'

'You speak funny ways, Charlotte Brontë.'

The doorbell chimed and they were swept by a cold draft from the opening door. Angharad Flett entered. The two lads with the Guy shoved their heads round the door and tried to slip-stream her into the cafe. Angharad pushed the door against them, slapping at their hands, trying unsuccessfully to keep them out.

'Penny for the Guy, missus?'

'Penny! I wouldn't give you nowt for that moth-eaten pile of old rags, and you wouldn't call me "missus" either if you knew what was good for ye.'

'We'll just sit out 'ere on yer steps then. No one's gonna come in yer mingin' café with us sitting outside, you should see how far 'r Billy can spit.'

'What!? You running some sort of protection racket ye little hoods?'

The boys laughed in sheer delight.

'I'll have you know I've got the police in here.'

'We know, 'e's already paid up.'

More delighted laughter from the boys.

'Give us the money or lose yer customers, missus.'

The potter grabbed two buns from off the counter and stuck one into a hand of each boy.

''Ere, you can have a bun each. Like it or lump it.'

'Thanks, missus.'

'Thanks, missus.'

'Don't call me, missus. Right, bugger off now the pair of ye, before I call your dad.'

'Where you gonna find 'im, missus? We 'ant seen 'im in bloody years.'

They ran off, laughing.

'Once you pay up they always come back for more,' said Brontë.

'Not with those, Inspector. They won't come back for any more of them, they're vegan scones.'

This time it was her turn to laugh.

'If you're as good at throwing pots as you are at throwing kids out,' said Brontë, 'you gonna have some good pots.'

A vegan scone bounced off the glass in the door, leaving a greasy smudge behind.

'And that, Mr Brontë...'

'Detective Inspector, if you don't mind.'

'And that, Detective Inspector, is why I don't have children.' She turned an appreciative eye to Yumi. 'However, I see that you do.'

'Yumi, this is Angharad. Angharad,' he gestured with his hand, 'this is Yumi.'

'My God, but she is too.'

Yumi smiled.

'So, Detective Inspector, how can I help? Or is this pleasure and not business.'

'Well, it's business. It's about your late father, if that's ok?'

'My late murdered father, you mean.'

'I so sorry. Your father was found in waterfall? I thought him was priest type "father" that was found in falls, not parent type "father"?'

'Not that one. Sadly, Angharad's father was found earlier in the week, in his cottage up the street.'

'I so sorry.'

'Don't sweat it, girl, we weren't close.'

'I shall be leaving you two to be talking peacefully.'

'There's no need, I have very little to say and the inspector has even less to learn.'

'No, I need go, now,' she stopped at the door on her way out, 'you, Charlotte Brontë, I see you later.'

'You will,' he said.

Ding!

And Yumi was gone.

'You never told me the full story about your father.'

'You've met our Lesley, then?'

'He told me what he did to you.'

'It were never me, love.'

'Not you?'

'I thought you knew; he didn't like girls.'

'It was your Lesley.'

'Could have been. He never touched me, I know that. Lesley also denied it ever happened to him. Either it did or it didn't; who knows. Maybe that's why he acts like such a butch bastard.'

'Well he certainly plays that part very well.'

'Was always such a little sweetie when he was a kid, poor little bugger.'

'I'd hardly call him a poor little bugger—he's as big as a brick shithouse.'

'It was the court case that split our family up, obviously.'

'Why obviously?'

'You remember it, Brontë. A load of paedophiles involving that care home up at Hewenden Bridge.'

'Highbatts.'

'Aye, that's the one. The lads were rented out to the rich and disgusting. Lads, Brontë, not girls. No evidence to say my father was involved, nowt was ever proved about anyone actually. The rich and influential tend to be... well, rich and influential.'

'What was his connection to the place?'

'He were the caretaker and boiler man up there.'

'And you don't know if he involved your Lesley.'

'Well if he did, that could've made him what 'e is today couldn't it?'

'A poor little bugger?'

Angharad threw her head back and laughed.

'Aye!' she said. 'A poor little bugger.'

*

Cecily Wyck woke wet, cold and naked.

She was lying in a pool of mucky water. She couldn't really see what it was as it was pitch black. It did, however, smell disgusting.

She couldn't work out if she was responsible for the puddle or if it was already there before she was thrown into it. For thrown she had been; she could tell by the pain in her knees, elbows and ribs.

The floor on which she lay was stone flagged, she could feel it hard and rough against her bare buttocks. Her back was pressed hard against a slimy stone wall, this also she could feel against her naked skin. She sat and shivered in the dark and listened for any noise to give her a clue of her whereabouts.

There was as much an absence of sound as there was an absence of light. No sound at all. Well no sound that is but the steady drip, drip, drip, of water into the pool in which she was sat.

Drip... Drip.

No light, no sound, no clues; but she could smell something. She could smell wet coal and wet stone. Her mind was befuddled and disorientated but she tried to make sense of the little information she had.

She could see nothing but she thought she had earlier heard a ringing. A bell. A familiar bell. A loud monotonous ring. It had been counting out the time. It was the church bell. She was somewhere on the main street she thought, near the church.

Drip... Drip.

Stone, water, coal and no light, the drip, drip, dripping from above.

She knew where she was, she was in a coal cellar. Somehow, she had got from the graveyard to a cellar up the cobbles. She had also lost her clothes on the way.

Cecily Wick began to shake more. Cold yes, but also afraid, very afraid.

Drip... Drip.

For the next hour or so, Cecily Wyck drifted in and out of consciousness. Sometimes she was aware of whether she was sensible or insensible, at other times she thought herself conscious when she was in fact out for the count.

At times she could feel snakes entering and crawling through her body, hissing as they squirmed inside her. She felt worms and insects that crawled over and under her skin. The creepy-crawlies on the surface grubbed down, deep into her flesh, and those underneath burst out, emerging on to her skin.

Her nose and mouth filled with the smell and taste of vomit, urine, faeces and rotting flesh, which made her gag and gip.

She wasn't sure if she saw a dark figure or not, a figure in a black cloak and hood. A figure with no face and no physical form, floating around her dead body that lay on the floor. Or was she in fact alive? The figure loomed over her and stared into the darkest areas of her soul.

The dark shaped hissed.

'Ssssssssss.'

She was uncertain if what she saw was reality or just a figment of her fevered brain.

'Ssssssssss.'

A crack of light appeared in what looked like a wall straight ahead of her. She was pretty sure this was real. It was accompanied by the sound of creaking hinges; the fracture grew slowly into a large rectangle of light. Into this stepped a hooded figure to be silhouetted against the bright light.

'What do you want?' Cecily's voice was quiet and quavered.

There was no reply. The figure tossed a pair of dirty trousers and wellington boots into the puddle in front of her. She stared at the items and then turned to look up at the figure.

'You want me to put them on?'

Silence.

Cecily Wyck did pull the trousers on. They were wet and cold and offered very little comfort, but they did cover her nakedness and this made her feel less vulnerable.

Next, a tattered anorak and gardening gloves were thrown across the room into the mix, Cecily slowly pulled these on too and she stood up on wobbly legs, her whole-body quivering. Although she shook and shivered, she was feeling the benefit of the clothing and they made her feel a little less petrified.

'Please don't,' she whispered, 'please.'

The silhouetted figure stepped further into the cellar and as it closed in, it took more the form of a body than an apparition. It pushed a wheelbarrow before it.

Squeak... Squeak... Squeak.

Almost visible now it approached the witch.

Cecily whimpered and burbled, making bubbles erupt and burst in the snot and tears which ran from her nose and eyes.

She began to jabber.

'No, no, no, no. Please, please, please, please.'

The creature gently placed a finger over the witch's slimy lips.

'Ssshhhh!!!'

It zipped the anorak right up tight to the woman's hairy chin and forced her to lie down in the wheelbarrow.

'Silence now,' said its sibilant voice, 'no one can hear you.'

'No don't... no don't... no don't...'

'Sssshhh!!! Save your strength. You'll need it. I am taking you to a party. A special celebration, you like celebrations.'

The dark creature looked down into the witch's petrified eyes.

'A special party where you will be the guest of honour.'

The witch's screams were once again stifled by an injection as the hypodermic was jabbed into her neck.

The witch was paralysed yet still fully conscious.

A roll of gaffer tape was produced from under the cloak of the assailant and with a swish they stripped off a good length, taped her mouth shut and attached a Guy Fawkes mask to cover tape, face and all.

It laughed and grinned manically into the mask. The mask grinned right on back.

'Remember, remember...' it hissed.

*

Back inside the police incident room, Brontë and his two subordinates were once more studying the timeline. The three officers pored like carrion over the sheet but couldn't make head nor tail of what little information they had.

'OK, here we go. You take down some notes, Rhiaz; you try not to be facetious, Pepper.'

'You know me, Brontë, always willing to help.'

He threw her a sideways glance, not sure if she was, even now, taking the mickey.

'Right, let's just look at what we've got, shall we?'

'I'll tell you what we've got, Sweet Fanny Adams, that's what we've got.'

'You're not trying hard enough, Pepper.'

'Am I meant to be taking this down?' asked Rhiaz.

'OK, you two, pack it in. It's like trying to work with Morecombe and Wise.'

'Who the hell's Morecombe and Wise?' whispered Rhiaz.

'They're a bit like Ant and Dec, but funny.'

Rhiaz nodded.

'Right, moving swiftly on, what have we got? We've got two deaths involving paralysis by injection, two penises sliced from bodies, one of which is still missing.'

'It should be a film, *One of Our Penises is Missing*.'

'Pepper.'

'Sorry.'

'Is it about sex?' volunteered Rhiaz.

'I suppose it has to be on some level.'

'What, like homoerotica? Bit much isn't it, cutting someone's dick off just to get your jollies?' said Pepper.

'It all sounds a bit like revenge and punishment to me,' added Rhiaz.

'You gonna kill someone for revenge,' said Pepper, 'but cutting their todger off, now that's something else.'

'Lady up at the stables, that's exactly what she came up with. She felt it appropriate punishment for a sex offender. Can't say I disagree with her.'

'She what?'

'Oh yes, claimed she would love to cut off an ex's meat and two veg.'

'You got her in the frame for this?'

'Well, it was her martingale that the priest was strung up with. She has a long black hooded coat and she threaten to cut someone's dick off. It's hardly a leap is it?'

'Then why isn't she in my cells?'

'All circumstantial; she's coming down later to do a written statement.'

'Well make sure she bloody does.'

'What about placing it in the mouth?' added, Rhiaz. 'What's all that about?'

'That, I think,' expressed, Brontë, 'is all about a message.'

'A message to who?'

'To whom,' corrected Brontë.

'To whoooom?' she emphasised the word like an owl might.

Brontë thought a bit about this, stood up straight and turned to the two officers.

'To us guys. It's a message to us.'

They were still chewing this over when a uniformed officer popped his head around the door.

'You need to come and see this, you three.'

'What is it?'

'You gotta come see for yourself.'

*

Outside on the main street, the preparations for the solstice parade were in full fling. Bunting and banners were going up everywhere and there were ghosts and ghouls being stuck in every window.

'What's the problem, Constable?' asked Pepper. 'This time of year the villagers always display their ghoulies in their windows.'

'Not the window displays.'

'If it's not the solstice paraphernalia, then…'

'Them!' he pointed up the road. 'It's THEM!'

And down the cobbles came the Wolves, slow and steady, filling the street from wall to wall, which was only three abreast as the cobbles were so narrow. They pulled to halt outside the incident room, all big, brash and cocky, looking for all the world like they didn't give a shit about anything; and to be fair, they didn't.

'Hey, 'Spector.'

'Hey, KickStart.'

''Lo, Lonely Hearts.'

''Lo, yourself, KickStart Bob.'

'So, warts t' feckin' craic, 'Spector?'

'Oh, you know, KickStart, protecting the people, enforcing the law, keeping the peace. What you lot up to?'

'Oh, you know, 'Spector, same old, same old.'

'Glad to hear it, KickStart. What brings you round my neck of the woods?'

'You do, 'Spector.'

'And what do you want from me?'

'Jus' listen to yerself will ya now, 'Spector? We want knotting. We've come to give you a present.'

'A present?'

'You'll see, 'Spector, you'll feckin' see,' and he laughed.

The Wolves moved off as a group, passing by the police and KickStart.

The leprechaun biker winked and slowly pulled away.

'Slainte, Brontë.'

'Cheers, KickStart.'

The column of bikes rode off, five deep now across the cobbles as the road widened. It took five minutes for every bike to have passed down the street, and another five for the exhaust fumes to be cleared.

Brontë and the three police officers stood alone on the cobbled street. Alone, that is, apart from an old, stained tea chest.

They stared at the chest and then looked at one another with raised eyebrows.

'It's a tea chest,' said Brontë.

'It is, or a packing case' said Pepper.

'It has something written on it.'

'What's it say?'

'It says *charity case*.'

Rhiaz lowered his head to the case.

'It's knocking,' he said.

'It's what!?'

'It's bleadin' knocking.'

'Why is it knocking?'

'I don't know why it's bloody knocking.'

'Well let's find out, then.'

It didn't take long to get the lid off the tea chest. It was only held in place with duct tape. Once the lid was off, the three officers peered into the open top.

Inside the box was a man, curled into a foetal position.

The man looked to be at least in his fifties, his hands and feet tied behind him.

'What's going on, Brontë?'

'I haven't a clue. You'd better ask him.'

'Hello,' said Pepper into the chest, 'what's going on?'

'Get me out,' said the chest.

'You all right, sir?'

'Help me, help me, please.'

'Ok, Rhiaz, get him out and get those cable ties off him. Pepper, go find him some food and a drink, that might stop him mithering.'

Pepper addressed the chest. 'Cuppa tea, sir?'

'Come on, you guys,' said Brontë seriously. 'No laiking about now.'

The two officers jumped to action.

'And treat him careful. He's had an awful fright, so get him a doctor to give him the once-over. I want him fit for interview, I want him happy and I want him ready for questioning. I want him in a frame of mind to answer questions, all right, Pepper?'

'Right, sir, but what if he doesn't want to talk?'

'Oh, he'll talk all right. By the nature of his arrival, he'll sing like Pavarotti. He won't want to see that lot again in a hurry.'

*

An hour later, the man from the tea chest was being questioned by Brontë and Pepper.

Pepper pressed the record button on the tape recorder.

'For the benefit of the tape, Wednesday the fifth of November at,' Brontë checked his watch, 'sixteen forty-five pm. Present are myself, DCI Charles Brontë.'

Brontë, turned to Pepper.

'Sergeant Jennifer Pepper.'

'Mr Andrew Murgatroyd Esquire, QC, duty solicitor,' said a pleasant looking skinny man in a grey suit, with a nice shirt but no tie.

They all looked at the figure in grey, who just sat there, silent and afraid.

'For the benefit of the tape,' said Brontë, 'can you please state your name and address.'

The man could hardly be heard when he spoke.

'Why am I here? I have done nothing wrong. I was kidnapped by a gang of hoodlums. I am the injured party.'

The man's head dropped to his chest and he began to very quietly cry.

'I have paid for my crimes.'

'Could you please give your name for the tape, sir,' said Pepper not unkindly, 'you are not under arrest, you are free to leave when you want, but we would really like your help… please.'

The man looked up at Brontë and Pepper, he managed to calm himself a little.

'My name is Kevin Forester, I live at twenty-two Moor View, Hewenden Bridge.'

Brontë took control once more.

'Can you tell us, Mr Forester, where you were on the evening of Friday the thirty first of October.'

'I was at home, and no I have no one to vouch for me.'

'You seem very sure.'

'I am very sure, Inspector, the thirty-first of October is Halloween. The night that children go from door to door, threatening householders with violence if they don't pay up with chocolate. It's basically extortion in my opinion.'

'You don't like kids?'

The man laughed ironically.

'So, the night of the thirty-first?' Interrupted Pepper.

'I locked my doors and closed my curtains. I did not answer my door. I have it all on film. My front door has CCTV. I have the door filmed all night. I never answered the door, I have the proof. I have film footage for every night.'

They sit in silence and they all looked at each other.

'If I could explain,' said the solicitor, 'my client has had his name changed by deed poll. He was, Inspector, in another life, Alfred Higgins?'

Pepper and Brontë looked sideways at each other.

'Who?' they said in unison.

'You may remember him from the Highbatts Care Home scandal. He is on the sex offenders register and has been punished for this crime.'

'I have taken my punishment, I have done the time, I have taken the physical attacks in prison and then the verbal attacks on the streets and at my home. And that is where I want to go now. I want to go home and barricade my door.'

They all looked at him.

'I want to go home,' he repeated. 'I just want to go home.'

'Let him go home...' Brontë's chair legs squeaked on the linoleum tiles. He stood and made for the door.

'No, tell Rhiaz to take him home... and tell him to use an unmarked car.'

'Thank you, Mr Forester. I'm sorry about the way you have been treated today, it was not of our doing. We may need to speak you again, and we may need to take a look at your tapes. If so we will phone in a request and send a taxi for you at your convenience. Thank you.'

'For the benefit of the tape,' said Pepper, 'Inspector Brontë has left the room.'

*

Back upstairs in the incident room, Brontë was being efficient and authoritative.

'Right, Pepper,' he shouted, 'I want the bloody Highbatts file, on my desk, like yesterday, OK?'

'It's right in front of you.'

'Oh. Right. Good.' He sounded somewhat deflated. He flicked through the file, his expression becoming stern.

'Brontë, wasn't our old friend Bonehead at Highbatts?'

'He was, Pepper. Coincidence, eh?'

'You don't believe in coincidences, sir.'

'You're damn right I don't.'

'You haven't got to the interesting bit yet.'

Brontë threw the file across the desk into her lap.

'OK, enlighten me.'

Pepper flicked through the file.

'Here we are. Not only was our tea chest friend, Mr Alfred Higgins, charged in relation to the Highbatts investigation… he was the manager of the home.'

'Well, I'll go to foot of our stairs!'

'What?'

'This all has to do with that home, it has to.'

'Shall I go get him back?'

'Nah, we know where he is, I want more gen on this before we interview him properly. I want to know we're asking the right questions, that we're asking about what we need to know. We'll go get him when we're ready.'

Brontë moved around the desk and lifted his jacket from off the back of a chair.

'You haven't heard the best bit yet, boss.'

Brontë stopped dead in his tracks and looked at her.

'I'm listening.'

'Nigel Flett was interviewed in relation to the case at Highbatts.'

'Flett worked at the home, that's right, we know that, his daughter told us.'

'Yeah, nothing came of it. No evidence in here about him at all.'

'Great,' he moaned sarcastically.

'Listen to this though, sir.'

'Go on, I'm all ears.'

'Father Patrick was a trustee. He was interviewed in relation to the case but he was never charged with anything, either.'

'Who was charged?'

'Only the manager, Alfred Higgins.'

'Scapegoat?'

'Could be, I suppose... and you are not gonna believe this.'

'Pepper, stop being such a bloody drama queen and spit it out.'

'You'll never guess who was the nurse up at the home...'

'Go on, who was it?'

'Only one Cecily Wick.'

'Get away, the old witch?'

'The very same.'

'Shall we pull her in?'

Brontë checked the time on his phone.

'Nope, I've got a prior engagement. We'll carry on tomorrow. She'll keep 'til then.'

Chapter Nine

The fifth of November. Bonfire Night.

Haworth Park hung on to the side of Haworth Hill for grim death. It was so exposed that locals believed that one day it would give up the ghost and be blown right across the valley. The leafless skeletal trees were dark and shiny with rain and the flowers in the usually well-maintained beds were withered, dead or gone.

This sombre scene, along with the dark and the fog, made this a perfect backdrop for plot night. Although winter was still a little away, Bonfire Night often seemed to be one of the coldest nights of the year. This year was no exception, and for this reason, the park was deserted.

Squeak... squeak... squeak...

The wheelbarrow wobbled its way unsteadily through the park gates, passed the bandstand and trundled across the path to a pile of wood. A huge pile of 'progging' built into a magnificent tepee of wood in preparation for the evening's celebrations.

It wouldn't be long now.

The cloaked figure pulled the wheelbarrow to halt beside the wood stack and sang quietly under its breath.

'Build a bonfire,
Build a bonfire,

Put the guy upon the top.
Stack the witch within the middle
And burn the bloody lot.'

To punctuate the end of the ditty, the wheelbarrow was upended to allow the body of the witch to slither on to the wood pile. To complete the job, the wood was arranged around and in front of her. Disguised in the old clothes, the witch was well hidden within the construction of the fire. If anyone did see through the gaps they would see only an old Guy Fawkes, not a person. A Guy deliberately placed to burn in celebration of the thwarting of the gunpowder treason. What could be more normal?

*

The witch was dazed, confused and drugged. She was certainly not aware of where she was and she kept drifting in and out of consciousness. Though disabled, frozen and unable to move, she could still smell. She could smell the damp wet wood around her, she could see and hear the partygoers starting to arrive. In her dazed state she couldn't remember why everyone was gathering. Somewhere at the back of her mind she remembered it was some sort of party.

Was it a Halloween party? No, not that. Was it an All Hallows party? No, that wasn't right either. Then it hit her like a sledgehammer.

It's a bloody bonfire party.

Oh shit, she thought, it's a bonfire party. And I'm the guest of honour.

Cecily Wyck tried to shout out, tried to scream for attention, but her mouth behind the mask was taped shut.

The fire had not yet been lit, but Cecily knew this would not be the case for long. Peering through and between the pieces of stacked timber, she could see families, waiting excitedly for the fireworks and fire.

FIRE.

She saw children with their sparklers and parking pigs. She saw the adults with their glasses of Cava and pies and peas.

She observed the policeman who'd interviewed her at home. Brontë, wasn't it, Inspector Brontë? He was talking to a woman and laughing with a couple of kids. She willed Brontë, to look in her direction, to find her and to save her, but he didn't.

The witch tried to scream but her mouth could not move and so no sound came out from between her lips.

Her mind screamed out but her mouth was still and silent.

*

Brontë turned to his ex-wife.

'So, who is this woman we're supposed to be listening to tonight and why on Bonfire Night of all bloody nights?'

'She is a visiting doyen…'

'Doyen!?'

'A doyen is a…'

'I know what a bloody doyen is, I'm just surprised you do.'

She hit him on the back of the head with her hand.

'She's been booked to talk at the parsonage on behalf of the Brontë society…'

'I have my own society?'

'You're not funny, Charlie, she's an expert on the Brontë sisters. She's here tonight because she is part of a planned series of events.'

'And why am I here tonight?'

'You are here tonight, Charlie boy, because you are keeping your ex-wife sweet; you don't want a disgruntled ex-wife, now do you?'

'Oh. I know which side my bread's buttered.'

'Grandma! Grandad! Mummy's here, Mummy's here.'

'Right loves, you go join her. We'll see you later. Come on, Charlie, we don't want to miss the start.'

'Don't we?'

Brontë, waved to his daughter and grandkids and followed his wife.

'Mummy, Mummy,' shouted the children, 'they're lighting the fire, they're lighting the fire.'

As their grandparents disappeared across the park, the children, along with the other revellers, turned towards the bonfire to watch it being lit. Some tall and wiry hippy dude, with greasy hair tied back in a ponytail, flared corduroy trousers and a tie-dyed hoody was trying, without success, to light his zippo lighter in the wind.

'For fuck's sake,' he said, almost under his breath, 'this thing's meant to be chuffin' wind proof.'

Mark (River) Hills had been nominated by the village committee as the official warden and fire lighter, a role that made him feel very important. He believed the fire brought him closer to, and connected him with, his own pagan ancestors. He knew the fires went a lot further back than most believed, way back before the days of Guy Fawkes and King Charles. His mind drifted back to imagine a time when the fires of the ancients were built to protect the families. When young men and women would ride horses between the flames to protect them from evil. He would love to have ridden horses between fires but tonight he couldn't even get his zippo going. Not only that, the wood was damp and was proving quite stubborn, even newspaper stuffed under the wood didn't help. Mark had flipped open the top of his lighter and was desperately spinning the flint wheel with his thumb. The sparks ignited the wick time and again but it didn't stand a chance against Yorkshire weather. The flame was always blown out before there was any danger of the paper and wood catching.

The struggling firelighter was looking thoroughly despondent with the whole situation, but he was not going to give up yet. He was made of sterner stuff than that. He would not be thwarted at this stage of the game.

He dipped his hand into the macramé handcrafted shoulder bag and retrieved a can of refillable lighter fluid. Not very green, or safe, he knew, but he was not willing to fail in his task. He doused the newspaper and surrounding wood with lighter fluid and once again began to spin the wheel on the lighter.

The fumes from the fluid lit easily and the wind fanned the flames into life. Mark watched as the fire spread, engulfing the scrunched newspapers and ignited the wood.

The fire was catching well now, the flames had spread almost the whole length of the wood pile. A piece of burning door and a chair fell with a whoosh, shooting a plume of flame and a cloud of sparks out towards the revellers. Mums and dads leapt forward and pulled their children out of harm's reach.

*

Cecily Wyck, on the lea side of the fire, could smell the lighter fluid, could smell the smoke, but she was incapable of doing anything about it. She couldn't move, she couldn't scream and now due to the smoke she could hardly breath, either. She could, however, feel the heat the flames now lapping at the wood surrounding her. When the old door fell away, it left a gap in the construction of the wood pile. A gap through which River could see.

He saw the shape of an old Guy standing in the newly exposed gap. That's a bloody strange place for a Guy, thought the warden. Guys are normally at the top of the fire strapped to a seat or an old plank. Not at the bottom of the fire buried and hidden from view.

The guy had a moustachioed and goateed plastic mask more in the *V for Vendetta* style rather than a traditional mask, and was made all the more frightening by the flickering flames. River watched the guy catch fire.

He saw the guy slowly ignite and the flames lick at the mask, which caught fire, melted and dripped away, revealing a second mask beneath. The mask of an old lady. The mask of an old lady with wide horror-stricken eyes. The mask of an old lady that began to melt. The mask of an old lady that was not a mask at all but a human face. A melting face with burning grey hair. The burning face of a terrified old woman. Mark Hill began to scream.

He screamed until he collapsed and then he stopped.

*

Up at the old parsonage, oblivious to the horrors of the park, Brontë was living through horrors of his own.

He was sat, shoulder to shoulder, with and in between rows and rows of women. There were young women, middle-aged women, old women, women of all shapes, sizes and colour. It was like his own private nightmare. It wasn't that he didn't like women, conversely, he loved women, he just found them intimidating in large numbers. There were no men in the room at all, apart from himself.

Brontë shuffled his chair a little closer to Margaret, who turned and looked at him.

'You're so predictable, Charlie.'

'What do you mean?'

'You've got such a glass head, I can read you like a bloody book.'

'Tell me, Margaret, why we don't live together anymore?'

Margaret adopted an expression of deep concentration, while she folded he arms and stroked an imaginary beard with the thumb and finger of one hand.

'Hmm, let me think, that's a difficult one, let's see. Is it because...' she counted the items off on her fingers, '...one: you work every hour God sends, irrelevant of whether it is a weekday or a weekend or a bloody holiday? Or is it two: because you come home late every night and sit in your greenhouse drinking beer and talking to your fucking dog till God knows what hour? Or is it three: because we grew apart while our kids were growing up. Or is it four: because life with you after the kids had left was just got so bloody boring, or....'

'OK! Jesus! I'm sorry I asked.'

'Shh!' hissed a woman behind them.

'Fuck off,' hissed Margaret under her breath, ensuring the woman couldn't hear her.

For a while they sat in silence and listened to the speaker.

For God's sake, thought Brontë, who actually gives a shit that the Brontë sisters wrote more words as children than in all of their published adult works all together?

'To be fair, Margaret,' he complained, 'we had nice holidays.'

'Nice holidays!'

'Sshh!' said the woman.

'Charlie, only you could say that. You took me to Whitby for a fortnight every year and to Filey for a long weekend every Whitsuntide Bank Holiday'

'I'm a changed man, I'm a totally reformed character.'

'Right, where did you go this last weekend?'

Shit! thought Brontë, *she's a sneaky bitch.*

'Sorry?' he stammered.

'This last weekend, where did you go?'

She waited. He desperately hunted for a lie but it wouldn't come.

'Whitby,' he answered sullenly but honestly.

'Ah ha! See, exactly as I said, just the same old stuff except now you take Obi-Wan-bloody-Kenobi instead of me. I must say I feel sorry for the poor creature.'

'Sshhh!' repeated the woman behind them and she tapped Margaret on the shoulder.

With relief Brontë turned to look forward and concentrate on the speaker before him.

'Many, many writers have used nom de plumes down the centuries,' said the red-haired woman on the speaker's podium. 'They are used as a sort of shield. They allow authors to conceal their identity and to write freely, but that's not the only reason... oh no.' She paused dramatically, took a sip from a glass of water and pushed back her strawberry blonde hair. 'The three sisters used the shared surname of Bell and keeping their own initials they became Currer, Ellis and Acton. However, this was not done with the intention of concealing their identity, rather to conceal their gender. Women would not be published so the pen name was essential. Her publishers did not know that Charlotte was a "she" and not a "he" until a year after *Jane Eyre* was published.'

'Excuse me...' Brontë said as he got to his feet and put his hand in the air.

The speaker smiled but threw daggers at him with her eyes.

'There is a time for a questions and answers session after I have finished my presentation, thank you. After I have finished,' she emphasised. She swirled her long red hair and returned her attention back to the group. Her smile became less fake. 'So, where were we? Ahh yes! The names chosen by the three writers were not particularly masculine. Ellis itself is a non-gendered name and...'

'But Charlotte changed her name to a man's to hide the fact she was a woman?' said Brontë.

'What part of "after I have finished" don't you understand, sir?'

'Sorry,' said Brontë as Margaret pulled him back into his seat.

'Sorry,' said Margaret to the speaker. 'He's just so into the Brontë sisters.'

The speaker looked over her glasses at them and after a short warning pause, continued.

'Initially Charlotte's work was seen as the struggle between the conventional expectations of women versus their sexual desires, the combat between the angel in the house and the devil in the flesh. Written by a man this was acceptable. When critics concluded that the mysterious Currer was in fact a woman, the book was attacked as being coarse and immoral.'

'Just like me, Charlie,' hissed Margaret into Brontë's ear.

'What, coarse and immoral?'

She slapped his shoulder.

'No, you swine, my struggle to get you to see me as a sexual goddess and not just a housewife.'

'Well...'

'I warn you now, be careful how you proceed, you could have been on a promise.'

'What, is this evening going to end with rumpy-pumpy?'

'You never know your luck, matey, just play your cards right.'

'I thought we were separated?'

'That doesn't mean I've got to be a nun,' she winked at him, 'I see us more as exes with benefits.'

Brontë distracted himself by looking around the room. The speaker had ground to a halt, and she seemed confused. There was a blue flashing light shining through the parsonage windows and the sound of a fire engine could be heard approaching.

Brontë saw a black creature rise from the audience, a creature all clad in black leather. He watched as Carol Redman ran to the exit.

'Charlie, It's a fire engine,' shouted Margaret.

Brontë was already following the pathologist out of the door.

'The kids are at the fire, Charlie. The kids are at the bloody fire!'

*

When Brontë arrived at the park, the fire engine was finishing extinguishing the last flames of the bonfire. Most of the merrymakers were gone and those that hadn't were now not so merry. There were a couple of uniformed officers talking to the stragglers and the pathologist was with Rhiaz. They were standing next to the remnants of the bonfire, which was now a pile of smoking cinders.

Brontë took in the scene and was surprised that there was a hippy guy throwing up into the rhododendrons.

'Rhiaz, you seen my...'

Rhiaz held up his hand.

'It's all right, chief, your daughter and her family are safely on their way home. I saw them off myself.'

'Anybody hurt?'

Rhiaz looked down at the smoking pile of ash.

'Just that one as far as we know.'

Brontë turned his attention to the pathologist, who was taking photos on her mobile phone.

'For pity's sake, Morticia, tell me that's not a body.'

'I wish I could, Brontë, but alas, that is a body.'

'What do we know?'

'I'm not being funny, Brontë, they're dead and that's all. If I wanted to tell you more I couldn't, not with the body in this state. You could always ask that guy, sorry for the pun, over there tossing his guts up into the rhodies.'

'Rhiaz, go get him.'

'So, if you've done with me, Brontë,' said the pathologist, 'I might just as well catch the end of the riveting talk at the parsonage. I'll organise the usual collection and I'll have this... mess... on the slab first thing in the morning. I'll let you know what happened. However, I don't hold much hope of finding out much, not with the body being in the state that it is.'

She walked away but after a few steps turned and called back to him.

'I'll tell your wife all's ok.'

Rhiaz arrived back with the VHB hippy who was wiping vomit off his face.

'This, sir, is Mr Mark Hill. He saw the body actually in the fire.'

The statement made the man gip.

'What did you see, Mr Hill?'

'Just the face, in the fire, covered in flame.'

'Male or female?'

'Old lady I think, I couldn't tell, really... the face was...'

Mr Mark Hill ran off back to his rhododendrons.

'Sir, look.'

Rhiaz was bending down over the smouldering ashes and pointing.

'What do you think?'

Brontë knelt next to him and observed a blackened silver disc on a bit of blackened silver chain. Taking a pen from Rhiaz's pocket he hooked the chain with the pen and held it up for inspection.

Rhiaz watched him.

'Dr Redman will give you hell for that, sir.'

'What Morticia doesn't see won't do her no physical harm.'

He held the disc and chain up before him.

'I think, Rhiaz me old love, that this is a pentagram. The last time I saw one of these it was bouncing on the cleavage of a well weird witch. You'd best get Pepper and the car.'

*

Pepper switched off the Astra's lights and she and Brontë stepped out onto the wet pavement. Brontë pulled his collar up to protect his neck from the drizzle.

'Right, let's go see which witch is which.'

'You're such a nerd, Brontë.'

'Thank you.'

'You're welcome.'

They made their way round around the house to the back garden, when they were halted by a strange sound.

Thunk!

The officers stopped dead in their tracks. Pepper looked at Brontë and brought her index finger up to her lips.

Thunk!

'What the hell is that?' hissed Brontë.

Thunk!

'I think,' she grinned, 'it's someone staking a vampire.'

Brontë gave her a look.

The two officers stood in the dark and listened.

Thunk!

'It's digging,' whispered Brontë.

'Digging? Who the hell does the gardening at this time of night?'

'Who the hell does bloody gardening, full stop?'

'Look over there. It's that weird vampire's familiar fella, what's his face... Eyesore, he's digging a hole in the lawn.'

'Shall I go see what he's up to?'

'No, leave him, one thing at a time. Let's go talk to the witches.'

'Remember, keep an eye out for hell hounds.'

'I'm ready for 'em.'

'What you gonna do? Give 'em a treat and tell them to sit?'

She opened her jacket and there was a flash of black plastic.

'I've got me a taser.'

'Christ, Pepper!'

'If those dogs show their slobbering chops round that door,' she mimed shooting with the stun gun. 'Kapow! And they'll twitching wrecks on their bloody backs.'

Brontë, shook his head at her and knocked on the door.

*

The two police officers sat on either end of the grubby velour settee. Two witches, the young one and her mother, stood staring at them.

'So,' said Brontë. 'Your mother, Mrs Cecily Wyck...?'

'Miss.'

'Sorry?'

'Miss Cicely Wyck, she ain't ever been married.'

'Right, yes, well, your mother, she didn't return home last night?'

'No.'

'You weren't worried?'

'No,' said the blonde woman, 'she's over sixty years old. She's been going out and staying out for at least fifty of them. We don't stop her.'

The girl giggled.

'Granny, liketh to thtay out.'

'And you've no idea where she went?'

'No, idea whatsoever.'

The girl giggled again.

'Inspector, why is it you came?'

Brontë looked at the older woman, Pepper looked at Brontë.

'We are really sorry to say… there's no easy way of saying this…'

They all looked at each other.

Brontë placed a plastic see-through evidence bag on the coffee table in front of him, the pentagram could easily be identified and was obviously a match to the ones hung around the ladies necks.

'I assume you recognise this?'

The women looked at each other.

'Is this hers?'

The girl gave out a little squeak.

'Is she dead?'

'We don't know, we will need something to check her DNA against. When did you last see her?'

'Last night,' said the younger of the two women, 'up at the graveyard.'

'The graveyard?'

'We'd gone to pay our respecth to the dead.'

'I'll come with you,' said the mother, 'I'll identify the body,' and she turned to get a coat.

'I'll come too, Mummy.' The younger woman jumped up excitedly.

'Ladies... Look I'm sorry... There'll be no need to attend just... if you could give the sergeant your mother's hairbrush or toothbrush?'

Pepper and Brontë stood and looked at the mother and daughter.

'We're sorry, we just need to do a DNA comparison.'

*

They walked back to the car and passed Caleb Smith, who was still digging in the garden. Getting back into the Astra, Brontë turned to Pepper.

'I want you to get a magistrate out of bed, and I want a warrant to search that garden first thing in the morning.'

'They won't be happy.'

'I don't care about our magistrate's happiness, just get me a bloody warrant.'

'Based on what? There's been no crime. So a guy's been midnight gardening, so what? People actually do that, Brontë, they plant their seeds by the phases of the moon. It's a thing. OK? I know it's weird but its only HB not even VHB. I can't prove that a warrant is necessary.'

'What about the screaming?'

'What screaming? There was no screaming.'

'The magistrate won't know that though, will they? Just get me a warrant, OK?'

'I bloody hate you at times.'

'Get me a warrant and then first thing in the morning get me a geophysics team. We'll find out why bloody Eyesore's nocturnal gardening.'

Chapter Ten

The sixth of November.

The following morning the investigators were standing around the Wyck's garden getting piss wet through. The curtains drawn across the windows overlooking the back garden twitched as the mother and daughter tried to sneak secret glimpses of what was going on.

The geophysics scanner was packed away, and the pathologist was ferreting around in a freshly dug hole. It was still raining and everyone was soaked through and splattered in mud.

'Not what you expect in a murder inquiry. I didn't imagine I'd come up here and find Her Majesty's coroner rolling around in the mud.'

'Is that a personal fantasy, Brontë?'

'OK, you guys, let's cut the crap, shall we? You want to know what I've found up here or not?'

'We most certainly do, Morticia. What've you got for us?'

'Graves, Brontë. Tiny little graves.'

'Little graves? What sort of little graves?'

'Well, these are pet burials. Nearly a dozen in fact and still counting. Cats actually.'

'Cats?'

'Exactly. Some quite old. They seem to have been in the ground for some number of years, but then some are quite fresh too.'

'Fresh?'

'Latest was buried within the last couple of days.'

'Last night?'

'Could have been.'

'You said "in these graves were cats", inferring something else was found in others graves.'

'I haven't got the evidence yet, Brontë. I can't commit.'

'Come on, Morticia, have a bit of a surmise. No one's gonna hold you to it.'

'I really can't, it's too sensitive.'

'Nothing's that sensitive.'

'Babies are that sensitive.'

'What?' whispered Pepper. 'What did you say?'

'It looks like it… could be babies.'

'Shit!' said Pepper.

'Very small babies.'

'How old?'

'Couldn't say.'

'Humour me.'

'Not till I know for sure.'

'How many?' said Brontë.

'Three.'

'Jesus Christ! OK, Pepper, get that moron that was digging up here last night down the station as quick as you can. And the mother and daughter, too.'

There was no answer.

Brontë turned to Pepper, who was staring, watching the removal of the little bodies, her eyes wet and shining.

Brontë raised an eyebrow. 'No jokes today, Pepper?'

'No jokes today, boss.'

They watched the removal of the last little bag.

'Sad little parcels,' whispered the sergeant.

'This job… it gets to you, sometimes.'

'It's a little close to home sometimes.'

Brontë didn't know what to say, so he said nothing. He just stood behind her and stared at her back.

Pepper wiped her nose on her sleeve.

'Dann it!' she said, trying to get her shit together.

Though she tried very hard she lost the battle with holding back the sobbing and one stray tear escaped over the lid of one eye, ran away down her cheek, dropped on to her coat and mixed in with the rain and mud.

'I was so, so young. My parents were shocked, it was all organised for me through the doctor.'

'You don't have to explain yourself to me, Pepper. I don't judge.'

'Some do.'

'Those who "do" though, would have to answer to me, wouldn't they?'

And then Pepper laughed. She laughed like a drain. She laughed through her tears and she laughed through her snot, both of which ended up across her face and sleeve.

Brontë handed her his handkerchief.

'Did I say something funny?'

'Funny!?' and she laughed some more. '"Answer to you", Brontë? That's hilarious. You that's hardly ten stone when dripping wet.'

'You get yourself off home, I'll take things from here for today.'

'Nothing wrong with me that a bottle of Shiraz can't put right.'

'You wanna come round my greenhouse?'

'Would love to, Brontë, but I'm OK. I'll be fine. I'll just sit and drink and stare at my wall.'

'Good plan. Might do the same myself.'

It was Pepper's turn to raise an eyebrow.

You haven't got a wall it's a greenhouse.

'Well, maybe I'll just sit and drink and stare at my dog.'

*

The interview room was sparse and grey, no pictures, no colours, no nothing. This was all planned, it was designed to be as oppressive and imposing as possible; make those being interviewed uncomfortable and wrong footed.

It didn't impress Caleb Smith, he rocked cockily on a chair, which he balanced on two legs, his boots planted firmly on the table and his hands planted deep in pockets. His baseball cap pulled back on his head making the peak stick straight up and point to the ceiling. He insolently chewed gum and stared at Brontë and Pepper in turn, for all the world looking like he didn't give a flying-monkeys about anything.

'Like to practice a bit of "moon planting" do we, Mr Smith?'

Caleb chewed his gum and sneered.

'I was a farmer in another life. I had to give it up, I can't stand pigs.'

'Ahh, Caleb love, you missed your calling,' said Pepper. 'You should 'ave been a comedian.'

'We've been doing a bit of digging ourselves, Mr Smith. Someone has been planting bodies by the light of the moon.'

'By the light, by the light, by the light, of the silvery moon…' sang the sneering man, and he laughed.

'Look, pal, cut the attitude, sit up straight, get your feet of the table and answer the fucking question.'

'Pepper!'

'Sorry, boss.'

'Right, sir, it is, as my sergeant so succinctly put it, time to start answering our questions.'

'We've found three graves in your midnight garden, Caleb.'

'It's not my garden, they're not my graves.'

'They're somebody's graves, Caleb.'

'Rubbish, they're 'oles. I did as I was told, I just dug 'oles.'

'So, tell us, Caleb… Who put the babies in the holes?'

Caleb sat up straight, looked from Brontë to Pepper and pulled the baseball cap from off his head.

'I don't know what you're on about.'

'The babies, Caleb, that's what I'm on about.' Pepper leant over the table. 'Who put the babies in the holes you dug, Caleb?'

'I don't know about babies. I only know about moth-eaten old moggies.'

Pepper leant right across the table, almost spitting in Caleb's face as she hissed at him.

'Three babies' graves, Caleb. Three dead babies.'

Brontë placed a comforting hand on her shoulder.

'I'll take it from here, Pepper.'

Pepper sat herself down and breathed heavily. Once she had calmed a little, Brontë returned his attention to the dog walker.

'Tell us about the little ones, Caleb.'

Caleb Smith's cheeks reddened. His brow grew little pearls of sweat and his words came out quickly, falling over each other.

'I know nothing about babies. I like babies. I wouldn't harm babies.'

'What would you hurt?'

Caleb looked back at him sullenly and kept shtum.

'I said what would you hurt, Caleb?

'Nowt. I wouldn't hurt nowt.'

'Did you hurt the Wyck's cats?'

'Them old dears, they've had 'uggins of cats over the years, dozens of 'em. They thought they were their familiars or summat, crazy bitches. When any cat died, they gave 'em to me in a sack to burry. I didn't hurt 'em.'

'What about the babies, Caleb? The babies you buried.'

'I told you, I buried cats.'?

The two police officers sat back and waited. They left a long silence and just sat watching him. It was what Brontë called his bear trap, leaving a big gaping hole for the interviewee to fall into. He sat back and waited for Caleb to fall into it.

'When they brought me a bag, I buried it... It were my job, right?'

Pepper moved slightly as if she was going to answer and Brontë placed a cautionary hand on her leg under the table, out of site.

They sat in silence.

'Look, once right, once I opened one of them bags, before I buried... before I put it in the hole. It had a dead kitten in it. Cats not babies!'

The room fell silent for what seemed an eternity.

'I want a lawyer.'

Pepper stood.

'Caleb, lad, you are so gonna need one, love.'

*

Later, in an adjacent interview room, Pepper was dunking digestives into a plastic cup of tea while Rhiaz questioned the youngest witch.

'For the sake of the tape, could you please state your name?'

'You're pretty, what'th your name?'

This knocked Rhiaz completely off kilter.

'Erm... I've already stated my name, it's Rhiaz Khan, Detective Constable Rhiaz Khan. You have to say your name... into the tape... please.'

'Well, Rhiath, my name ith, Elthpeth Wyck, but you can call me Ellie.'

'Well, Ellie, if you could...'

'For the benefit of the tape,' interrupted Pepper, 'Detective Constable Khan will be addressing you as Miss Wyck, and if you wouldn't mind you just address him as Detective, OK?'

'Oh my God, you're a thtroppy cow aren't you, love?'

'Miss Wyck, we would like to ask you about, Mr Caleb Smith.'

'Yeth, Detective.' She winked at him. 'How can I help?'

'Do you know Mr Caleb Smith?'

'Ooohh, I do, love.' She turned to Pepper and smiled. 'Well, that wath an eathy one.'

'Just concentrate on the detective constable please, miss.'

'With pleasure.' She returned her attention back to Rhiaz. 'Chritht what'th her chuffin' problem?'

'How is it you know Caleb, Miss Wyck?'

'Duh! Hello! I know him becauth he workth up at the houth, doethn't he?'

'He does odd jobs?'

'Yeah, he doeth like... thtuff, ye know.'

'Like what sort of stuff?'

'Like walking the dogth and well... thtuff.'

'What other stuff, Miss Wyck?' asked Pepper. 'What other stuff does he do? Does he do gardening? He tells me he just fills in holes.'

This delighted the young woman no end and she laughed like a loon. She laughed so much she struggled to control herself.

'What's so funny, love?

'You are,' said the girl, 'you're bloody pritheleth you are. "He fillth in holeth." That'th bloody funny.'

Elspeth Wyck looked from Pepper to Rhiaz and back again. She tried to control her laughter. She wiped tears and makeup from her eyes.

'Why's it so funny?'

'I'll tell you what'th tho bloody funny, he's my baby daddy. That'th what.'

Pepper spat tea and biscuit out on to the table.

'He's what!?' she gasped.

The girl giggled.

'Are you saying he's your unborn baby's father?'

'Yep, Granny callth him the thperm donor.'

Pepper and Rhiaz looked slightly relieved.

'He donated the sperm so you could become pregnant?'

'He did.'

'Did he donate it to a clinic or something, or did he...' Rhiaz ground to a halt, lost for words.

'You mean did he put hith thing in me, wath that part of his hole filling dutieth?' She started laughing again.

'Yes, that's exactly what the constable means, Elthpeth. Did he?'

'He did, Thergeant. Granny said I would hopefully catch firtht time, tho we would only have to do it the oneth, but I wouldn't have minded coth I really liked it. Have you ever done it, Constable?'

The young witch giggled. Rhiaz opened his mouth but before a word could come out Pepper interjected.

'I think it's best that Constable Khan sticks to asking questions and not answering them.'

'Grandma said Mummy had liked it too.'

'My God. Grandma organised a sperm donor for your mother too?'

'Oh yeth. Caleb'th been the family hole-filler for quite thome time now.'

'But not Grandma, surely?'

'No thilly, she's far too old. She had her own donor a long time before Caleb came on the thene, if you pardon the expression.'

'So not Caleb?'

'No, Granny thaid it wath Caleb'th dad, but we never met him or nothing.'

'For the benefit of the tape, the interview is being terminated.' Pepper checked her watch, and clicked the tape machine off.

'Well, this is a bit of bugger.'

*

Morticia, hosed down the pathology slab. She was ready for home, ready for a large glass of Chablis and a hot bath. She sighed as Brontë entered the lab.

'And whose little girl are you?'

'Piss off, Brontë. I'm not in the mood, I'm off home to get the right side of a bottle of white.'

'A quick update would be appreciated, and think on, you never give enough information for my satisfaction. Once I'm happy you can trot off and drink wine till it comes out your ears.'

'Right, here we go. Pin back your lug holes. The body in the fire is that of an elderly woman and I have confirmed what you surmised, it's the body of Cecily Wyck.'

'Cause of death? Or is that a stupid question?'

'No, not a stupid question... for once. It looks like she wasn't dead when she was burned. Could have been unconscious, could have been drugged, but certainly not dead. I'll let you know when I get the lab tests back.'

'How do you mean drugged?'

'Same injection mark on the neck.'

'Same as the railwayman and the priest?'

'More than likely. I'll let you know when the lab results come back.'

'So, the three are connected?'

'I let you know...'

'Yeah, yeah, when the results come back from the lab.'

'Ah, at last, he catches on.'

'What about the bodies from the garden?'

'Two babies...'

'Two not three?

'No just the two, the rest were cats.'

'Right.'

'So, there are two babies' skeletons. There could have been many years between their births. I'm waiting on lab results on them, too.'

'How old?'

'What do you mean how old? They're foetuses.'

'How long have they been in the... How old would they be now?'

'I couldn't say, yet.'

'Hazard a guess.'

'Brontë, I'm the coroner's pathologist, I don't guess.'

'Humour me, I won't quote you.'

'One could be twenty years, the other could be fifty.'

'Bloody hell!'

'But that's not the strangest thing, Brontë.' She turned to the detective. 'You are so not going to believe this...'

'Both children are related to Cecily Wyck and both are related to Caleb Smith.'

'Hey! Get a load of you, Brontë. Now you have impressed me. How the hell did you know that?'

'Good old-fashioned police work.'

'OK, smartarse, I'll tell you something you don't know. You don't know that when I managed to work out which end was which—which way was up and which way down...' she paused more to annoy Brontë than for effect '...I found something in the mouth.'

'Well it can't have been her penis cos presumable she never had one.'

'It was somebody's penis, though.'

Brontë was struck momentarily dumb.

'Hah, you didn't bloody well know that now, did you?'

'I didn't, no.'

'Guess, who it belonged to.'

'I haven't a clue.'

'You're no fun, Brontë. Go on, guess!'

'Well, it would be kind of appropriate if it was Caleb Smith's, but I'm sure he must still be in possession of his.'

'Neeerrh-urrrrrrh! Wrong answer.'

'It would be poetic though. I bet it wouldn't have been the first time...'

'Ok, Brontë, enough.'

'Go on, you know you're dying to spill the beans.'

'It was Father Patrick Murphy's... And that certainly is not poetic.'

*

Back in the incident room, Brontë and Pepper sat around drinking vast quantities of Nescafé and eating their own bodyweights in McVitie's chocolate digestives.

They pored over the makeshift timeline and between them cooked up impossible theories.

'Right, let's stop and go through it all again. What have we got?'

'We've got the weirdest case I've ever been on, that's what we've got.'

'Weird or not, Pepper, there must be a way through it.'

'We have the three dead bodies...' She counted them off on the fingers of one hand. 'Number one: the railwayman, Nigel Flett, paralysed by some sort of injection and his cock cut off...'

'Pepper, can we try stay a little more professional and use appropriate vocabulary and terminology.'

Pepper let her eyes roll to the ceiling.

'OK! Paralysed by injection and his penis removed with a sharp implement...'

'Better.'

'...and said penis placed in his oral cavity.'

'You're taking the Michael now, Pepper. Mouth will do fine.'

'Number two: the priest, Father Patrick, paralysed by injection, penis removed with same or similar sharp instrument. Could have bled to death but more than likely drowned. Penis not found in mouth, or anywhere else for that matter.'

'Good.'

'Number three, Cecily Wyck, probably...'

'Possibly.'

'Sorry, *possibly* paralysed by injection and as yet no cause of death. Could be the fire. The witch, however, had had no dickus of her own to disectus,' she looked at Brontë and he ignored her, 'but it was discovered that the priest's dismembered sausage had been deposited in her witchy mouth.'

'You were doing so well until then.'

'All of which smacks of some sort of homoerotic sadomasochism involving penises.'

'You're thinking a male perpetrator?'

'I certainly am. A woman could whip the old wedding tackle off a fella but not like this. This is not a woman. I know women don't get off on that sort of shit.'

'And what about the elements?'

'Come again.'

'The elements?'

'You've lost me.'

'The four elements?'

Pepper, raised an eyebrow.

'You know. Earth? Air? Fire? Water?'

'Are you talking in tongues?'

Brontë stabbed the wallpaper timeline with his finger.

'Look, the priest was killed in water. The witch was killed in fire, OK?'

Pepper dunked a digestive in her coffee.

'And what about the railwayman?'

'I'm working on that.'

'Would have to be earth or air.'

'The starlings could be air.'

Up went the eyebrow again.

'I know, it's a bit of a stretch, it's a work in progress, but what if it is? If it is, we've definitely got another murder to come, or more if they repeat the pattern.'

'What about the bodies in the garden? Could be earth.'

'Nah, not connected.'

'Why not?'

'They're going to find out there's too many years apart. Once the DNA corroborates what the lovely Elspeth admitted to in questioning.'

Pepper nearly threw her drink all over herself when the door suddenly burst open.

Crash!

'What the…!'

Crupper charged into the room like a caricature of a rampaging bull, face red and sweating, steam blasting out of his ears and nostrils.

'You arrested that pervert yet, Brontë?'

'And which pervert would that be?'

'That pervert, Brontë, that's been cutting people's dicks off, that pervert. Which other pervert did you think I meant. Have you got another one?'

'Well I suppose there could be any number of perverts out there, couldn't there… sir?'

The chief constable paused to breathe and tried to gather some composure before continuing, slowly and deliberately.

'I want that baseball-capped pervert arrested and charged.' He stormed across the room but halfway across he stopped and spun on his heels. 'And I want him locked up. OK, Brontë?' He thought for a second. 'Today!'

'Well, we don't know if it's him or not, now, do we? And we can't just arrest him because of the way he looks.'

'Don't give me any of that bleeding hearts bollocks, Brontë, just get him arrested.'

'We don't have any evidence; we can't prove he's done anything.'

'Can't prove he's done anything? I know in my stomach that he did it. That's what we good police officers call gut instinct. Your problem, Brontë, your problem is you don't have any guts. But what you do actually have is enough circumstantial to twist together to get that fucking gay bastard sent down. So, do it!'

'I don't think he's gay… sir'

'Does it matter? He looks gay and he acts gay. Nail him.'

Crupper continued to the door, where he stopped again.

'Oh, and Brontë, if you pause insolently, just before you call me "sir", ever again, I'll banjo you, my lad. I'll banjo you so hard and you'll be back into uniform as quick as… just wait and see how quick, that's all.'

Pepper placed a hand over her smirk.

'Also, we discussed the whole "banjo" thing earlier on if you remember… sir?'

This time Crupper did exit before he had the chance to do, or say, anything he might later regret. He slammed the door behind him.

Crash.

'I just love the way you bring out the best in people, Brontë.'

'It's my superpower, Pepper.'

*

Constable Rhiaz Khan was a couple of floors below down in the interview room. Sat opposite him was Kevin Forester.

'So, what can we do for you Mr Forester?'

'I've been thinking... well I wasn't thinking, earlier was I? I mean my head was up my arse wasn't it? After being kidnapped an' all by them bleedin' monsters and then being stuck in a tea chest and everything... well I wasn't thinking.'

'And now you are?'

'No, I have been. I've been thinking ever since I went home.'

Rhiaz sat and looked at the guy opposite him. He was sweating and his hands were shaking. Rhiaz felt for him.

'And what is it that you have been thinking about, Mr Forester?'

'I've remembered the name of one of them lads that was up at the home.'

'A name?'

'This is very hard for me to do, Constable, I find it almost impossible to talk about my... about that time.'

'But you are here to help us, yes?'

'If I can do just something... anything that will... it's Steven Livesey. The name is Steven Livesey.'

Rhiaz wrote the name down in his notebook.

'I remembered the boy, Stephen Livesey, was adopted by a local family.'

Rhiaz scribbled some more.

'That is helpful, sir. Hopefully we can trace the child.'

'No child now, I think.'

'No, you're right.'

'You won't trace him round here either, Constable.'

The police officer stopped taking notes and looked up at Kevin Forester inquisitively.

'Shortly after the trial the whole family fled to America, hopefully a new start for 'em all I suppose.'

Rhiaz sat back in his seat and stared at the man before him.

'Chuffin' 'eck!'

*

Brontë and Pepper were still going over the timeline when Riaz burst in on them.

'Sir!'

'Woah there, Rhiaz, me old son, hold your 'orses, lad.'

'But sir...'

Brontë held up his hand.

'Now then, Riaz, just the man. You're a Pakistani right?'

'Sorry, Riaz, your superior officer is yet to complete his Equality and Diversity Training.'

'You don't wear a turban or anything, I know, but you are a proper Muslim?'

'We don't wear turbans.'

'Course not, but do you worship earth, air, fire and water?'

'What's he on about, sarge?'

'Humour him, Rhiaz.'

'Can't say the elements are a big part of it. Back in the day though there was a lot about heat, dry, cold and moist.

'It's not the same, Brontë,' said Pepper.

'It's something to bear in mind.'

Brontë turned to Rhiaz.

'So, my little Muslim-mucker, why you grinning like the cat that got the cream?

'I've been talking to Kevin Forester, again. He's remembered the name of one of the lads from Highbatts.'

They sit in silence and stare at Rhiaz.

'The name he remembers is,' he read from his pocketbook, 'a certain Stephen Livesey. I looked him up and he has no police record and I can't find any history...'

'Come on, Rhiaz, spit it out, man.'

'He emigrated to America with his foster family. Now stick that in your pipe and smoke it.'

Brontë and Pepper looked at each other and replied simultaneously.

'Where to in America?'

'I looked it up... South Carolina!'

'Shit!' replied the two officers.

'Get the American hack back on the phone. Now!'

*

It felt to Capability Goldman that he had only been asleep for a few minutes when his landline woke him.

He had got to bed late after a long day at *The Post* writing up a shooting. Two guys dressed as Buffalo Bill and Annie Oakley pulled out American long rifles in a theme bar and randomly shot three people and their pet dog called spot. To be fair it wasn't what he liked to write about, he would have rather driven rusty nails into his eyeballs, but he'd been told to cover the story so cover it he had.

His bedroom was unbearably hot and humid so he had not slept well at all. He let the phone ring on to answerphone. He couldn't be bothered to get up. After another half dozen rings or so the answer message did indeed kick in and he could hear his recorded voice quite loud in the silence of the bedroom.

'Y'all listening to the answer machine of Capability Goldman, which means I'm out or in the sack, which is basically one and the same. If it's early, I'm at the office so catch me there; if its late I'm in bed and it's where you should be, so what the crap are you phoning me for at this time of the bleeding night? Call me back at a more reasonable hour, say after seven. However, if it's Columbia University with an offer of a Pulitzer Prize, then you are about ten years too late, amigos.'

Beeeeep!

The machine went silent for a second then burst into life, and Capability was listening to some limey.

'Sorry to bother you, Mr Goldman, this is DCI Charles Brontë again. We spoke earlier in relation to a recent execution and we may be privy to further information.'

Capability shouted at the phone.

'Privy!? Who the heck says "privy". Isn't a privy a John over there in good old Blighty?'

'I would like to speak to you again if I can. Please call me at your convenience.'

'More bloody toilets, ye weird limey fecker.'

'Thank you for your help,'

Beeeeep!

'Speaking in English coulda helped, compadre.'

Capability Goldman looked through the gap in his blue curtains and saw the sun was just rising, he moaned and rolled over away from the dawn, desperate to catch a few more hours shuteye before he had to face the day. A trickle of sweat ran down the centre of his back and made him shiver.

'I'm gonna have to change them curtains,'

*

Brontë had parked the Monster in a layby up on the moor near Top Withins. There was no colour today, none of the greens, purples or oranges of yesterday. Now all was grey, hazy and blurred. Just as dramatic and beautiful though, he thought. It wasn't raining or drizzling as such but Brontë was still getting wet through. The water condensed on the collar of his leather jacket, ran down his neck and down his back, making him shiver.

His bike, propped up on its main stand, enabled Brontë to sit side-saddle in comfort while he waited patiently by the side of Brian Bolton's butty-van.

A voice called out from inside the van.

'Spam and brown sauce on a white teacake.'

Brontë collected the breakfast bun from a big chap, who was bent double so he could fit inside the van. His hands were as big as frying pans, fingers like sausages and a head as bald as an egg.

'You're not so busy today, Arthur?'

'Nah, Charlie, weather's only good for ducks.'

'Might cheer up later.'

'Nah, the telly sez it'll be silin' it down by this aft.'

'Well, I hope not, Arthur. Cheers.'

'Cheers, Charlie.'

He sat and munched on his sandwich and watched as a blob of Daddies sauce, dripped out of the sandwich and splashed down his white t-shirt.

'Bollocks,' he said out loud.

'You all right?' asked Brian.

Brontë saluted him with his teacake while he attempted to suck the brown stain from the shirt, but that only made matters worse. He sat on his bike in the mizzle and looked out over the mist-blurred moorland and counted his blessings. He hated his boss and had to spend most of his days with the man. He loved his wife beyond anything but didn't spend enough time with her at all. He spent the majority of his time with and old motorbike and his soulmate, a white mongrel dog. He had no friends to…He was dragged from his reveries by the Bond movie theme tune. *Thank God*, he thought, *I was just about to throw myself in the bloody reservoir*.

'The name's Bond,' he said into the phone, 'James Bond.'

The person on the other end of the phone hesitated.

'I'm sorry, buddy, wrong number. I'm trying to get hold of a Detective Inspector Brontë.'

'That'll be me.'

'I'm sorry, I thought you said Bond.'

'Just my little joke.'

'Oh, I see,' said Capability, but he didn't really. '*Buenos dias*, Inspector, Capability Goldman at your service. I hope I haven't disturbed your breakfast?'

'Nah, you can't really disturb a spam butty. Their disturbing enough as it is.'

'A what?'

'Forget it, what you got for us, Capability?

'No tengo nada, mon amigo.'

'I have a funny feeling that means you've got nothing.'

'Spot on, Detective Inspector, sir. Your Spanish is better than your English.'

'I phoned you last night...'

'Yeah, I got your message.'

'I've got something I want you to check for me.'

'Fire away, sir.'

'It's a name, someone who emigrated to South Carolina some twenty years ago or so. We'd like to get a trace on him, see what he's been up to, where he is now.'

'What's the dude's name?'

'Stephen Livesey.'

There was a pause from the Carolina end.

'What?'

'Leave it with me.'

'What!?'

'I'll get back to ye.'

Brontë was left hanging on the phone.

They're bloody strange people, these Americans, he thought as he wiped his greasy hands down the legs of his jeans, leapt on the Monster and rode off into the cloud that was quickly turning to rain.

*

Caleb stood in the magistrates' court and awaited the result of his bail hearing.

He had removed his cap, which he now clenched firmly in his dirty hands, and his chewing gum was left stuck under the table top in the police interview room.

Caleb would do anything to avoid seeing the inside of a cell again. Even if it meant crawling to a magistrate.

'Mr Smith, your solicitor informs me that you have been crime-free for over fifteen years?'

''Ave been to prison for one mistake in my life. I never want to go there again. So, I 'ant done nowt wrong since. It's a plan, Your 'Onour.'

'I have yet to reach the dizzy heights of being an "honour" Mr Smith, you may address me as "Your Worship".'

'Yes, Your Honour... Worship.'

'The police seem to think you pose very little danger to others, is that right?'

'Yes, Your Worship.'

'And I wonder if you are a potential flight risk, Mr Smith.'

'I'm sorry, Mam... Your Worship.'

'Are you likely to flee before the case comes to court, Mr Smith? Are you likely to up-sticks and bugger off?'

A snigger passed around the court.

Caleb did not snigger. Caleb did not even crack a smile.

'No, Your Worship. I have nowhere to go. I have things still to sort out here, at home. I have my plan.'

'Not to go back to prison.'

'That's right, Your Honour. I'll go straight home. I'll keep to myself. I have to do what I have to do.'

The magistrate hardly looked at him as she passed judgement.

'Bail granted, Mr Smith. You may leave.'

Caleb left the court room and crossed the entrance hall towards the exit as quick as he could without looking too eager. Sitting outside another court room were the two witches. He noticed them but he managed to pass them without being seen himself. They sat close to each other on a small bench, huddled together and whispering.

Whispering and sniggering.

Oh yes, he thought, I have to do what I have to do.

*

Caleb had indeed gone straight home. He wanted to be nowhere else. He wanted to do nothing but to sit in a darkened room. Hide himself away from the world.

This he did for a few hours, crouched naked on the floor, faced into the corner, rocking, and as he rocked he hummed.

One arm hugged his head, the fingers and hand stroking his stubble. His other hand was clenched tightly into a fist, rhythmically thumping the wall at the end of each rock. His mind whirled, his thoughts going round and around, spinning like a top.

And as he pitched backwards and forwards he chanted.

'Babies... Cats... Babies... Cats...'

Over and over again.

'Babies... Cats... Babies... Cats...'

*

Hours later, still naked, he sat at the kitchen table, chair turned to the wall and desperately chain smoking. There were two empty cigarette packets in front of him and an overflowing ashtray. Caleb reduced to searching through the ashtrays, sorting out some of the bigger tab ends that were still smokable, relighting them and smoking them down to the filter. He was now muttering rather than chanting. Muttering under his breath.

'Who's the daddy...? Who's the mummy...?'

Inhale. Exhale.

'Who's the daddy...? Who's the mummy...?'

When the dockers were gone, all burned right down to the cork, Caleb crossed the kitchen and took a knife from the wall-mounted knife rack. His favourite knife. His sharpest knife. The knife he used to slice through muscle. The knife heavy enough to chop through bone. The knife with the jagged double edge that glided easily through sinew. His good knife.

Caleb threw his black stockman coat over his naked body and drew the hood over his head, pulled the collar tight around his neck and stepped out into the night.

The knife in his fist flashed silver in the moonlight.

Out in the dark the truth kept hitting Caleb in mind-numbing waves of anxiety, fear and pain. It made his head hurt and his mind spin.

He stumbled to a stop every few steps to stifle the screams building up within him, biting down on the soft flesh between his thumb and finger, the physical pain combatting the mental turmoil.

Tears ran down his face as the blood ran down his wrist, but the screams stayed silent.

He made his way forward in this manner towards the witch's house, towards those he hated, those who abused him. But it was his father that had first introduced him to this horror, this hell.

'Who's the daddy...? Who's the mummy...?'

Caleb retched and threw up over a wall.

He knew as he approached the house that the Alsatians would not betray his presence. He'd known the dogs since they were pups and he knew how to control them. Cruelty and love. A kick and then praise but not in equal measures. Just as his father had trained him. Pain and pleasure. Brutality and love. Not any more though, not any more.

Caleb entered the house and headed for the bedroom.

Slowly he climbed the stairs. He placed his feet carefully on the outer edge of each step to reduce any creaking. He knew the mother and daughter had been bailed and he didn't want them being warned of his presence.

He'd been up to the bedroom a number of times before, when his services had been required, and he had admitted this to the police. But he also told them he knew nothing of babies in bags. Where could babies come from? How could they be babies? Babies needed daddies; babies needed mummies.

He started talking to himself now as he made his way up the last few stairs.

'Who's the daddy? Who's the mummy? Which is the mummy, witch is the mummy.'

He stopped on the stairs and doubled over in agony. Biting his hand again to smother the screaming inside his head.

'No, no, no, no, no…'

He made his way across the landing towards the girl's room, where he stopped and listened, his knuckles white as his fingers gripped the handle of his good knife.

He held his breath as he stepped towards the bedroom door willing himself forward, each step a battle of the mind.

The door to the younger girl's bedroom was slightly ajar and there was the soft glow of a light seeping around it.

This was the bedroom.

'Who's the daddy?' he whispered. 'Who's the daddy?'

He had to force himself to breathe as he went. He stretched out his hand and pushed the door further open. The room was musky with the smell of smouldering josh sticks and was lit with the light of flickering candles.

The young, pregnant woman lay naked and spread-eagled on the bed before him and he could not only see her but he could smell her too. Her large stomach and breasts were plump and shiny with oil and they seemed to move independently of each other under the flickering candlelight.

'I've been thinking about you, Caleb.'

Caleb's grip tightened around the handle of his knife.

The witch continued to lay on her back. Her hand stroked between her legs in slow circular movements that made her gasp.

'I hope you're going to be a good boy, Caleb.'

He stepped nearer to the bed, his throat dry, his heart thumping.

'Yes,' he croaked. 'I'm going to be a good boy.'

'Come and thee what I've got for you.'

He took a step towards the bed, his mind reeling, his senses shot to hell, his brain filling with doubt. The feel of the cold blade that he now had pressed against his thigh gave him the resolve he needed and he lifted the knife shakily above his head.

'Who's the daddy?

'Well you are, thilly.'

'Who killed my baby.'

'Well we did, thilly.'

He heard a noise behind him, but it was too late. Before he could turn, his head exploded with a mixture of horrendous pain and mind-shattering lights.

He was dead before he'd toppled across the young woman's naked body.

Elspeth giggled as she tried to wriggle out from underneath him.

Carrie Wyck smashed his head twice more on the crown with the heavy brass poker, his skull making a terrible, sickening sound as it cracked open.

The naked woman on the bed laughed.

Chapter Eleven

The seventh of November. Seven-thirty in the morning.

The sun rose over Haworth Village and reflected dramatically off the wet roof tiles, exaggerating their beauty and complimenting the myriad of smoking chimney pots.

After beautifying the roofs, the sunshine slipped between the cottages and bounced off the silver and gold geometric cobbles making them steam magically.

The whole village sparkled.

As did Angela Morson, the milk lady. She'd been up and working for what felt like an age and she had witnessed the first rays of the sun coming up over the moors. Sunshine, she thought, was good for her soul.

The rain had only just stopped so water still trickled down between the sets, adding depth to the drama. Sunshine and rain was just the best she thought, she loved it. This was when Haworth was at its best. The streets washed clean and the tar shining like mercury running down the hill.

Angela, drove her battered Nissan flatbed up the street, the cobbles causing the milk bottles, crated in the back, to rattle out a happy clinking commentary as she went.

She had just dropped a couple of green tops off at Snicket End House when she noticed a red tint to the water that ran down the street. Curious, she followed the flow up the hill to the pavement flags between the pub's entrance and the church gates. Here the red tint was becoming considerably brighter.

Somebody's dropped an ice lolly in the road, she thought, *it's melting and turning the runoff to red.* She wished the bloody visitors would pick their litter up and take it home with them, or at least stick it in a bin.

And what the hell was that bundle of crap at the top of the steps in front of the church gate, more bloody rubbish? She held her milk crate in one hand balanced on one knee and bent down with her spare hand to investigate the pile of rubbish. She grabbed a handful of stubbly skin before she had chance to check herself.

She held in her hand a severed head.

A head with shocked staring eyes and a mouth open wide in a silent scream, blood that dripped gloopily from the shreds of skin that hung from the tattered neck mixed with the rain water and ran off down the street.

Angela's facial expression mimicked that of her gruesome find: eyes open wide in horror, mouth opened wide to scream. The scream, however, when it came, could hardly be described as silent.

She dropped the crate, the milk bottles smashing on the stone, spilling milk to mix with the rain and blood. Angela may have thought, if she were not too busy charging down the street, that the flow had now taken on the appearance of strawberry milkshake.

Angela Morson would never enjoy wet sunny mornings ever again.

*

In the pathology lab, after all had been cleaned and tidied, Carol Redman sat with a steaming mug of tea. No matter what the time of year, the pathologist's tea always steamed as the lab was kept very cold for obvious reasons.

Brontë entered through the heavy plastic curtains.

'Hi again, what's new?'

'Cats or babies?'

'Let's start with cats.'

'I've not put too much effort into the cats. Some were kittens, with just the odd adult. They seem to age from about a couple of days...'

'Could it have been as early as last night?'

'Could've been, I suppose.'

'Bollocks, that confirms Smith's story.'

'There seems to be a body every six months or so going back for years. Could go back thirty years, there's quite a number of them.'

'And the babies?'

'Only two...'

'Well that's two too many.'

'The foetuses,' she waited for a response but there was none coming, 'have some years between them.'

'Jesus! Where the hell have they come from?'

'It would seem the first is Carrie Wyck's offspring and has been in the ground a minimum of fifteen years. The second is the girl's, Elspeth Wyck's. Been there about a year. There's about sixteen years between 'em.'

'And the father?'

'Looks like your friend Caleb Smith has been a busy boy.'

'Both!?'

'Oh yes.'

'I don't know if I can get my head round this.'

'And...'

'Go on.'

'They are both males.'

'Both boys.'

'Correct.'

'This is weird.'

'Well try this for size, it looks like one is Elspeth's brother and the other her son.'

'Jesus!'

'Exactly. Which means one is Carrie Wyck's son and the other her grandson and to Cicely Wyck they're grandson and great grandson.'

'How the hell did they do the abortions?'

'Wasn't the grandmother a nurse?'

'Bloody hell, she was.'

'And the weirdest thing is they're both Caleb Smith's.'

'Son of a bitch, Caleb, you old dog. Where is he by the way?'

'Well, his body's in that drawer and his heads in this fridge here.' She opened the fridge and removed the head.

'What do you think did it for him, the removal of his head?'

'Hacking his head off certainly wouldn't have done him any good but no, decapitation was post-mortem.'

'Whoever did it, did they know what they were doing?'

'Good God no, very poorly executed. They made a right bloody mess of it, if you'll pardon the expression, but it seemed they had a very sharp knife and maybe a cleaver.'

'Go on then, enlighten me, if he was dead before he was butchered, what initially killed him?'

'Sorry to be boring, Brontë, just our old friend the common or garden, blunt force trauma to the back of the head.'

'A hammer?'

'No something thinner and oblong.'

'Do you think he knew what was happening to him?'

'What you getting at?'

'The others knew what was about to happen to 'em, knew they was about to cop it. The killer wanted them to know. Wanted them to look death in the eye. Wanted them to suffer.'

'You linking this to the other murders?'

'Of course. They're all sadistic murder with mutilation?'

She picked up the head and put a finger in a whole at the back of the skull.

'Look.'

Brontë forced himself to look but wasn't happy about it.

'He wouldn't have known a thing. The first blow killed him outright. He never knew what hit him. They came up behind him and...' she demonstrated by miming striking the head '...WHAM! He would have been dead before he hit the deck.

She turned the grotesque head in her hands.

'The other two were not needed. They were just to make sure. Wham! Wham! Maybe for pleasure even, certainly brutal and merciless.'

'You think the murderer is one and the same person?'

'Whoa there, Brontë boy, hold your 'orses, that's your job. I come up with the what and where. You come up with the who and the why.'

'Thanks a bunch,' said Brontë as he meandered his way across the lab.

'Do you want my two-penny worth, Brontë?'

'Fire away.'

'The foetuses were self-aborted by the women themselves.'

'Why would they do that?'

'You're asking me whys again. Think about it. The main reason for abortions is that for one reason or another a child is not wanted.'

'I'm listening.'

'The unwanted children from the garden are boys, the Wyck family are all girls. They didn't want the boys, Brontë.'

'They stopped procreating once they had a girl apiece. So Elthpeth,' he lisped the name, 'Wyck, must be pregnant with a baby girl…'

'…and so our old mate Caleb has outlived his usefulness.'

'The women could have done for Caleb, but did they do for the others?'

'Then tell me, did Caleb Smith still have his todger intact?'

'He did, he lost his head but not his how's your father.'

'Then they're not connected. If the woman were the cock croppers, Caleb's old fella would have been a prized memento, they would certainly have whipped that bugger off pretty damn quick. You, my little mortician, are a star.'

He marched back across the lab, grabbed her head in his hands and kissed her on the forehead.

'Carol Redman, bless your cotton socks.'

'Brontë, if you hadn't noticed I'm a goth. I don't wear cotton socks, I wear black stockings and suspenders.'

'Now that's a first from you... too much information for once.'

*

Elspeth Wyck was unperturbed about being in the interview room again. In fact, she thrived on the attention. She had already been processed, her samples taken and along with her clothes packed off to toxicology. The SOCO paper boiler suit she had been provided with she'd unzipped to reveal as much flesh and cleavage as possible. The duty solicitor sat next to her was po-faced and bored.

Brontë entered the room and clocked the girl's naked flesh.

'Ms Gallagher, advise your client to make her clothing more appropriate or this interview will not happen and she will go back to the cells and wait.'

'Chritht!' said the girl in the boiler suit. 'He'th a piece of work ithn't he?'

The sulky solicitor silenced her client with a wave and they talked in hushed voices for a while. With a look at Brontë that could fell a pig, the girl zipped her overall up to the neck and folded her arms across her chest.

'What'th wrong with 'im anyroad, ith he gay or what?'

Brontë found it expedient to ignore her.

'Can we state our names for the tape, please?'

'Ms Sally Gallagher,' said the solicitor, 'duty legal representative.'

'Detective Inspector Brontë.'

All eyes fell on the girl.

'Elthpeth,' she lisped sullenly.

Brontë lifted his eyebrows enquiringly at the girl, who took in an exasperated gasp.

'Wyck... Elthpeth Wyck, I mean it'th not as if we all don't' know, ith it?'

'Miss Wyck, can you confirm, for the benefit of the tape, your relationship with Caleb Smith.'

'Yeth.'

They waited for her response.

'Well...' she said while rubbing her tummy.

'He's your baby's daddy?'

'Yes, the babieth daddy...' she chewed on her finger nail, 'and my daddy.'

Sally Gallagher perked up a bit at this and looked interested in her work for a change. She turned to her client and spoke.

'I think at this point it might be best—'

Elspeth giggled.

'And he'th my brother, too.'

The solicitor nearly fell off her seat.

'I think I need to speak to my client.'

'And,' continued Elspeth, ignoring the legal adviser, 'I killed all three at onth.'

She laughed.

'Miss Wyck, I strongly suggest you...'

Brontë held up his hand to the solicitor.

'Are you saying you murdered, Caleb Smith?'

'I wouldn't thay murdered as thuch, but I did kill him.'

'And then beheaded him?'

'Oh no, not that; Mummy did that becauth she thought it would be more... dramatic!'

'Dramatic!?'

'She thought everyone would think the killer wath the "Vampire".'

She wriggled her fingers in front of her face and wailed like a ghost.

'OooOOooo!'

'Why Elspeth? Why did you kill your... Mr Smith?'

'He toyed with my honour, Inthpector Brontë,' she smiled coyly, 'and me five month pregnant with hith daughter, too. Grandma thaid it was dithguthting that he thtill wanted to... well do what he wanted to do.'

'So?" Said Brontë

Elspeth sat and looked enquiringly

'Tho,' she said, 'whatth a girl gonna do?'

*

In the incident room, the three detectives deliberated once again over the woodchip timeline. Brontë tapped the paper with a red sharpie.

'There's something else, there has to be.'

'We've been through it all, boss. If it's not the Wycks, we're right back where we started, with nothing.'

'Unless it was Caleb. Could still have been him,' said Pepper, throwing in her two-penny worth.

'I don't see it, Pepper. It doesn't fit.'

'We still need to keep him in mind, he's better than anything else we've got. If the killings stop now it'll point the finger right at him. He's all we've got.'

'Except,' said Rhiaz 'there's still the American connection.'

'Yeah, well that's producing sweet Fanny Adams, as well.'

Brontë drew a circle on the paper around Capability's name.

'What time is it in South Carolina?'

Rhiaz checked his watch. 'About nine o'clock, boss.'

There's two nine o'clocks in a day, Rhiaz, which nine o'clock are we talking about?'

'Breakfast time, Inspector.'

'Hey, breakfast in America. Anyone for syrup and pancakes?'

'It may be nine-o-clock in Carolina, Pepper, but here, it's just past, catchthefuckinpsyscho o'clock. So, stop thinking about your stomach and start thinking about who it is.'

'Yes sir, boss, sir.' She saluted him.

'Rhiaz, get that Competence Goldsmith fella on the blower, he should be out of bed by now.'

'Capability, sir. Capability Goldman.'

'Yeah whatever, let's see what the fat Carolinian has to say.'

'You've only ever spoken to him on the phone, Brontë, what makes you think he's fat?'

'He's American, isn't he?'

The door in the back wall smashed open and shook the room.

BOOM.

'Brontë!'

The three officers held their breaths as Superintendent Crupper marched across the room.

'If you'd have locked up that baseball-capped perv when I said, he'd still be alive today.'

'He didn't do it.'

'No, then who did?'

There was a beat as Brontë thought about that.

'We don't have anyone.'

'See,' Crupper heaved a great sigh, looked up at the ceiling and held his arms out beseechingly, 'Smith would have been as good as anybody, wouldn't he?'

'You can't just twist the law around to suit yourself.'

'Don't be ridiculous, man, of course you can. That's exactly what you can do, you bleedin' idiot.'

Brontë was saved from further harassment by Rhiaz's ringing phone.

'Inspector Brontë, sir,' Rhiaz jumped up, clutching the telephone to his ear, 'Carolina's just got back to us.'

Brontë turned to the superintendent.

'It's important. I need to take it. It's Carolina.'

'I don't really give a chuff what you do, Brontë, I just want this sorting and no more bloody messing about.'

Crupper barged his way out of the room and Brontë turned to Rhiaz.

'Put him on speaker.'

'Good morning, Great Britain. Capability Goldman here at your beck and call.'

'Good morning, Mr Goldman. You are speaking to me, Inspector Brontë, with Constable Khan and Sergeant Pepper, we spoke this morning'

'Sergeant Pepper!? You gotta be pulling my leg? What is it with you English dudes? Hey, Sergeant, I suppose you'll get by with a little help—'

'So, Mr Goldman, tell me what you know about Steven Livesey.'

'You are so going to love this.'

'Go on then, I need a bit of love in my life.'

'Stephen Livesey, the guy you wanted me to trace. Well I traced him. I thought I recognised the name, I had to check to be sure.'

'And?'

'Initially you were after some guy who turned out to be a female psychopath, the Ice Maiden.'

'We all know this.'

'Name of Currer Bell, also known as...'

'Spit it out, Capability.'

'Stephen Livesey.'

The three police officers froze and then looked from one to the other.

'Shit,' they said in unison.

'Simon Livesey and the Ice Maiden are the same person. He came here to South Carolina about twenty years ago with his foster parents.'

'Go on, what else?'

'Studied at the USC...'

'Which is?'

'Which is the University of South Carolina. He majored in physiology but dropped out, petitioned the local authority, changed his name and became a female stripper name of Currer Bell.'

'But Livesey was a boy. You know, like a male type boy.'

'Hey, welcome to America.'

'He had a sex change?'

'She had gender reassignment.'

'He became a she?'

'Slam dunk, Inspector.'

'And this stripper become a killer why?'

'Christ, she was a frigging sociopath. What other reason did she need?'

'Tell me, Capability, do all serial killers receive the death penalty in South Carolina?'

'Only the real bad ones.'

'Like the Maiden.'

'Oh yes, I'll say. She was a real doozy. Viciously skewered five people with an ice-axe and relieved them of their wedding tackle. Well she did the men anyway.'

The three police officers looked at each other.

'Jesus,' said Pepper, 'it's the same MO. We've got us a bloody copycat.'

'What happened to the penises? Where were they put in the victim's mouths by any chance.'

'Oh no, nothing so simple.'

'You purposefully being enigmatic, Mr Goldman?'

'You haven't heard the half if it, Inspector.'

'OK, let me have it, and I know you're a reporter but can we try cut out the melodramatics eh?'

'Hello, who's helping who here?'

'Ignore him, Mr Goldman, he's a miserable old bugger. What is it we don't know?'

'She stuck their Bratwursts right up their tukhus.'

'Tukhus?'

'Where the sun don't shine, mam.'

'Well that's different,' said Pepper.

'And I'll tell you something else you don't know: only the judge, the district attorney and myself knew that bit of information. So, if you've got a copycat killer over there, Inspector Brontë, it has to be Supreme Court Judge Arnie Jefferson or District Attorney Pat Cooper, cos it certainly ain't me, that's for sure.

'It's all too much of a coincidence. Someone else had to know.'

'Not a chance, not even the chief justice knew that snippet. Well I think I've just about covered everything I know, I've got an appointment with griddlecakes and fresh orange juice if you don't mind.'

'Thank you, Mr Goldman. Keep in touch.'

'Hey, officers, catch you next time.'

The phone went dead.

'Right, Rhiaz, grab your felt-tip and update your timeline. One, Livesey was at the Highbatts. Two, he moved to America. Three, he became a she. Four, she hacked to death five random Americans. Put a circle and a big question mark around the word "random". Five, she was executed by lethal injection. And finally, number six, her restless spirit returned to Yorkshire to wreak vengeance on all those that abused him as a child.'

'A spirit?' laughed Pepper.

'Well if not a spirit, bloody who?'

'I'll tell you what boss, we never asked Mr Goldman if he had the lowdown on the death row visitor.'

'Lowdown?'

'Sorry, information.'

'How that'll move us forward? God only knows.'

*

Brontë and Obi-Wan sat in the greenhouse, lost in their own thoughts. Brontë was somewhere in Southern Carolina tracking down turban-clad murderers who rode Harley Davidson motorbikes.

God only knows where Obi-Wan's head was. His feet constantly twitched, so he was probably chasing rabbits somewhere, but probably not in the Americas.

A shadow fell across the windows and Brontë turned to the door to see who was coming. Obi didn't bother. He already knew who it was.

'Woof,' he said.

The door swung open revealing a hand holding a bottle of Shiraz, which was followed by the head of Margaret Brontë.

'Anyone want wine?'

'I wouldn't mind a gill, but the dog's already had enough.'

'I thought as much.' She entered, pushed Obi off his seat and took his place. 'I brought two glasses.'

'What about Obi?'

'He can drink out of the pond like always.'

'What brings you round here anyway? Not just to drink wine and be mean to my dog.'

'I've come around to get the goss on your new girlfriend.'

Brontë looked at her.

'It's all over the village.'

'Chance'd be a fine thing.'

'Oh, come on, you've been seen, Charlie.'

'I can assure you, I have not been seen with anyone and particularly not our local pathologist.'

'Good God, who mentioned the walking dead? You have been spotted with our new visitor from America.'

Brontë laughed. 'I know of, nor have been seen with, no Americans. I have, however, spoken to one on the phone.'

'Well, Charlie boy, Shirley from the hairdressers saw the both of you up on the cobbles. Shirley spoke to her and little old Yumi took great pleasure in describing how you chased her butt naked round our cottage.'

Obi lifted a quizzical eyebrow. Brontë couldn't tell if he was shocked or impressed.

'She's not American; she's Japanese.'

'Rubbish, she's as American as apple pie.'

'Japanese.'

'Brontë, I spoke to her on the phone when she booked her stay at the cottage. She's as Japanese as Dolly Parton.'

'She even looks Japanese.'

'Barak Obama looks African but he's not. She may look Japanese but I bet she hasn't ever been up to the Golden Wok Takeaway never mind the east. She's been pulling your leg, Charlie.'

Brontë jumped to his feet and threw down the last of his wine.

'Where you going?'

'I'm off to find out who Yumi really is,' he kissed her on the mouth. 'You are a star.'

'Bit late to work that out.'

'Call Pepper and tell her to meet me at the cottage.' He thought for a moment. 'And feed the dog if you would.'

'What did your last slave die of?'

'Sexual exhaustion.'

Yeah, in your bleadin' dreams.

He slammed the door behind him.

*

Pepper stood at the cottage door being spot lit by the outdoor security light. She had already knocked three times and then had held her finger on the bell-push for an age.

Brontë pulled up on the Monster and after killing the lights and the engine he joined her on the steps.

'She's not here.'

'Ok, move out of the road.'

'What you doing?'

Brontë unclasped the front of the key-safe and tapped the appropriate number into the combination lock. The lid sprung open and the key fell into his palm. It was only when he was opening the door that Pepper spoke up.

'I believe, Brontë... if we are sticking to proper police procedure we need a warrant.'

'I believe, Pepper, that this is my house, so proper procedure is I can do what the chuff I want.'

'There's no need for bad language.'

'Isn't there? Let's go in and 'ave a look, shall we?'

Brontë pushed the door open, stepped inside and switched on the lights.

The pair poked around the downstairs of the house for a bit, being careful not to disturb anything. However, there was nothing to disturb. It looked like no one was staying at the cottage at all. They found nothing, only some dead headless flower stalks in a vase. Pepper entered the kitchen but here too found nothing. No pots, no dirty dishes, no rubbish in the bin, nothing. Then her gaze landed on the fridge and she moved towards it.

'The fridge? What do you expect to find in a bloody fridge?'

'Ah now Brontë, you wanna find out anything about a woman just have a dekko in her fridge or her handbag.'

He gently pushed her out of the way and opened the fridge door; it was empty.

'Empty,' he moaned.

'OK, shall we look upstairs.'

'I'm right behind you, Pepper.'

They searched two cold and empty bedrooms and found nothing. They used their torches as the lighting was poor and they worried things may be overlooked in the dark corners of the rooms.

'These rooms don't feel like anyone's slept in 'em since Heathcliff was a lad,' said Pepper.

Brontë ignored her.

In the third and largest of the rooms, Pepper switched on the light and found the bed unmade and the curtains closed. In one corner stood an old oak wardrobe. The door was hanging ajar.

Pepper whispered to Brontë as she stepped a little nearer.

'I hope that she isn't gonna jump out like some little vampire-ninja.'

She opened the door by stretching forward and tapping it with her size-four Dr Martens.

'Oh fuck!'

'What is it?'

She turned to him and displayed a black hooded cloak and a long black wig.

'Looks like Bride of Dracula attire to me, I'd stake my badge on it. Stake... get it?'

'You're not funny.'

'Oh, but I so am.'

Brontë crossed to a washbasin and picked up a pink disposable shaver. 'There's dark hairs stuck to the blade and some in the basin.'

Pepper waved the wig at Brontë.

'Of course! She shaves her head. Damn it! That's why she covered it when I chased her naked round the cottage.'

'I just love it when you drop these bombshells into conversation.'

'It's a long story but it wasn't her naked arse she needed to hide, it was her bloody head. Makes you wonder who the little bald Asian guy was who visited the Ice Maiden.'

'Look!'

'What is it?'

Pepper pulled a plain packet from out of the wardrobe and peeped into it.

'It's a file.'

'Containing what?'

Pepper flicked through the papers.

'Well?'

'It contains,' she read a bit more, 'an account of what happened at Highbatts: names, notes, descriptions and some other stuff.'

'Put everything back where it was, we'll come back in the morning with a warrant .'

'I'll get a couple of uniforms to watch the place tonight just in case she comes back and wants to do a runner. I'll go back to the wife and a bit of left-over Shiraz. We'll sort everything in the morning when we have a warrant.'

Chapter Twelve

Back in Haworth. The Eighth of November.

The following morning found Brontë and Obi on their favourite morning walk, across the Hewenden Viaduct. Obi had had a private poo somewhere on the old railway bank while Brontë stood face into the wind and rain to wake himself up. Water ran down his cheeks. Both man and dog were aware of the shenanigans of the night before, and it was hard to tell who was the most embarrassed.

'I know, all right,' said the man to the dog, 'least said soonest mended.'

Obi raised his eyes to the heavens and looked out of under hooded hairy brows.

'I've told you, I'm not talking about it, and if you bring it up again you can forget about sausage for breakfast.'

Obi continued to stare and to wriggle his brows.

'What can I say? It's exes with benefits, but you're right, someone's gonna pay for it.'

The night before, Brontë's ex-misses, had already finished the last of the Shiraz before Brontë got back, but he'd got more wine in his secret store so they'd attacked that too.

They had both got hammered and she had stayed the night.

They woke up late, entwined in each other's arms and tangled up in bed sheets.

After taking Obi back home and sticking him two sausages in the frying pan, he placed a mug of Yorkshire tea on the bedside cabinet next to the ex's head. He kissed the mat of blonde hair that was protruding from under the covers. The only bit of her that was visible.

'I'm off to work,' he said to the untidy pile of bedclothes, 'let yourself out.'

The pile stirred and an attractive but makeup-smudged eye peered out from the depths.

'God, I feel like shit.'

'Yeah! You look like shit.'

'Charmed, I'm sure.'

Her arm snaked out from under the covers and she grabbed her tea.

'I'd have your babies for a bacon sandwich.'

'That boat's well sailed. I'm off to work now; look after the dog.'

'It's not 'the dog' like its ours; it's 'your dog' like it's bloody yours, Charlie.

She groaned and disappeared back under the covers, taking her tea with her. Obi jumped up on the bed and flaked out on top of her.

'Bloody hell, he's spilt my tea. Can't you take him with you?'

'This is his house. Get your arse out of bed and feed him his sausages… Oh and close the door on your way out.'

'Go bollocks, Charlie.'

Brontë stood for a second and watched the pile of bed clothes.

'What the hell are we gonna do, Margaret?'

The pile of bedclothes wriggled and disturbed the dog.

'Climb back in here and you'll find out.'

On his way to the door he noticed a conspicuous contour under the duvet. A contour that more or less coincided to where his wife's backside should be.

He smacked it as he passed, a grin spread across his face.

'And make the bloody bed when you get up.'

'You're such a twat, Charlie.'

Obi-Wan barked in agreement.

'Woof.'

*

Brontë parked the Monster at the bottom of the cobbles. He hit the stop button and pulled off his lid. Up the street, people were opening their shops and preparing for the day ahead.

A mother and three boys were bickering over the state of their shop window.

'What ya think?'

'It looks pretty.'

'It looks pretty… weird.'

'I like it, Mummy.'

'Oh, I like it OK. But it is a bit weird.'

'Oh, for God's sake,' said the mother as she stormed off into the shop.

The boys followed her, looking particularly unperturbed.

Brontë continued up the cobbles, passed their shop window and glanced in.

The shopfront boasted a mannequin of a young girl dressed in coat, hat and scarf and strange red wellingtons. She was carrying a huge pumpkin.

'Bit weird,' he said out loud, 'but I like it too.'

As he made his way past the Fleece Inn, he noticed through the windows a number of young women stripping off and rubbing bizarre black makeup on their faces. There was lots of laughter and shouting.

Brontë knew these were the local mummers, an amateur dramatic society who revelled in local festivities. At this time of year they executed impromptu performances up and down the cobbles. Performances that included dance, music, drink and a lot of showing off. Passers-by would try guess the mummers' identities by poking and prodding them or by interrogating them. To make this more of a challenge, the mummers would stuff their costumes into weird body shapes and wear masks or paint their faces.

What fun was had.

Brontë entered the incident room and found Pepper and Rhiaz sipping coffee and eating sausage sandwiches. Rhiaz offered him a brown paper sandwich bag as he crossed to the timeline.

'Sarnie, boss?'

'No, I'm good, thanks.'

'Never again,' said Pepper, 'never again will sausage pass his lips until this case is well and truly over and well forgotten.'

'I don't think we'll ever forget this one, Pepper.'

He slapped the wallpaper timeline with the palm of his hand.

'You will remember, Rhiaz, my little buddy, when I said don't start the timeline with the railwayman right at the beginning of the paper.'

'I do.'

'It all started way before,' he rolled more paper across the wall, 'all the way back here, years and years ago.' He jabbed the sheet with his pen. 'Right back here where the children of Highbatts were abused.'

'You think the murders are acts of vengeance.'

'I do. Someone who knows of the abusers and what it was they did.'

'Which is where we come unstuck. We 'aven't got a bloody clue.'

'The only person we can come up with that seems to have been connected to the Ice Maiden is an unknown American Asian male and we have got nowt like that.'

'Apart from the beautiful Yumi, who is a Japanese female.'

'Well we do know a man who might 'ave a clue. Get on the blower again, I need to check something with our friend in America.'

Rhiaz waved his mobile in the air.

'I've got him on speed dial.' He pressed a button on said apparatus and held it to his ear.

'Put him on speakerphone.'

'What time is it over there? What if he doesn't answer?'

'It's about five o'clock in the morning. Ten quid says he doesn't.'

They stood in silence listening to the phone ring.

'Keep it ringing till he answers.'

However, it stopped ringing after the first six rings or so, and a tired voice drawled out of the phone.

'Y'all, better have a good reason for calling at this godforsaken time or I'm gonna be madder than a puffed toad.'

'Capability, it's Brontë. Good morning, sir.'

'Is it Brontë? Is it a good morning over there on your little septic tiles, because my morning hasn't started good at all. Over here in the good old US of A I've been dragged out of my pit at the crack of a pelican's fart by a limey feckin' copper.'

'Sorry about that, Goldman, I seem to have painted myself into a corner and I need a bit more help from you.'

'What I know, Brontë probably don't amount to a hill of beans... but I'll do my best.'

'I'm still interested in the visitor that the Ice Maiden had at her execution.'

'The skinny Asian dude in the cheap suit.'

'Exactly. You are sure about the "Asian" bit... and the "male" bit for that matter?'

'You mean my whole goddamned observation?'

'Pretty much, yeah.'

The phone went quiet.

The three police officers looked from one to the other. Pepper mouthed, *Is he still there?* to the other two officers.

Brontë and Rhiaz shrugged.

'Hello?' said Pepper into the phone.

'Yes, don't worry I'm still here, I was just thinking... The dude was very slight, wore a man's suit and had a shaved head, I didn't see a lot more. And like I said before, this is America. Could have been a boy or a girl or any other variation in between.'

'What about being Asian?'

'Now that, Detective Chief Inspector, I'm one-hundred per cent sure about.'

'You sure of that? You're sure he or she was Indian or Pakistani?'

'What you on about? I never said anything about India or Pakistan.'

'You said—'

Rhiaz snapped his fingers. 'He said Asian.'

'And...?'

'In America that doesn't mean people like me, sir; it means Chinese.'

'Exactly,' said the phone.

'Could that also mean people from Japan?'

'Yes,' said the constable.

'Japanese, Korean, and anywhere else from that part of the globe,' said the phone.

'So, we can safely say that the visitor at the Women's Correction Institute rather than being an Indian male could have been a Japanese woman.'

'I think that just about sums it up.'

'Right, Capability, listen,' said Brontë, grabbing the phone and speaking directly into it. 'In the Ice Maiden's case, was there a Japanese woman with a name like Yumi?'

The officers waited impatiently.

'Oh shit, Brontë, that's who it was, that's who the feck it was. When Livesey bombed out of university to became a drag queen he shacked up in a couple of rooms, with a Korean striptease trapeze artist...'

'Striptease trapeze!?'

'You better belief it, Brontë, glorifying under the stage name of Yumi Mummi, and the Ice Maiden was her counterbalance when she flew her trapeze out over the audience.'

'You couldn't make this stuff up, could you?'

'She was the world's only exponent of the Naked Double Straddle Snatch.'

'Where on God's green earth did she learn that trade?'

'She was an orphan, claimed she was abused by her foster parents...'

'Here we go.'

'...and a number of high-ranking dignitaries in the care system. They all denied it of course.'

'Of course.'

'No one believed her, she ran off before she could be, as she put it, imprisoned in a care home. She resurfaced a few years later as the flying stripper.'

'They had a lot in common, the two of them, Yumi and Livesey.' Said Pepper.

'They sure as hell did, mam, and bizarrely...'

'Bizarrely what?' asked Brontë.

'Bizarrely, two of the Ice Maiden's victims were Yumi's foster parents.'

Brontë jumped to his feet.

'Shit!' he said. 'Shit, shit, shit, shit. Shit!'

'Inspector, you have a mouth dirtier than a racoon suckin' coal.'

Brontë slammed his hands down on the desk.

'Strangers on a Train!'

'What!?'

'None of the murders were on a train,' said Pepper, 'they were all around the station but none were on a train. And strangers very rarely murder, right?'

'*Strangers on a Train* is an Alfred Hitchcock old black and white psychological thriller.'

'Psychological as in psychopathic.'

'Two strangers meet on a train and they work out they each have someone they'd like getting rid of.'

'As you do.'

'The psychopath says they should swap murders, so that the police won't suspect either of them.'

'Like that's gonna work.'

'It's a good plan. Like you said, strangers don't kill strangers.'

'Did it work?'

'Watch the film.'

'Ha, it didn't work.'

'The Ice Maiden took on Yumi's abusers, slaughtered, humiliated each of them by removing their privates et cetera. No one suspected her because she had no connection to the victims whatsoever. The only reason they got her was because she was caught red handed.'

'I'll get on to it,' chirped the phone. 'I should have seen this. I'll find her faster than a speeding ticket, Brontë, don't you worry.'

'It's too late, Capability. You won't find her in Carolina, she's over here. In God's own county.'

'You've seen her?'

'Oh yes, I've seen her all right, and I've even witnessed her infamous Naked Double Straddle Snatch.'

Chapter Thirteen

Hewenden Bridge Railway Station.
The ninth of November.

Albert Ackroyd locked his cash into his safe, damped down the stove, closed up the dirty old ledger and grinned at his reflection in a mirror, the glass of which was stained darkly with soot.

'You're a good-looking bastard Albert Ackroyd,' he winked at himself. 'That Fanny Funnel is one lucky lady.'

He'd been meeting his paramour in their secret love shack nearly every day for nigh on twenty years. He pulled a foldable trundle-bed out from under his desk and removed his blackened and smoky overalls and his blackened and smoky underwear. The next part of the ritual was to lay naked in the dark and wait for his lover.

The sound of her entering the van made him wriggle in anticipation.

'Is that you my little, Funny Fanny Funnel? I hope you've brought the ginger biscuits,' he giggled.

The only response was heavy breathing coming out of the darkness. God, she sounds up for it today, he thought.

'Stop fannyin' about, Fanny and get your hot bod over 'ere.' This time he laughed out loud at his coarse humour.

The catch on the door snapped shut.

'Oooh! That's my girl.'

More heavy breathing from the shadows. Albert was now not so sure who had entered the carriage. He was now sounding a little apprehensive and was feeling quite vulnerable in his nakedness.

'I'm too long in the tooth to be afraid of noises in the dark, my love.'

The only response was more heavy breathing.

'I've no money, there's nothing here worth having. You may as well just turn right round and go fuck right off.'

A large lump of coal flew from out of the dark, shot through the air and struck Albert square in the face, nearly knocking him senseless. He screamed out and his hand shot up to his injured nose and cheek.

'What the fuck!?'

'You should have reported what you saw,' said a voice in the dark that wasn't Fanny's.

'Jesus!'

Another piece of coal flew out of the dark and struck him in the chest. He staggered backwards, stumbling over buckets and sacks, only just managing to stay on his feet.

'You should have reported what happened to the boys.'

A third chunk of coal shot through the air, striking Albert once more on the head, causing him to shout out again and blood to run down his face.

'Shit...'

'You could have protected the innocents.'

He was once again smashed by coal, this time being knocked down, and he measured his length out on the carriage floor.

'I am comeuppance,' said the voice, 'and this is retribution.'

*

Brontë and Pepper were once again studying the timeline, Brontë now wielding the black marker pen and Pepper reading from the file confiscated from the missing Yumi, running through the victims.

'OK, we know it all leads back to Highbatts,' said Brontë, 'kids being abused by paedophiles. First the railway volunteer.'

'We found no traceable connection with Flett to the home but this file compiled by the Ice Maiden says he abused the kids up there.'

'And now he's dead,' Brontë executed a flamboyant tick through Nigel Fletts name. 'Tick!'

'Next, the good Catholic priest himself...' said Pepper in a really pathetic Irish accent.

'That's an oxymoron if ever there was one.'

Pepper referred to her file.

'The father provide pastoral care for the boys,' she looked back up at Brontë. 'He must have known about the abuses.'

'More like he was an abuser... and now he's dead. Tick.'

'And last but not least, Cicely Wyck, a nurse at the home.'

'And now she too is dead. Tick!' Brontë chewed on the end of the pen. 'But we don't really know if she's the last or not.'

'There could be more, and if there is who's next?'

'God only knows.'

'God and Yumi Mummi. Possibly, but there ain't no more information in here.'

'Shit!' shouted Brontë in frustration, and he threw his pen at the wall.

'Temper, temper,' admonished Pepper, 'and you know what Capability thinks of your potty-mouth.'

Brontë froze for a second and stared at the black mark he had made on the wall.

'You all right, boss?'

Almost in a trance Brontë turned slowly and looked at her without seeing her. He spoke, not to her but to himself.

'I do know what Capability thinks of my mouth...' He broke free of his trance and addressed Pepper again. 'Get me the old Highbatts police file.'

'The one with nothing in it?'

'That's the one, the one that's been almost completely redacted.'

She went to the filing cabinet in the corner of the room, leaving Brontë to his thoughts.

'Dirtier than a racoon sucking coal.'

Pepper threw the file across to him. 'Here it is for what it's worth.'

Brontë flicked through the sheets in the file, '...a 'racoon suckin' coal.'

'There's nothing in there worth the paper it's written on. Everything's been burned or buried. The stuff that remains is worse than useless.'

'No there's something here, something I've seen but discounted.'

He rummaged some more in the file, laughing as he did.

'A 'racoon sucking coal...' He dramatically brandished a sheet of paper above his head. 'A-ha! And here it is!'

'Here's what exactly?'

'It's a copy of an old council lease. A lease on a council coal yard that has been signed over to public ownership.'

'You've lost me.'

'Right about the time Highbatts was being investigated, the station coal yard was signed over to no other than a Mr Albert Ackroyd. Our very own, friendly neighbourhood coalman.'

'You think they're connected?'

'Well it's either that or it's a huge coincidence, Pepper, and you know the first mantra of the Brontë school of policing.'

'Always take credit for your sergeant's hard work?'

'There's no such thing as coincidence.'

'Of course.'

'Remember what he told us at the yard, "I've delivered to every school, hospital, shop and factory in this 'ere neighbourhood" and "it's amazing who you see shunting whom when out on yer deliveries". He's seen someone shunting somebody they shouldn't have been and he's cashed in on it. Was given a bung to keep his trap shut.'

'It must have been something mega to warrant a whole coal yard.'

'It must that. Let's go see if he can enlighten us.'

'Let's go see if he's still alive!'

'Christ, I never thought of that. Go get the car and be quick about it.'

*

The naked trapeze artist was presently not naked. She wore a black jacket, black tutu, black tights and knee-high Dr Martens. She cut a bizarre figure standing over the battered body of the coalman, which was bleeding and smeared in coal muck.

'I don't know who you are,' his voice week and wavering. 'I don't know what you want.'

'But you know Highbatts?'

Slowly Yumi lifted a large lump of coal directly above his head.

'You know Highbatts. You know the boys.'

'I never touched a boy.'

'Your silence caused much pain.'

'I would never hurt a child.'

She let the coal drop and it smashed down on to the side of his head and he lay still. Removing the silver blade from its sheath she kicked the old man's legs apart.

'Your silence was very expensive...'

The knife flashed in the darkness.

'...expensive for too many boys.'

Yumi, wiped her coal-soiled hands over her face, completely blacking out her features.

*

The battered Astra pulled out on to the cobbles, Pepper driving, Brontë riding shotgun and Rhiaz in the back.

The mummers, all dressed in black strappy things with big boots and stockings, had blackened up their faces into macabre black skulls. They were blocking the road and danced in a weird zombie-like robotic manner.

'Get 'em out of the bloody road, Pepper,' said Brontë, leaning across the steering wheel and fisting the horn.

'Brontë!?'

'Get out of the bloody way,' he shouted at the revellers.

With a lot of shouting and swearing the dancers reluctantly moved to let the car through.

Pepper swung the car into the coal yard and pulled up beside the railway shed. The three police officers leapt out and made for the railway carriage door, which suddenly slammed back against the side of the carriage with a huge bang.

Bang!

Fanny Funnel shot through the door and down the steps as fast as a speeding train. Brontë guessed she had not moved that fast in many a year. She leant against the side of the carriage, her arm supporting her and she threw up a load of ginger biscuits all over the wheel arch.

'This doesn't look good,' said Rhiaz.

Brontë entered the carriage while Rhiaz and Pepper comforted Fanny.

Inside it was as dark and sooty as ever, Brontë stepped carefully as he moved into the carriage to search. For what? God only knew, but he was sure it wouldn't be pleasant.

Though he was fully prepared for the worst, when he fell over the body of the coalman he was shocked. The naked white skin glowed slightly in the dark and the blood ran like black streaks across it. He crouched by the side of the body and put his fingers on the dirt ingrained neck; there was no pulse.

Pepper entered quietly behind him.

'Has his penis gone?'

'It has.'

'And?'

'And there's blood around the mouth so we can presume…' He thought better than putting his thoughts into words. 'Mind you, there's blood everywhere, I suppose.'

Pepper took her phone and tapped in a number.

'I'll call it in and get SOCO and a hearse.'

'Not a hearse, Pepper. Call an ambulance, I can feel a pulse.'

She ended her call and dialled another number.

'Ambulance,' she said, 'Hewenden Railway Station… you'd best make it quick.' She turned to Brontë. 'If they make it quick, he might be saved.'

Brontë looked down at the bleeding groin.

'He might, but he may live to wish they never got here.'

'What now?'

'If he dies we call Morticia. If he lives,' Brontë shrugged, 'he goes to the hospital and we book him.' He stood in silence and looked down at the bruised body.

There was a polite cough which made Brontë turn to see Rhiaz in the doorway, silhouetted against the sky.

'What is it, Rhiaz?'

'Mrs Funnel, sir. I think you need to come and speak to her.'

'Right, you come up here, Rhiaz,' he pointed at Alfred Ackroyds groin, 'you stop that from bleeding him out.'

'How the hell do I do that!?'

'The police manual says apply firm pressure on the wound.'

Rhiaz wasn't a hundred per cent sure they weren't winding him up. He looked into their faces but their eyes were giving nothing away.

'The manual says to use a pad and apply pressure, maybe use an article of the casualty's clothing.'

'He's bloody naked!'

'You better whip your shirt off then, Rhiaz me old son.'

'He's going to bleed to death, Rhiaz, just hold the wound together.'

Brontë and Pepper were happy to leave the carriage and leave the very unhappy constable administering first aid. They found the equally unhappy Fanny Funnel leaning against the carriage. Thankfully she had stopped tossing up her cookies.

'Sorry about that, Brontë.' She wiped her mouth using the bottom of her pinny. 'I thought I were made of stronger stuff.'

'It was a big shock.'

'Yeah well that's as maybe but I would of sworn I wunt of battered an eye lid.'

'What happened?'

'I came to see Alfred. We were gonna...' she thought for a second '...eat biscuits.'

'He was naked, Fanny.'

'Nowt to do wi' me, Inspector. He was like that when I arrived and that... thing was standing over him.'

Brontë and Pepper looked at each other.

'Whoa there Fanny, say what?'

'Who was stood over him, Fanny?'

Fanny Funnel stared back at the two officers.

'Who, Fanny? Who'd you see?'

'I don't know, Mr Brontë, sir. It looked like one of them bloody mummers that are parading up and down the village.'

'What did they look like?'

'Like a black swan.'

'A what!?'

'A ballerina like in *Swan Lake* but the black one. Everything black, tutu and the full works.'

'What's this swan look like?'

'I couldn't tell. They was blacked up, you know... with makeup or summat?'

'That was what Capability said happened in Carolina. The visitor at the correction facility disappeared into the Mardi Gras crowds disguised as a dancer.'

'Shit,' said Brontë.

Brontë and Pepper worked their way up the cobbles, checking all the mummers. They spun them round and prodded and squeezed them. They checked males and females alike, pulling their clothes in attempt to identify Yumi. They pulled at people's masks and hoods and wiped makeup off their faces, looking for soot.

The mummers were not happy.

'Oi, what the chuff you playing at?'

'Hold on, fella, you want a smack in the gob.'

'Oi, get off, will you? What the fuck you doing?'

The police officers excused themselves, waving warrant cards in the faces of those they had upset or offended.

'Cool it, mate. We're the police.'

'I don't care who you are, get your bleeding hands off.'

'Hold it, boss, she's not here. These are all villagers, she is not here.'

'She must be here.'

'She's gone.'

'Where?'

Brontë took a deep breath, turned in a circle and looked up and down the street, exasperated. He took in the revellers and the candles and lights. He saw the cottages, the shops and the cafes. He saw Gobble on the Cobble and he remembered his time with Yumi.

'I know where she is.' He set off up the cobbles at a quick trot.

*

Yumi ran along the Hewenden Viaduct footpath, the sweat running down her face leaving channels in the sooty disguise, the disguise which enabled her to sneak past Brontë and his colleagues. It made her smile, the thought of Brontë's desperation as he drove passed in the car shouting at the mummers. She didn't want Brontë upset—she quite liked him—but she was worried he could stop her before she had fulfilled the promise she had made to her lover, Currer. She knew Brontë was getting close to sussing her out, if indeed he hadn't already, but there were still two left on her list.

She ran a little faster.

Halfway across the span of the viaduct she stopped, took a deep breath and climbed on to the parapet wall.

The view from one-hundred and twenty-three feet above the ground was amazing, Pen-y-ghent to the north, Pendle capped in cloud to the west and to the east the now smokeless and lifeless mill chimneys of Bradford.

'I can help,' said a voice.

Yumi turned. Brontë was on the viaduct path looking up at her.

'Don't jump.'

'Why, Inspector, you gonna take me in your arms and save me from myself?' There was no need now for the faux Japanese accent, so she used her natural voice, a deep Southern drawl.

'I know everything.'

'Nobody knows everything, Inspector.'

'I know enough.'

'If you know enough, Inspector, you know I'm going to jump.'

'I can help.'

Now she looked annoyed.

'Two more, Brontë, that's all I had left to do. Two more and it would have all been over. If you wanted to help me you could have let me finish.'

'You know I couldn't do that. That's not justice.'

'We wanted revenge, Inspector, not justice. We were never going to get justice.' She turned on the parapet and looked over huge drop. 'And it all ends here.'

'Wait!'

Brontë jumped up on the wall beside Yumi. His legs wobbled uneasily and his head span. Although he did not look down, his vertigo detected the open expanse and void over the side of the wall and he felt faint.

'So, you're not Japanese, then?'

'Nah! Possibly my ancestors were.' She waved her hand over her head gesturing to behind her. 'Way, way back.'

'I really can help.'

'The only way you can help is to let me carry on.' Yumi turned to him and threw her arms around his neck. 'You gonna let me kill the bad guys, Inspector Brontë sir, and cut off their little weeners?'

Brontë looked like he was trying to form an answer in his head. Yumi placed a finger over his lips.

'Don't bother; it's all over.'

'Please!'

Yumi, smiled and kissed him on the cheek. 'You're not bad, to say you're FIVE-O.' She stroked his hair. 'I'd give it up if I was you.'

'Get off of the wall, I'll sort out the bad guys.'

'Hey, Brontë, I'm the bad guy here remember. Here,' she placed two crumpled sheets in his hand. 'These were the last two.'

She kissed him on the lips.

'See you later, sweet potata.'

Yumi shoved Brontë's shoulders with all her might and the force toppled him backwards over the side of the wall; Yumi was propelled backwards over the other side.

Brontë fell hard onto the viaduct causeway path and the last thing he saw was Yumi disappearing into the abyss. Brontë fell only a few feet on to the stone path, but his head connected with the stone slabs and he was knocked clean out.

Chapter Fourteen

November the ninth.

Keighley Royal's assessment ward had three beds but in reality it only had room to comfortably fit two. Margaret sat on the edge of the bed that contained a sleeping Brontë.

One of the other two beds was occupied by an old man who burped along to the reassuring beeping of his heart monitor.

Burp... Beep... Burp... Beep... Burp... Beep... Burp...

If that wasn't bad enough, the last bed held a man who lay on his back snoring like a drowning pig.

Snort... Grunt... Squeal... Snort... Grunt... Squeal...

The resulting cacophony was driving Margaret to distraction.

Snort... Burp... Beep... Grunt... Burp... Squeal... Beep... Snort...

Brontë had been brought to the hospital the day before and diagnosed with mild concussion and kept overnight for observation.

He was fast asleep and dreamt of Yumi falling backwards into the fog. He watched her swallowed up by the dark and mist as she fell to her death. She was smiling. He woke with a start as she smashed on to the rocks below.

Snort... Burp... Beep... Grunt... Burp... Squeal... Beep... Snort...

'What on earth is that God awful noise?'

Margaret looked down at him.

'Well, you've woke up in a delightful mood.'

'You been and knocked yourself bloody unconscious recently?'

'You been to bloody charm school recently?'

'What time is it?'

'Ten.'

'Then it's time to get up.'

'You think, huh?'

Brontë swung his legs over the side of the bed, groaned and held his head.

'Jesus H Christ!' he flopped back on to the bed. 'I feel like I've been kicked in the head by a cow.'

'Yep, you look like that.'

'I've got to get out of here.'

'I'll go find the registrar.'

Margaret made her way to the door, it was blocked by a tattooed, denim-clad biker. She turned back to Brontë.

'There's a tattooed, denim-clad biker blocking the door.'

The biker stood to one side and she passed.

'Ah! Missus 'Spector, how's yourself? Eye ear Holy Joe's been acting the maggot?'

He stepped out of her way.

'I'm really sorry, young man, but I haven't a clue what you're on about. But if it's Brontë you want, he's over there between the belcher and the snorer.'

She exited, giving him a wide berth.

'What brings you round this neck of the woods, KickStart. Come to hand yourself in?'

'Hugh lock shite, 'Spector.'

'I've been better, KickStart.'

'Common joiners, 'Spector. You'd 'ave a reight craic.'

'I'm a police officer, KickStart not a biker.'

'The company of wolves is better than the company of pigs.'

'You didn't come all the way down here to invite me to come and run your charitable section, KickStart.'

The biker sat down too hard on Brontë's bed, making the policemans head move and so wince in pain.

'Bone sez it's all over.'

'Oh my God I hate being dumped.'

'Bone sez yer quits.'

'Which, is a shame, because I need one more favour from him.'

'Snot gonna 'appen, 'Spector.'

KickStart went to leave but stopped at the door.

'Jeesus, 'Spector, what's the feckin' favour?'

'I need someone to see a man about a clamp.'

'The councillor?'

Brontë nodded.

'I want him to have a chance to pay his dues.'

'I'll tell the boss,' and with that he left.

Brontë's phone played the Bond theme and vibrated on the bedside table.

'Brontë!'

'It's me,' said the phone.

'I know it's you, Pepper.'

'There's something you need to see.'

'What is it?'

'Just get your arse over to the viaduct as soon as you can.'

*

When Brontë polled up on the bike Pepper was sitting on the viaduct wall, swinging her legs impatiently and tapping out stuff on her phone.

'You took your bloody time.'

'Do you mean "good morning, sir"?'

'Good morning, sir, you took your bloody time.'

'What is it?'

'Follow me.'

She led him up the path across the viaduct and stopped near the parapet where he'd fallen on to his head earlier. She looked at Brontë, winked and started hauling on a rope, a rope that was bound in strong black fabric.

'What the hell is it?'

'Brontë, you ain't seen nothing yet.'

She hauled the rest of the rope up and piled it haphazardly at her feet. She waved the loose end in Brontë's face.

'What on earth is it?'

'It's a bungee. Your little naked trapeze artist bungeed off the viaduct buttress.'

'She's not dead.'

'It would appear that after a quick tussle with you,' Pepper threw the bungee back over the viaduct for effect. 'Yumi leapt to freedom on a big bleedin' elastic band. She bounced around on the end of it for a little while as she cut herself free and then fell a short distance into the beck below. Splash!'

'I don't believe it.'

'You better believe it, sunshine. And what's more, there's even more that's harder to believe down there.' She pointed over the side.

*

Standing under an arch and looking up at the dangling bungee that hung from the viaduct, water droplets splashed down on to the faces of the two officers. They looked at the spot where Yumi must have dangled like a spider on a silken thread.

'So, what's to see up there?'

'It's not what's up there, Brontë,' she pointed to her feet, 'it's down here.'

Brontë looked at the ground.

'Tyres tracks?'

'Motorbike tracks, Brontë. Motorbikes! It looks like your little leather-clad mates have whisked away our prime suspect.'

'Well bugger me backwards,' said Brontë.

*

Brontë rarely entered Crupper's office, and when he did it was because he had been summoned and not out of choice. Today it was his pleasure. He threw the door back on its hinges and marched straight up to the desk: no knocking, no messing. Crupper didn't look up from his keyboard.

'What do you want, Brontë?'

In answer, Brontë threw a case file on to Crupper's desk.

'What's that?'

'Highbatts file.'

Crupper slid his pen between the covers of the file and flipped it open, revealing the sparseness of information inside. He sneered at it.

'Lots of shoddy admin work back in the day Brontë, lots of files went missing. Looks like most of this file went missing too. The case is closed, long forgotten.'

'You were the investigating officer.'

'Does it say that in there?'

'Nope.'

'No, it doesn't say it anywhere, so get out of my office, before I... just get out, Brontë.'

Brontë threw a second file on to the desk.

'Now this file is different; this file was written by one of the Highbatts victims, a Simon Livesey. It makes for very interesting reading.'

Crupper reached out for the file; Brontë pulled it out of his reach.

'Events, names, dates... the whole kit and caboodle.'

'I never went to Highbatts... ever. So, with the serious risk of being repetitious, Brontë, get out of the bloody office.'

'Nope, not one visit. Strange that. Not one visit, even when you investigated the kids' allegations.'

'The allegations were proved to be malicious.'

Brontë ignored this and thumbed through the file.

'Your golf partner, however, he was quite a regular.'

'He was interested in the boys welfare.'

'I've made a promise to a friend... that the councillor's going to get his just deserts.'

'You have nothing on the Councillor Swain.'

'I don't need anything... You're going to jog up the stairs, walk right on up to the chief's office and spill the beans.'

'Yeah! Like that's gonna happen.'

'If you confess to covering the whole Highbatts affair before anyone discovers it, you might get away without prison time. Police superintendents don't tend to go down well in a prison. Well actually that's not true, they go down quite a bit, but that's a whole different kettle fish.'

'Why on earth, would I do anything so mind numbingly stupid?

'Well, when I leave here, I'm off up to visit the good councillor with this file.' He waved it triumphantly. 'I will advise him I can make it disappear, as long as he confesses his sins. I'll explain, like I've just explained to you, that if he takes the first step it would make a difference.'

'He's not going to confess to being a paedophile, you idiot.'

'Oh, he might, I am pretty sure he'll manage to play down his role in the affair a great deal, while probably exaggerating yours. That's what councillors excel at: twisting lies to sound like truths.'

'He won't fall for it.'

'Oh, won't he? When it's either that or the chance of a long stretch in Armley as a kiddy-fiddler. He'll bite my bloody hand off.'

The two policemen stood in silence and stared at each other across the desk. Crupper broke the impasse and snarled at Brontë.

'What happened to Detective Charles Brontë, Inspector Honest of the yard?' Contempt was smeared across his face.

'I took a leaf out of your book, sir. "Get the result no matter what."'

*

A crocodile of bikers meandered up the moor road and two by two they entered the falls car park. The heavies scurried into the hut as the car park filled with chrome and leather. Councillor Swaine came to the door of the hut and watched as the bikes circled his property. The racket they made destroyed the peace and their exhaust fumes fouled the air. One by one the bikers drew-up to form a semicircle before the councillor and his hut. At the front of the pack were Bonehead and KickStart, each carrying a helmeted pillion rider. As one the bikers cut their engines, leaving the councillor standing in silence.

'Who the hell are you lot?'

'Us, Counslaw?' said KickStart. 'The Pagan Wolves. Funny really, you with all that money you'd think you could keep the wolves from the door.'

The pack laughed dutifully.

'I have men of my own,' threatened the nervous councillor.

'What's he say, KickStart?'

'E zed e has is girlfriends inside the hut.'

The pack thought this was funny too.

'I don't want any trouble.'

This made them roar.

'Ha! Just listen to the fella, Bone. Head dozen whan tenny trouble, four fecks sake.'

'It's a bit late for that.'

Everybody laughed again.

'Dew whan meat two eggs plain?'

'Leave it to me.'

'That's right,' said the councillor, 'I'm not going to deal with you, you little Irish fucker.'

'Hey!' hissed the Irish mechanic. 'Less of the "little" if you don't mind?' He laughed and the pack joined him.

Bonehead nodded to KickStart, who pulled his bike away.

'You can deal with me, Councillor.'

'You better hurry up. My lads are on the phone, the police will be here any minute.'

'We won't be staying long, Councillor. We've come for a refund.'

'Now that is funny.'

Bonehead's bike pulled back into position. His pillion pulled a helmet from its head: it was Jeanne Hepworth.

'Good afternoon, Councillor.' She waved at him. 'My friends and I have come for a refund.'

'You see, Councillor,' added Bone, 'you don't want us bad boys hanging around here all weekend now, do you? You won't sell another ticket and that'll cost you at least an arm an' a leg. May as well pay the refund. It'll be cheaper in the long run.'

'You can't threaten me.'

The packed laughed again.

'But that's exactly what we can do. We might have to come back every weekend. In fact, we might set up camp and stay till until, ooh let's think… next Pancake Tuesday, that should just about break you.'

'You don't know who you're messing with.'

'It's not that we don't know. It's that we don't actually give a rat's arse.'

There was a pause as the councillor chewed over his limited options.

'How much does the old cow want?'

'Jeanne, how much did he charge?

'It was seventy-five pounds, love.'

'So, Councillor, I believe that's a hundred and fifty quid you owe the lady.

'She just said seventy-five.'

'Yeah well there's an interest charge and an extra fifty quid for the "old cow" comment.' He turned to Jeanne. 'That do you, Mrs Hepworth?'

'That'll be lovely, dear.'

The councillor stuck out a wad of ten-pound notes towards Bonehead.

'I don't want your money, arsehole.' He gestured to Jeanne, 'It's the lady you owe.'

The councillor handed the money to Jeanne, breathing angrily and muttering under his breath.

'Thank you,' said Jeanne to the councillor and then repeated it to the two bikers.

'Thank you, thank you.'

'And now, Councillor, I think it's time to say you're sorry.'

Silence

'Come on, say you're sorry, and then we'll be off.'

Councillor Swaine spoke the words to Jeanne through gritted teeth. 'I'm sorry.' It was all he could do to stop himself spitting.

'You should be ashamed of yourself,' she told him. 'I don't know how you sleep at night.'

'We're real bad bastards,' added Bonehead, 'and we sleep. Do you remember me at all, Councillor?'

'I've never met you in my live, I don't associate with scroats.'

'You must remember Highbatts?'

The councillor hesitated only slightly. 'I don't know what you're on about.'

'There's a vampire on the moors, Councillor, you heard that?'

'Rubbish, man.'

'Been going around killing anyone involved with the Highbatts incident some year ago, apparently.'

'Look, you've got your money, now bugger off.'

'This bloodsucker is killing them and then whipping off their privates. So, if you value your life... and your cock, you better take care.'

A lone bike swung off the moor and pulled up beside the group. The councillor was forced to step back to make room. All eyes were on the lone biker as they removed their helmet.

'Brontë!?' said the councillor and he laughed. 'I don't believe it, I don't bloody believe it. Hail fellow and well met.' Councillor Swain took a step towards the angels. 'These louts and,' he waved his hand in Jeanne's general direction, 'Ma Baker here have just exhorted from me my hard earned. Arrest them, Brontë.'

'Hard earned!?'

'All right, Brontë, easy now. Don't forget I know your boss.'

'Now then, Inspector Brontë.'

'KickStart.'

'Hey, Brontë.'

Bonehead saluted the police officer.

'Hey, Bonehead.'

Councillor Swain was shocked by the familiarity.

'You're not telling me you're with these reprobates.'

Brontë ignored him and returned his attention to the Wolves.

'All done?'

'Aye, 'Spector, are wok ears done.'

Bonehead turned and nodded. He kicked his bike to life, winked at Brontë and pulled away, Jeanne Hepworth clinging desperately to his back.

'Goodbye, Detective Inspector,' and she waved politely.

The pack kicked their bikes to life and moved off, each of them high-fiving Brontë as they passed until there was just Brontë, KickStart and his pillion left.

The pillion removed their helmet and rubbed a leather-gloved hand over their bald head.

'Hiya, Charlotte.'

Brontë looked into Yumi's smiling face.

'I see you've fallen on your feet.'

'You're so funny.'

'Oh yeah, I'm a right barrel of laughs, me'

She giggled.

'I have a warrant for your arrest.'

'Not worth the paper it's written on,' KickStart added. 'Bone pro miced Yumi safe pass age out the count tree, 'Spector.'

'Bone told me he didn't do charity work.'

'T'isn't charty wok. Yumi paid in spades, dis is victim support.'

'Well you better get on with it then, the cavalry will be here any minute.'

KickStart looked up across the moor. He could just about hear the sirens and see the blue and whites winding their way towards them. He fired up the old chopper.

Yumi blew Brontë a kiss.

'Sayonara, Charlotte.'

And there they were, gone.

'Well that's that,' laughed the councillor. 'Well done, Brontë. Your mates in blue will soon 'ave the bastard.'

'They're not coming for him... They're coming for you.'

'Bollocks. Crupper's in my pocket. He won't send anyone after me.'

The sound of the sirens increased as the police cars drew closer.

'You may well have had Crupper in your pocket, Swaine, but very shortly he'll be spilling his guts to a room full of gold braid.'

'Bollocks, he hasn't the balls.'

'He's gonna be telling everyone about your nasty little habits.'

The councillor looked around, frightened and confused the sirens now almost deafening.

Councillor Anthony Swaine set off across the car park as fast as his chubby little legs had ever carried him, but it still wasn't fast enough.

An incident response vehicle skidded to a halt across the car park entrance and spewed out uniformed officers, who stood and watched the councillor struggling up the side of a heather-covered bank. Brontë pointed at the escaping councillor.

'There's your man, fellas, he has a bit of a head start on you.'

The uniformed officers ran after the gibbering councilor.

'Lovely,' smiled Brontë. 'I do love a good game of 'Hare and Hounds.'

He put his hand to his mouth and blew an imaginary hunting horn, blasting out a series of quick notes.

Tat..Tat...Tahh!

Epilogue

Hewenden Moor. The First of December.

Brontë shot across the moor road on *the Monster* and he clocked ninety-nine miles an hour as he hurtled into the Mad Mile, and he sang 'Born to Run' into his helmet at the top of his voice.

Brontë wore his oldest jeans and scruffiest leather jacket and the new biker vest he had got courtesy of KickStart Bob. The vest was emblazoned with a wolf's head, with a rocker below embroidered with the words 'Lone Wolf'.

When he hit the bend at one-hundred and ten miles per hour, he howled like a wolf.

'Ah-hooooooooo!'

Coming soon

THE BRONTË WAY

The second novel in the INSPECTOR CHARLES BRONTË THRILLER SERIES by TOM MARSH.

Email - tommarshrul@gmail.com
Web - www.tommarshwriter.co.uk

Milton Keynes UK
Ingram Content Group UK Ltd.
UKHW040234031224
451863UK00001B/32